HOW OTHER PEOPLE MAKE LOVE

Made in Michigan Writers Series

GENERAL EDITORS

Michael Delp, Interlochen Center for the Arts
M. L. Liebler, Wayne State University

A complete listing of the books in this series can
be found online at wsupress.wayne.edu

HOW OTHER PEOPLE MAKE LOVE

Stories by Thisbe Nissen

WAYNE STATE UNIVERSITY PRESS
DETROIT

Lyrics from "Kathleen," composed and written by Josh Ritter, reprinted by permission of Rural Songs.

ISBN 978-0-8143-4836-9 (paperback)
ISBN 978-0-8143-4837-6 (e-book)

Library of Congress Control Number: 2020947079

Publication of this book was made possible by a generous gift from The Meijer Foundation.

On cover: "Laurel," *The Thousand Dollar Dress Project*, Sonya Naumann.

Cover design by Lindsey Cleworth

Wayne State University Press
Leonard N. Simons Building
4809 Woodward Avenue
Detroit, Michigan 48201-1309

Visit us online at wsupress.wayne.edu

For Jay and Sonne

CONTENTS

.

Every heart is a package tangled up in knots someone else tied.

—Josh Ritter

ALONE AND CLAPPING

In memory of Kimberly Grace Langford (1963–2006).

About her presence at the Klish wedding Genie Spahr feels somewhat duplicitous. Shelly is an old friend, yes, and there *is* something beyond their shared past that binds the Aerobox girls, even nearly twenty years after the rise of the Reebok, the battle of the bulge, and the ascendancy—and nosedive plummet—of Dr. Robbie Wax and the Powerout! They'd clung and clustered through the trial, but once Wax went to prison, the displaced girls resorted variously to waitressing, temping, personal training, lifeguarding, escorting, eldercare, stripping, and, in Genie's case, returning to college—pre-med—with an infant Björned to her breast. A round-robin letter circulated for years, a letter Genie has occasionally hauled out to prove her involvement—her *centrality*, really—in what amounted to a landmark case in the statutory rape prosecution of an aerobics guru/cult leader. She was not the plaintiff, though she testified on the girl's behalf. Genie herself had been a perfectly legal almost twenty-year-old by the time she'd lost enough weight to render herself desirable to Dr. Robbie. He had them all on the pill, of course, but Genie'd been one of the statistical outliers—or, if she were completely honest regarding her pill-taking diligence (as she well knows few women ever are) she has to admit she'd been a typical woman who took her birth control with typical regularity resulting in a typical efficacy rate of 91 percent. Genie Spahr, teenage 1980s aerobics-video-weight-loss minor celebrity, had not been—as Dr. Robbie claimed, and took credit for, in the infomercials—"perfect." Genie is now, and has only ever been, "typical."

If she'd gone through with the abortion, Dr. Robbie would have gladly kept her around, for typical as she may have been, she was also *Genie: An Aerobox™ Success Story* (the most successful video in the Powerout!™ Series, as Genie is sometimes disturbingly compelled to remind herself).

But that was ancient history—before Tyler's birth, before the trial, before Powerout! VHS tapes were in demand only as kitsch, gifted as gags at white elephant parties across middle America. Genie's video opens on a photo, a snapshot still of her arrival at college, freshman year, then cuts to video, a year later, to find its heroine, age nineteen, lumbering out of the dining hall licking a soft-serve, rainbow-sprinkled cone, a good forty pounds flabbier, cheeks like a blowfish, thighs saddled like a pack llama. Thus begins the chronicle of a ferocious year of workouts, our heroine shape-shifting through kicks and punches into a svelte little Aeroboxer™, moving up to a spot at the front of the "class" behind Wax, competing for the favor of the master, and finding herself, by video's end, sporting a coveted headset mic, counting aloud and whooping and grunting in endorphin-addled ecstasy. Understandably neglected is any on-screen depiction of Genie's concurrent assumption of a spot in Wax's bed, which turned out to be more temporary even than the weight loss, hardly exclusive, and far less enviable than her place on the Aerobox arena floor. During the trial, Genie liked joking about a sequel—"Genie II: Knocked Up & PoweredOut!"—but nobody else ever thought it that funny. Recently, though, there seems to be interest in a *Powerout!: Where the Girls Are Now*, a proposed follow-up that would find Genie morphed yet again, into Eugenia Spahr, MD, former secretary of the PTA in the Iowa town where she makes her home.

Tyler, Genie's Aerobox love child, is a gay seventeen-year-old student at the School of American Ballet in New York City where he lives with four teenage ballerinas in an unclean apartment in Hell's Kitchen. In a few years, if he remains—knock on wood—uninjured, he'll be soloing with the City Ballet. Tyler is the geode core of Genie's life and the source of her gravest anxieties. No number of safe-sex videos and condom conversations will ever truly put her mind at ease with regard to her son's safety. Also, she misses him. Her Iowa nest is not big, but it's proverbially and literally empty without him, and Genie is—proverbially, literally, existentially, and physically—lonely. The has been virtual talk on the updated, tech-savvy round-robin (now at www.aeroboxgirls.com, and, wisely, password protected) about finding a man for Genie, and Shelly has promised her a wedding-reception seat at a table with an apparently eligible one named Bob Boule. By way of description, Shelly has offered that Bob is "forty-five," "single," a "good man," who "likes children," and is "smart." This is all it took to get Genie on the plane, about which she feels slightly embarrassed of—and frightened for—herself. Genie is thirty-seven years old. Sometimes she thinks she would like to have another child.

The Klish ceremony is held at a business plaza church off the Pennsylvania Turnpike. Genie pans the sanctuary for a man who might reasonably be Bob Boule; she has no idea what he actually looks like. Debbie Beatty, the only other Aerobox alumna present, is in the wedding party, so Genie sits by herself to watch all fourteen bridesmaids float by, each delightfully fatter than the last, as though they've been arranged according to dress size. Debbie's near the middle of the lineup, no heftier or svelter than Genie these days. Shelly looks good, Genie thinks, if somewhat orange from tanning, and about as butch as ever, despite the wedding gown and the groom. *Biceps like Shelly's wither all forays into femininity*, Genie will tell Tyler on the phone later tonight or tomorrow. Real life, Genie feels at this point in her own, is infinitely inferior to the version of it she relays in amusing anecdotes to her son. *Now she's Shelly Klish*, she'll tell Tyler. *With a name like that, the woman will never cease to be an object of every lesbian's desire, husband be damned.*

The Klishes don't force their guests through a receiving line; they simply disappear after the ceremony as though they've been whisked off to a janitor's supply closet to hastily consummate the marriage while their guests move, en black-tie masse, to an adjacent office park where a businessmen's Ramada convention center will be the site of the reception. But, upon arrival, it is discovered that the hall's not yet done playing host to a bar mitzvah bash—soft-skinned boys in suit pants stealing each other's yarmulkes, and thin-wristed girls, hose bagging at their knees, checking one another's braces for trapped food—and the Klish party can't get into the room for another hour, so the wedding guests make their way to the Ramada lobby sports bar. Amstel Light is on special, and they conduct their predictable conversations ("Bride's side?" "Groom's?") beneath life-sized Steelers and Pirates posters while fourteen games play simultaneously on fourteen mounted consoles around the bar. All interaction is punctuated with upward glances at every flash of a screen. *We looked like a pack of paranoiacs watching for Big Brother*, Genie will tell Tyler, *or sinners checking for God.* This, she feels, is funnier than the fact of a bunch of adult strangers relying on televised team sports to quell their crowd-borne anxiety. Genie smiles at every passing man between thirty and sixty-five, just to be safe, and though her smiles don't go entirely unacknowledged, there's no Bob Boule coming back at her with a, *Genie Spahr?* The double takes come mostly from women who, consciously or not, must recognize Genie as the girl from the videos. Genie feels fundamentally incapable of deciding whether it thrills or depresses her. Anyway, if Bob Boule's seen the videos, he's not making that connection across twenty years and fifty-odd pounds.

By the time a side wing of the banquet hall opens for cocktail hour, the guests are already hammered, tearing at the hors d'oeuvres table like stoned adolescents. There's cruise ship opulence to the spread—tremendous crystal bowls of fern- and moss-colored dips, surfboard-size giant salmon catching waves of ornamental kale, ice skating rinks of wraps and rolls, mosaics of crackers cobbled like great Italian piazzas, a botanical garden of crudité. The help, in white *Iron Chef* costumes, wield their steak knives and sauce ladles like majorettes, and Genie's instinct is to duck and cover every time a blade catches the chandelier light. She would not mind, just now, spending some time underneath a banquet table; she's drunk far too much on an empty stomach and piles her cocktail plate high with booze-absorbent tidbits. Sadly, for all the flash, everything tastes like everything else: bland and chewy and oiled.

When the ballroom doors fly open at last, Genie is not only still drunk but also stuffed so full she can't bend at the waist. Upon finding her table, she's forced to perch on the lip of her chair in a sort of a deep knee bend to ensure the integrity of her straining dress seams. Tablemates arrive, introducing themselves as they claim their assigned seats. There's a pair of lesbians, Corey and Angie: one in a tux; the other exquisitely beautiful, fine boned and shimmering, her head shaved clean to the scalp. And there's Jilly and her developmentally disabled older brother, Craig, both siblings chinless with pronounced underbites. Craig's suit is of a tan stain-resistant material—though stained nonetheless—and woefully inadequate of length in both leg and arm. Jilly's got an aqua blue blazer over a navy-blue elastic-waist dress, and earrings to match her plastic-beaded bracelet. Everyone stands to shake hands across the table—piled with more china and glassware than an Oneida showroom—but then, once they're seated, they can no longer see each other over the mounded centerpiece: donut-sized hot-pink roses and enough baby's breath to choke a baby. Last to arrive at table number seventeen are the photographer and his assistant who make a brief appearance, not to take their seats, but to unload a small arsenal of black ripstop camera bags, tripods, screens, umbrellas, and an antique glass-plate field camera that might have been fresh from the battle at Antietam. All this gear serves to block the table's view of the rest of the room, and vice versa, which lends to the sense that the guests at number seventeen are more like stagehands in the wings of this reception.

Genie finally picks out Bob Boule from across the room, this recognition accompanied by a twisting abdominal cramp, like the squirm of an intestinal parasite. As Bob Boule comes toward her, the wrench in Genie's gut gives way to nauseated exhaustion. There's a wave of heat, and Genie has to fight every impulse in her being not to simply lay her head down on her place setting and die. A tulle and satin goody bag of mints and mini champagne bottles would serve as a headstone. Her epitaph: *Do not open in close confines. May cause serious injury.*

When Bob Boule arrives at table number seventeen, sweaty and winded from his cross-ballroom journey, he smiles down, ducking humbly, almost bowing, and says, his voice warm and full and disarmingly kind, "You must be Genie," and Genie thinks, *god, can't I please be someone else?* She is no actress, does not mask disappointment well, so perhaps it's a purely autonomic response that makes her approximate a smile, stick out her hand, and say, "Bob," in a way that makes it sound like she's been waiting her whole life for Bob, and here he is, Bob, and her relief at finally meeting Bob is beyond her wildest fairy-princess imagination. Only this *isn't* the Bob Genie's been waiting for. Her Bob is taller, she's sure. Her Bob may be balding, but he's balding like Bruce Willis, not like someone's Aunt Myrtle. Her Bob is nothing like this Bob! Where is *Genie's* Bob? The Bob who's like her, but male: the slightly sad, once-handsome, now aging-but-still-sort-of-handsome Bob in whose faded beauty her own will begin to glow anew. Who is this man, Genie wants to know, and what has he done with her Bob?

Well, Bob Boule may be an imposter, but he's not an idiot. The man is well aware that an existential vacuum has just slurped up every trace of anticipation from this meeting: *shwoop*, gone. In its place is a corporeal weight landed with the thud of indisputable news: you're pregnant, you're bleeding, you're caught, guilty, dead. Nonetheless, what's a Bob to do but take his seat beside Genie and plow on down the dead end of this night? As he's settling in, though, he stops himself, suddenly remembering his manners, and says, "Can I get you drink?" He's desperate to flee, it's clear, but Genie's no less desperate, if just for a few moments alone to regain her bearings in the face of this disappointment. "Great!" she chirps, and off he spins toward the bar, speedy as a busboy newly promoted to waitstaff: green as celery and eager to make waiter of the year. He hasn't even asked what she's drinking.

Bob's flight is accompanied by a voice, booming from everywhere. It's God, in Dolby: it's DJ Dan! Gangly, double-jointed, on a mic with too much bass, perched on a platform above the dance floor, he's the emcee, the party-master-meister, and he's starting things off with *pizzazz*! He's motherfucking Bob Barker calling, *Come on down*, only it's "Ladies and gentlemen"—and the disco beat's a-thumping—"Ladies and gentlemen, let's hear you give it up for the *wedding party*!" And everyone in the ballroom is clapping and swaying, singing right along to "Celebrate good times, come on," as one peachy-pink bridesmaid after another gallops in from the double doors marked EXIT, trailing behind her a rental-tuxedoed groomsman. Below DJ Dan's platform they gather like feudal subjects, dancing in place while he contextualizes each entering pair, painfully mispronouncing every name out of his mouth. "Now, why don't you all give it up for Miss Sharon Gan-e-shan-e-than, who's known the bride since junior high, and Mister Jim Nach-a-mie, who works in the cubicle next to the groom!" And they dance on down the parquet, filing in to wait and clap and cheer for the next couple down the aisle, like the setup for some elaborate square dance that just keeps on setting up, DJ booming, "Celebrate" giving way to "We Are Family," Shelly's husband's mom and dad blundering down the aisle like Dorothy and the straw-legged Scarecrow. DJ Dan says their last name so it rhymes with *leash*. Mom and Dad *Kleesh*: a *cliché* that's lost its accented *e*.

When it's finally over—first dance segueing into group dancing, conversation rising in the ballroom once again like ants from a rain puddle—Genie's sufficiently distracted from the letdown of Bob that she thinks she can cope like the adult she's supposed to be. He returns to the table with a drink so absurd it might as well come with a garland of orchids and the kiss of a grass-skirted native girl. "I asked for something festive," he explains. The drink is blue, the swizzle stick plumed. Bob's drinking scotch, and from the smell and weave of him Genie's guessing he put away a few while the bartender alchemized her Sapphire Sizzler. She sips and toasts simultaneously by way of *thank you*. It's spiked Kool-Aid. It could be worse.

Bob's finally about to actually sit when he freezes mid-knee bend at the sight of something across the table. Genie's eyes follow his. "*Jilly Nader?*" He gawks, incredulous.

Jilly snaps to attention. "*Bob Boule?*"

And what do you know: Bob Boule *babysat* for Jilly and Craigy Nader lo so many years ago back in Tipp City, Ohio, and *my god, what are the chances?* Bob crosses behind Genie, laying an apologetic and conciliatory palm on her shoulder as he moves, to kneel by Craig's chair and greet that blank-eyed face. He steals the photographer's assistant's empty chair, pulls it over so he and Jilly can catch up. Oh, they'd *loved* him, Jilly tells Bob: does he remember how he'd also worked part-time at the Frostee Barn and he'd give them free jimmies on their extra-swirly cones of vanilla-chocolate twist? Genie drains her Blue Voodoo in three sips and heads for the bar without a word to anyone. Bob and Jilly will be married within a year; she's willing to put money on it.

Even before the meal is served, Brother Craig is led away by elderly parental types. Bob Boule and Jilly Nader get up to dance and hardly return the rest of the evening save to wolf down bites of chicken Kiev and braised baby carrots and gulp Pepsi products before they lunge back to the dance floor as though the job they have to do out there is so important, so *vital*, so *incredibly rewarding*—like missionaries or disaster relief workers—they can't bear to be anywhere else.

"*That* seems to be going well," says Angie, the beautiful, bald, glimmering dyke. Genie understands her to be some sort of counselor or social worker.

"And he was *my* blind date," Genie confesses. "Well, wedding fix-up person. Whatever."

"I'd say you got the best end of that deal," says Corey, the butchier, tuxedoed one. She's got thick, dark, cropped hair, and a sharp jut of jaw. Her smile is crooked and sly as a gangster's.

"That's kind of you," Genie says.

"Can I . . . ?" Corey starts, then begins again. "We were just trying to figure out . . . are you . . . Do you know Shelly back from Aerobox?"

"My youth," Genie admits, "in spandex."

"I knew it!" says beautiful Angie, eyes flashing under blue mascaraed lashes.

"In the flesh," says Genie. "Substantially *more* flesh, but . . ."

"Oh, feh!" Butch Corey swats playfully. "That wineglass has more flesh than *any* of you in those videos." She drops her voice then, like someone might overhear. "Did he starve you?"

"Oh no," Genie tells them, "we starved ourselves."

Angie says, "It was *years* before Shelly admitted *any* of it to Corey."

"So you guys knew her *after* that all, then?"

"I met her in church," Corey explains. "Late eighties."

"Corey used to be Born Again," Angie adds.

"Please excuse my wife," Corey says. "That's her favorite thing to say."

"Shelly and I weren't in much contact then," Genie says. "I never knew quite what to do with her whole Jesus thing."

Angie rolls her eyes in commiseration.

"Well," says Corey, "if it helps explain anything, I was straight back then too."

"Thank god for growing up," Genie says.

"Praise be," Angie says, then adds, "Just for the record, *I* was never a Jesus freak, cult aerobicist, *or* straight."

"Which is why *you* get to have cancer!" Corey booms. Her false cheer is even more devastating than Angie's look of admission.

"Nice segue, honey."

"Thanks," Corey says, "I've been working on it."

"I'd've never guessed you weren't a natural bald," Genie says. Angie palms her scalp, demurring. "*You're* very kind."

"Are you through with chemo?" Genie asks hopefully.

"Oh, no," says Corey. "Not hardly."

"We're on a break, me and chemo," Angie says. "Hey, you should come out with us tonight—I don't know if you do dyke bars . . .? We're meeting friends after this. It's not far from here . . . Sisters'? Sometimes the DJ's decent, and they make a *strong* cosmopolitan . . ."

"Sold," Genie says. She is nothing if not easy.

"Hey," Corey begins, "so, what do you do now, post-Aerobox?"

"Ob-gyn."

"No kidding?" Corey gapes.

"No, why?" Genie asks. "You too?"

"Oh, god no, I just . . . wow." Corey's stammering like she's starstruck.

"You," Angie smacks her, "are *such* a lesbian."

Corey shoots her a look, then turns back to Genie. "So, wow, so what's that like?"

"Well . . ." Genie's unsure how to proceed.

"I mean, like not *really* knowing people, but knowing these really intimate things . . ."

"I guess it's that way for any kind of doctor, I suppose," Genie says. Angie elbows Corey. "You're pestering our new friend, honey. They take oaths against those kinds of questions."

"It's fine, really," Genie says. "I do like what I do." She's fumbling. "I like being a resource for women, someone they can tell things to."

"I bet that's amazing," Corey says, "to hear the ways people talk about sex . . ."

"She's not Dr. Ruth!" Angie chides.

Genie laughs. "Sometimes it's more amazing what people *won't* say. The words people can't bring themselves to use. I've got a hand on their cervix, and they'll do just about anything to avoid the word *vagina*."

"It's not an *easy* word," Angie allows.

"Ex*cuse* me?" Corey balks.

"I mean," she qualifies, "I can imagine it's difficult for some people."

"Well that's just sad," says Corey.

"I can only imagine what it must have been like for Kinsey," Genie begins, but she's not wholly sure of her audience. "Alfred Kinsey? The sex studies of the forties . . . ? Hearing people's stories, their excuses . . . I mean, of course, you always get the *Our Bodies, Ourselves*ers, talking like the future of the women's movement rests on how often they can use the word *labia*." These are lines Genie's practiced to perfection at this point in her career.

"Okay," Angie declares, "I'm never saying anything to my gynecologist ever again."

Genie laughs, but feels the need to defend or clarify. "No, no, but there are ones who make it worth it . . . When someone's in tears at the relief of being understood. They're like displaced persons waiting to meet someone who understands their language. Then I get to feel like I'm their kinswoman from the old country, or something. And that's the trade-off for the hundreds of sorority girls who come in wanting to go on the pill because they don't want to carry a purse out to the bars and there are no pockets for condoms in their minidresses."

Angie claps a hand on Corey's back. "My wife, you may be interested, was a Tri Delt."

"Must we air *all* my dirty laundry right here, right now?"

"Honey," coos Angie, "Genie's a professional."

"Hey, what time is it?" Corey asks.

"Eight thirty-ish."

"We should probably go . . . we told . . ."

"Should we say goodbye to Shel . . . ?" Angie peers around the photo gear, scans the dancing crowd for the bride, and there she is, throwing down to Gloria Estefan.

"I haven't even said hello yet," Genie tells them.

Corey is already up, stealing goody bag mints for the road. "We'll think up something to tell her later," she assures Genie.

And then—easiest thing in the world—they're crossing the parking lot asphalt toward a white Civic. Angie politely offers Genie shotgun. "No, no," Genie says, climbing in back. "Cancer before age . . . beauty before age . . ."

Corey raises an eyebrow over the hood of the car, shooting Genie a complicated look. It says, *Hey, watch whose lady you're flirting with, lady,* but says it proudly, like she's tickled, though there's admonishment in it, too, not for the flirting, but for the self-deprecation. Genie's sure her own look back at Corey is too convoluted to convey much of anything at all.

The night is warm, a musky breeze coming in through Angie's open window. She turns back in one sudden motion, craning around the seat. "You tell me if it's blowing too much."

"It's perfect," Genie says, and wonders if there will ever come a day when she just accepts that life's a lot better when you stop trying to force yourself on aging bachelors and give in to blaring down the highway in a beat-up Honda with a pair of cancer-fighting lesbians. There *are* sperm banks, for god's sake; there are many more ways than one to have a child. She fights the longing to take out her phone and call Tyler in New York.

Angie tilts her head up singing, "Oh, how I love to feel the wind in my hair . . ." and flittering a hand through imaginary tresses that flow out the window. She leaves her arm outstretched, fingers rippling.

Genie does her nerdy doctor voice, "So, when did it . . . when did you lose . . . ?"

"What?" Angie spins round again, waves a hand at her ears, the window.

"How long have you been . . . follicle-ly challenged in this way? Differently follicled?"

Corey pipes up, projecting her voice into the rearview mirror, eyes on the road. "She was looking like a damned cancer patient until three days ago when the Mach III and I got to her."

Angie nods sagely, miming razor-to-the-scalp. "Sudsed me up and went to town."

In a bigger city, a coastal city, you might get a choice: lesbian biker bar, swank lesbian cocktail lounge, microbrew pub for knitting lesbians in polarfleece. But this is it, the only place in town, and they're *all* here. Corey and Angie's friends are the we-used-to-be-hippies-joined-Peace-Corps-Taught-for-America-got-MSWs-had-kids-work-in-local-government-are-usually-asleep-by-ten-but-still-smoke-a-joint-every-so-often crowd. In a flurry of handshakes Genie meets a dozen women, their names a continuous song: Leilani, Ramala, Fonda, Nadine—she has no idea who's who. Angie takes charge, herding them through the congested entrance. "Coming through. Make way, coming through—"

"What does she think she has, cancer?" calls one of the friends, and the rest let out slow snorts of breath through their noses, shake their heads, follow their leader.

Inside is not half so crowded as out. The dance floor's empty. The DJ is a tiny Asian woman in a white leotard and circulation-defying jeans, wearing headphones as big as Princess Leia buns. Corey and Angie's friends drag together all the tiny round tables they can, swivel up stools beside them, then order cosmos all around. And there's much talk and laughter, photos taken of newly bald Angie, much oohing and aahing over her beauty, all of which seems to Genie like it should have happened outside, upon sight of her, and now feels somehow false and conciliatory, if still inarguably true. But Angie doesn't seem to mind: she's the life of the party, everything rolling off her, joke after joke after joke, and the cosmos arrive and the jokes come faster, ceaselessly, until they're all exhausted by laughing. Someone heads to the bathroom. Two others break away to play *Ms. Pac-Man*. Conversations faction off into twos and threes, volumes level out. Angie and Genie are at a table sticking off to one side that affords them an unimpeded view of the other tables semicircled, cabaret-style, around the empty dance floor.

On their left is a coed group of friends: two guys with goatees in baggy shorts and visors, a few girls who look no gayer than Genie, probably college kids who wandered into the wrong bar and decided to stay. Standing beside their table is a woman who strikes Genie as the embodiment of every new PFLAG parent's sad vision of their lesbian daughter's future: an apple-bodied woman in Dockers, still wearing the pearl stud earrings she got for high school graduation. Her hair is thick and blonde and as styleless as it was in her ruddy-cheeked Catholic school field hockey days. And here she is, hovering on the periphery of the only straight table at a gay bar, stepping back and forth in her Adidas like there's a dance step she's trying to remember, swaying and clapping offhandedly to a rhythm all her own.

"You know," Angie says into Genie's ear, "when this cancer stuff starts really getting me down, when I start feeling sorry for myself, from now on I'm going to think: Angie, it could be worse, you could be alone and clapping. That's the kind of thing that'll follow you to the grave. RIP Jane Doe. Alone and Clapping." She leaves off talking a second, and though the bar is loud, there's a silence like an absence between Angie's mouth and Genie's ear. And then, in a voice totally devoid of the sarcasm that's buoyed her—buoyed all of them, all night—Angie says, "I'm going to be cremated, myself." And then it's back to the ironic, facetious, self-protective swagger. "I'm in full support of this new movement, actually—have you heard about it? The whole carry-me-out-and-dump-me-in-the-woods-to-be-eaten-by-wild-animals-and-decay-into-the-earth thing? They've got some kinks to work out yet in the whole"—she waves her fingers, searching for a word—"System," she finally says, though it's clearly not the word she was looking for. That seems to deflate her, and Genie wonders at what point you stop trying for the right word because you could die before you find it, and why bother?

The seasickness of sorrow swells in Genie's jaw, fills her ears, closing off the outside, but just then the DJ segues so miserably from one beat to another that everyone in the bar seems to lurch a little, sloshing their drinks. It's like in the old Aerobox videos, painful to watch as the girls falter—suddenly flailing, tragically clownish in their faux paint-splattered, strategically slashed, off-the-shoulder sweatshirts, with their two-tone legwarmers and asymmetrical hairstyles, their glitter tights, Madonna bows, trapezoidal neon earrings—improvising until Robbie Wax revises his count, picks up the new beat, and sets them back on their aerobic course. The girls weren't dancers; they were metronomic, maniacally smiling, Sun In–headed storm troopers. And, god, if they didn't think themselves the hottest things around! Such a delusional confidence, though. Heartbreaking in hindsight, and train-wreck devastating to watch on video.

In Sisters' bar, someone has finally taken the dance floor. The song is by Prince, the lights infused a hot, dense purple. The dancer is terrifically tall, wearing highwater overalls, a good half foot of shin and ankle in sagging black hose protruding from the cuffs. At first it looks like she's shirtless under the overalls, but then a pose reveals a gold-lamé bodysuit hugging a pair of pillowy breasts attached not to the body but the leotard. There's a long cord hanging from the dancer's neck, to which is attached a 4 × 6 laminate index card—a convention-type ID badge in a protective plastic sleeve that keeps slapping her, annoyingly, in the face.

The dance continues—ecstatic and spastic, then mellowing to a Pentecostal/Grateful Dead shimmy-twitch—until the song is over and the dancer takes a girlish skip-gallop to her table, flops exhausted into a chair, and kicks up one long leg to fling it over the other like she's one of Toulouse-Lautrec's prostitutes, all ruffles and crinoline and nineteenth-century bravado. Self-consciously, then she smooths the hair from her face with a look of prideful, prim annoyance. She's absolutely aware of every eye on her.

Angie leans to Genie and says, arch and disparaging, "She's ready for the fucking paparazzi." It's kind of mean the way Angie says it, and the sort of thing you're not supposed to *say* aloud about a person so obviously developmentally compromised, and Genie wonders if that's a political correctness that flies right out the window when you're dying. Because it's clear to Genie, in that moment, that Angie doesn't just *have* cancer; she's dying.

Genie turns to whisper something back—she doesn't even know what, just something—but winds up colliding instead, her mouth swiping Angie's chin, or her cheek, Genie can't quite tell, but it flusters her into a kind of cover-up, pretending like it hasn't happened, or that it's so inconsequential she hasn't even noticed. She comes off, she knows, as childish, like one of her own patients, employing that illusory protection of magical thinking: *Well, I guess I knew my period stopped, but I figured I was stressed out with school or something, because that can happen, right? It doesn't always mean you're pregnant.* Fumbling stupidly, Genie makes it to Angie's ear and says, "That's exactly how I look in the Aerobox videos, like I'm trying to seem so absorbed in the workout I don't even notice the cameras."

Angie pulls back, eyebrows crinkled in; she hasn't heard. "What?"
But Genie shakes her head, waves the words away. It doesn't matter,
she doesn't really want to have said it, or anything, in the first place. From
down the cobbled-lesbian table Corey's watching them, Genie and Angie,
her gaze more suspicious now. The words Genie imagines behind Corey's
look are something like, *Why flirt with* her? *She's dying.*

And that's just about when the back door of Sisters' swings open and is
held there by a barrel-chested woman in a wifebeater as an electric wheelchair buzzes up a makeshift ramp. The wheelchair driver's got a Dorothy
Hamill bowl cut dyed Bozo-the-Clown carmine. From her ears dangle
papier-mâché chili peppers big enough to be Christmas tree ornaments.
Her skirt is ankle-length, a florid chili pepper motif, and propped in the
wheelchair's footrest are two fuzzy, leopard-print booties sewn with huge,
red, ice skate pom-poms. With bells. The wheelchair takes a purposeful
survey of the room, turning a stealthy pivot then locking into position, full
speed ahead, around the corner and toward the bar with a determination
that makes Genie wonder if such a gaudy and brave-seeming entrance
actually requires a substantial steeling of will, and if this woman now
needs what Genie would need in her place: a scotch, and fast.

The wheelchair gets swallowed from view by the bar crowd, and the
DJ starts spinning Madonna, which draws Genie's attention back to
the dance floor where the overall-clad woman has begun, in all earnest-
ness, to vogue. Her poses are practiced, choreographed, and memorized,
every cant of the hip, each thrust of bony shoulder. She's frozen in a kind
of Warrior One archer's stance, long fingers spread before her face like
she's clearing her path of spiderwebs, when she seems to catch her first
glimpse of Angie, and once she's laid eyes on Angie's beauty, it's like
she's immobilized. She doesn't move, just stands frozen in her vogue
in the middle of the floor, no decorum mediating her transfixion: mouth
open, face awash with the inner glow of someone dying in a Lifetime
movie and seeing the faraway white light. And then she begins to move
toward Angie, drawn as if to eternity's beaming lamp. Five feet from their
table, the dancer stops, bares a set of great, horsey teeth, and, in a high-
high falsetto directed right at Angie, says, "You're *beautiful* . . ." Genie
can almost read her neck placard now: *Emerging Feminism*, or maybe

Entering Femininity, an insignia of intertwined woman symbols, and a name, printed smack in the center, bold, all caps: **BRITNEY**.

Angie doesn't respond, and Genie finds herself looking down the table for guidance from Corey, who's already caught wind of the situation and is standing, setting down her drink, and sidling over with the proprietary look of a sheriff coming to set things to right.

"You're beautiful," Britney repeats, oblivious to all but the object of her desire.

Angie has meanwhile regained enough composure to smile back—magnanimous as Miss America, patient as a caseworker—and thank Britney, to say, "That's very nice of you."

Britney barely hears, eyes glazed, like nothing exists but the force of her want. "You're so beautiful." Her voice is breathy with desperation. "I want a beautiful girlfriend like you."

Angie's silent, but Corey slides in then, wraps an arm grandly around her wife's shoulders, and plants an unsubtle kiss on her temple. Then it seems Angie can speak again. "Lots of beautiful girls *here* . . ." she finally says, sweeping a hand over the crowd.

Britney looks out as if surprised to discover other people in the club. She returns her eyes to Angie. "But I want a girlfriend who's beautiful like *you*."

"Don't we all . . ." Corey says, more smugly than Genie thinks the situation seems to warrant. *This is a threat?* Genie wants to chide her.

But Corey's swagger also kicks off something in Angie, who plunges into full-on social worker mode. "Meeting someone," she tells Britney, "someone you find attractive, who you really like and really connect with—it's not easy for anyone. Relationships are a lot of work—"

Britney scowls, twisting a ponytail coquettishly on one finger, then whips around to Genie like an ostrich about to spit, as if to say, *And what might* you *have to contribute, lady?*

"Don't look at me," Genie says, drunk enough that her tongue's on its own. "I'm as bad off as anyone, and straight to boot."

Angie giggles, and Corey snorts a good-natured cowboy laugh, but Britney just keeps staring, like Genie's truly the most pathetic creature she's come across in a long time, and the whole situation's uncomfortable enough that Genie's honestly grateful when an awful, grinding, mechanical screech turns everyone's heads to the dance area where the chili-pepper-wearing woman's wheelchair has gotten hung up on something—some glitch, like a bottlecap caught in a gear—and it squeals as it works past the snag. In the chair, the woman's shaking her head violently as if to say, *Stop looking at me!* Or maybe, *Don't look at me now! Not like this! Look at me when I've got it together, not now!* And Genie has a flash of herself, from the news footage, leaving the courtroom after the Wax verdict, shaking away the reporters, Tyler clutched to her chest in a swaddle, her eyes pinched shut, head wagging like she might be able to make them disappear if she concentrates hard enough. It was so hard to explain: how sometimes all you desired was to be up at the front of the class, the camera's eye focused on every flex of your enviable abs, everyone in the video audience aware of the style of your unitard, the generation of your sneaker, the gleam of every perfectly glistening droplet of sweat on your tan, taut, hairless flesh. And then sometimes you wished you were gone. Out of the spotlight entirely. Not anonymous, not unfamous, and not never-famous, but just gone from view, out of sight and wondered after, ever after. It was complicated. Sometimes Genie imagines Tyler as a star, a famous dancer, and she relishes—deliciously relishes and savors—the idea that she'd be mentioned occasionally, as his mother, a 1980s aerobics VHS luminary, and she feels no small amount of shame at what she knows is undeniably her own narcissism.

Genie's aware of movement nearby: it's Britney springing in a gallop toward the dance floor, her fixation on Angie suddenly supplanted. The woman in the wheelchair is making her way back across the club. In the hand that's not maneuvering her wheelchair's joystick, she holds a brandy snifter frothing over with seafoam-hued foam. It's stuck with a straw too tall for the glass and about to topple, and Genie's seized with the same anxiety she'd be feeling if it were her own special-occasion skirt about to get splattered. Everything we put ourselves through by way of preparation, and all of it ever at the mercy of our inevitable human floundering.

Britney bends to speak to the woman with her rump stuck high in the air, boppy as a cheerleader, and though the exchange isn't audible, the wagging of chili pepper earrings renders their wearer's decisive "no" apparent to anyone watching. Rejected and visibly peeved, Britney pops upright again and stalks away while the woman in the wheelchair, her face a plane of mild annoyance, seems to be shaking off the encounter and moving on to find herself a table.

Beside Genie, the talk between Corey and Angie has grown close and private, their heads touching, bodies blocking off the outside. Genie stands, reaches for her purse. Here she is: drunk, middle-aged, hopelessly straight, and sneaking off to call her son from the dyke bar restroom.

Genie's waiting in the bathroom line when the ruddy, blonde woman emerges, still alone and still clapping, still grooving to that inner beat. She aims for a baby-dyke college girl in a Pitt cap sitting alone across the dance floor at a table for two. Dropping to one knee—the squat-stance of a coach before a benched player—she sticks out a hand of introduction. What follows is a clear and painful rebuff, but then she's climbing back to her feet again, sway-clapping away as if she only stopped and knelt to rest a second. Because what can a person do but move on?

Corey joins the bathroom line, leans against the wall beside Genie and follows her gaze, then elbows her in the rib. "Go on, be a gentlewoman. You're a dancer—ask the poor gym teacher to dance, why doncha?"

Genie is seized with panic, which emerges as sarcasm. "The most I could do," she tells Corey, "is ask her to aerobicize. If it doesn't have an eight-count and isn't targeting a specific muscle group, you put me out there and I look about like *that*." She nods toward Britney, back on the dance floor flailing madly, she and her imaginary adoring audience the only people in the world. As soon as it's said, Genie's overwhelmed with remorse, horrified—shocked, even—by her own callous cruelty. She wants to take it back, to apologize, to make Corey see that what she feels for Britney isn't mockery, it's envy. Genie will never, ever, be that free to move her body in the space of this world. But the words won't come out fast enough, and right there, in the bathroom line, Corey's leaning at her, ready to lunge, and Genie understands: Corey's about to slug her. Genie is about to get publicly belted for being the pathetic, hypocritical asshole she knows she is. Involuntarily, she closes her eyes, awaits the blow, almost wants it: a fat lip of physical pain, so much more straightforward

to contend with than a head fat with existential agony. Genie waits for
the slam of Corey's fist, but feels only hot breath on her face, Corey's
hot cotton candy–cosmo breath by Genie's ear, Corey's body leaned
in conspiratorially close as she's saying, "I've had too much to drink.
And my wife is in the fuck-everything-I'm-dying stage of things. The
I-can-say-whatever-the-fuck-I-want phase? It's a little contagious." This
is a preface, Genie can tell, but she doesn't know to what and gets a rising sense of panic that what's coming is a proposition, some version of
the, *I know you all were into some kind of aerobic orgy-type thing back
in the day and I was wondering . . .* come-on she's fielded more times
over the years than she'd care to admit. Corey's so close now, on the
verge of spitting it out, and Genie thinks maybe she's almost hoping for
the ask. Maybe what's walloping in her own chest and in her pelvis isn't
dread, but desire. Maybe the pull of Corey's teeth on her earlobe, the
glutted shock of Corey's hand wedging inside her—maybe these are things
she wants, or maybe, at least, they are things that might quell the
want. But what Corey's saying, now, in her ear, isn't, *Come back to
the hotel and fuck me and my dying wife*, she's saying, "I always wondered, you know—because Shelly didn't ever really know—why you
decided to have the baby. Why you didn't have an abortion. Was it a
religion thing or something? It's like no one ever really knew *why*."

Genie rearranges her brain, accommodates the question—unexpected
in the moment, but nothing she hasn't been asked before. Nothing she
doesn't have a stock answer for: a stock answer that's also true. "I was
twenty," she tells Corey. "I was twenty, and he was enough of a father
figure, and I was immature enough that when he said 'Abort,' I said, 'No.'
I'm not sure it was much more complicated than that. I think I'm someone who's always worked harder when I had something to work against.
Clearly I wasn't aware of it at the time, but looking back it seems like it
all set me up to go back and plow through college and med school with a
kind of determination I don't know I'd've had otherwise. Like I *had* to
do it, then, because the odds were so stacked against me: young single
mother, blah blah blah."

Beside her, Corey's nodding thoughtfully, eyes squinted in appreciation of the conjured vision. She should, Genie thinks, have a length

of dry grass tucked in the corner of her mouth to chew on ponderously. "Intense," Corey finally says. "In-tense."

Genie shrugs. "I guess. Or just, you know, life."

"Yeah." Corey snorts softly. "Yeah, life. It's intense." She looks over to Angie, momentarily alone across the room, and peels herself from the wall that's propping them both up. "I'm just—" she begins, and then is gone, sentence ever unfinished, gone to Angie, to their life, while it lasts. And only then does Genie think of the real answer to Corey's question. The answer is Tyler. She didn't abort because: Tyler. She couldn't abort because then there wouldn't be Tyler. She knows very well there's a flaw in her logic, that this answer isn't an answer, but it also somehow means there is no question. It's a tautology, a Zen koan, an impossible unpossible paradox. It's a chicken and an egg and an omelet all at once. It just *is*.

In a dirty bathroom stall the gray-pink hue of an old Caucasian crotch, Genie sits on the toilet lid and takes out her phone to call her son. But there's a voicemail from earlier tonight she didn't know was there, ring lost in the music of one dance floor or another. It's Tyler.

"Ma, don't you dare. This is a prophylactic message, dearest Mom—a condom of a message! This is your son, and I am not taking your call tonight—I am calling you first, to tell you that wherever you are, when this message is over, you need to hang up the phone, kick off whatever ridiculously uncomfortable shoes you're wearing, walk up to the nearest DJ, and make them put on whatever crazy eighties lunacy is going to make you get your ass onto that dance floor, you mad Aeroboxing legend, you. If it has to be the motherlovin' *Dirty Dancing* soundtrack, by god you will not be alone on that dance floor. Go. Now. Do it. Patrick Swayze loves you. *I* love you. Get the fuck out there and shake that fabulous middle-aged ass like you know you want to! There is no excuse. Because I *know* that if you're looking at your phone, Bob Boule did not turn out to be the love of your life, and who the fuck cares? Get out there and dance, Mama. It's good for the endorphins. Or the endorphins are good for you. Or something like that. It's good for you. Get out there and dance—it doesn't matter if you're the only damn person on the dance floor. Get the fuck out there and shake that ass! Okay, this has been a public service announcement. Head to your nearest dance floor. DO not pass go. Do not collect $200. Follow the aisle path lighting to your nearest dance floor and move that boo-tay, Mamacita! You hear me. That's an order from your doctor, Doctor."

She is nearly crying and laughing at the same time, lunging out of the bathroom toward the DJ. She doesn't know what will come from her mouth when she gets there. She doesn't know if Tyler's drunk tonight, too, out at some bar in New York City. What kind of a mother is she? It takes faith to let your child go—faith in what you've taught him, faith in the person he's become, that he'll keep himself safe. He is the best man she knows.

You Were My Favorite Scarecrow

Calista Wertheim was, in her time—as most people are, in their times, I suppose—lovely. She had a propensity toward all things batik and slashed her way through life with that mane of frizzled yellow whipping behind her. Garry loved her, and I assume she him, with a devotion and a level-headedness I admire and understand. We were close friends, the four of us—Calista and Garry, me and Witold—for many many years. There were countless dinners in Chinatown, summer barbecues, Sunday brunches on the terrace. We attended each other's events: Witold's openings, Calista's benefits. I use the past tense: Witold is dead, and though Calista has not yet passed, she is gone from us in most ways that merit use of the present. When she was alive, she ran a nonprofit center for the arts with a will of iron. And I laugh just thinking about Calista and iron! Some years ago, she commissioned a piece by a young sculptor—an artist whose work I'll admit I actually admired, to a point. But a point decidedly shy of having a gigantic foot erected on the lawn of your Marin County home! A giant iron foot to serve as the backdrop for your daughter's wedding, countless showers and graduation galas, and two monumental anniversary parties: Garry and Calista's tenth and twentieth. The thirtieth will be this summer, but there will, in the end, be no party. We think (and I have been an instrumental part of this decision process) that Calista would have preferred not to celebrate anything just now, under the circumstances, and she's the one we have been trying to do right by.

The most recent lawn party was just a year ago, and I think we all knew it might be the last. Garry and Calista's son, Patrick, had graduated from high school. I drove out from the city the day before, a sheet cake the size of a small nation sprawled across the back seat. I was so terrified of crushing it I went forty-five the entire way. The Wertheims lived in the loft below ours before their kids were born, then moved to the suburbs to raise them, a move that made sense, for them. Witold and I pooh-poohed their flight eternally. Not a decision we'd have ever made ourselves, something that showed the differences in who we were and who they were. For all we liked one another, we weren't similar in the ways that friends often are. Witold and I could never have imagined leaving San Francisco; Calista and Garry dreamed of—and did it. Their kids are good people: Sarah, in dental school; Patrick—who's the spitting image of Calista, the wide-set eyes, broad jaw, that shock of blond, too towheaded for his age—now just finished his first year at UCLA. I like these kids, am proud of them in the way I imagine one might be of one's own. Children were not important to Witold and me, and though everyone wants to know if I regret that decision now that Witold is gone, I am more bothered by their questions than I am by my childlessness. *Just to have a part of him still here*, they suggest, and I think, *A part of him? I want all of him.* They want to know if I have missed seeing children grow up, and I say, *I have seen children grow up.* Do not be under the impression that I have glommed myself onto Garry and Calista's kids to vicariously experience the joys of parenthood. I have not. They know me, but not so well. I have been present, but not hovering. I did not want children. That has not changed.

So, the lawn party. Patrick's graduation. An early summer day just made for a garden party, all of us drinking the first gin and tonics of the season, feeling very Gatsbian in our floral dresses, our pale, lightweight slacks, shirts rolled up and open at the collar. As a graduation gift I had given Patrick a small painting of Witold's, a study he did for a landscape in the Sierras back when we were first married more than forty years ago. Witold's work stunned me when I first encountered it, and him, and still does now: such subtlety, so little representation, everything in the suggestion of what might be, an impressionistic haze of what actually was. Patrick thanked me for the gift profusely. Later, I was nursing my G&T in private, out of sight of the milling guests, on the far side of the garden shed when Garry came to me, a proffered spanakopita wedge bleeding grease onto a cocktail napkin. "He loves it, Lindy, *loves* it. I mean, *of course* he does—it's Witold's . . . Of course. But it's so special. Thank you." He pressed the hors d'oeuvre into my hand as if it were all he could do. Garry is an exceedingly earnest man.

"I'm so glad," I told him. "I thought he might."

"You know," Garry said, "you know what else?"

"What else?" I teased him. Getting to the point is not Garry's strong suit.

"You know what else he said? He came to me, totally unsolicited, totally on his own, out of the blue, he came up to me, just standing there by the bar, I was talking with Merle Buschbaum, and Merle wandered off and just Patrick and I were left, and he said, just looked right at me, like he knew, I swear, like he knew and he was somehow trying to say, 'Dad, it's okay, I know and it's okay, okay?' He said, 'Lindy's a really amazing woman.' Just like that. I think my jaw must've dropped into my drink. If he didn't know before, he had to know then."

I was smiling—a smile I hope conveyed what I was going for: love, mixed with sympathy and understanding, but not just *sympathy and understanding*, all full of priestliness and free love. I was trying for knowing understanding, with a dose of sagacity, for which I think Garry looks to me.

"I didn't know what to say," Garry continued. "It was like he knew, but how was I supposed to be *positive*? And how would he know anyway? Is it written on my face? Is he just a perceptive kid, just a super-perceptive kid who's figured it out somehow? We're not obvious. I know we're not obvious. There's no way we're obvious." He looked around him. No one was there. On the other side of the garden shed, Patrick's still-adolescent friends chatted it up with their parents' set, as if graduating from high school had suddenly made middle-aged men of them all. Their acne-scarred faces were puffed with self-importance that day. There was no one in the world who cared where Garry and I might be.

"We're not obvious," I said.

"I know," he said, "you're right. You're right. I know you're right. So I asked. I said, 'Patrick, what do you mean?' And he just answered, straight, honest, nothing to hide, just said, 'She's great. I just really like her.'" Garry was famous for impersonating his children's speech. "'She's always been around, and I guess I always knew she was great, but it's like it was just something I knew, like a family thing, like just something I knew was true because I knew you and Mom thought she was great but not because I knew myself that she was great. And then today she gave me the painting, and I just understood I guess somehow, that she really is great, and I understood why you and Mom love her so much.' And that was that, and then he saw some friend and he skittered off to talk to them, and that was it, and I still don't know what he knows or if he knows or what he was trying to tell me, but I swear it was like permission. Is that crazy? That's what it felt like. Is that absolutely crazy?"

"Maybe he was?" I offered.

"Giving permission?" Garry asked. "I don't know. Maybe he was." And I could tell the tears were welling then. He has cried in my presence enough that it was as if I could see the tears crowding up the back of his throat, thick and salty and all at once, the way tears come. We used to tease Garry; two things move this man to tears: *The Wizard of Oz* and marathons. I kid you not. The whole *there's no place like home, there's no place like home*, and the goodbyes to the Tin Man and the Lion and the Scarecrow, who she says she'll miss most of all—which I always thought was rather horrible, there in front of the rest of them, just to come right out and say that: you were my favorite, Scarecrow, my favorite one of all. But then at some point I suppose I understood that, too. Of course he was her favorite. And of course she could say so, and it wasn't callous, not really, it was just true: she loved him most. That scene, it sets Garry sniffling and snorting, the tears rolling down his cheeks—big, fat, wonderful tears. That and a good marathon. Something about the sheer exertion of it. Those guys careening past as we huddle behind the police do-not-cross lines cheering them on, and you can see their limbs working, pumping, more force than you've ever *seen* in the body of a human being. We teased Garry relentlessly, year after year: was it his long-lost dream to be a track star? *Garry*, we'd rib, *what is it, a repressed memory coming back? Were you forced to flee some childhood home? Hypnotized and made to run the 10K?* Only now do I think I understand that it is the power, the sheer power in those bodies flying past. And I love that about Garry: his unabashed love for things greater than himself. He is moved, deeply, by his own sense of awe, and I find myself thinking that such amazement and wonder are rare things to find in a man, a man his age in this jaded and cynical world. Witold was a wisecracker, a snubbing and stoic old bear, but now I see something Witold got from Garry: access to a vantage point less considered. I know what Witold loved.

Garry is Witold's oldest childhood friend, a psychologist. Calista is dying. Alzheimer's, early onset. Not like Witold's, which came with the age that expects it: he was ten years my senior, just past his seventy-sixth birthday when we buried him. Calista is fifty-five, looks ninety, and no longer knows what you mean when you sit her down on a toilet and tell her it's okay to go. We joke, morbidly, Garry and I, as people in such situations are bound to do, that there must be something in our water, but who knows, maybe there is. I know seven women—seven!—whose husbands have prostate cancer. Seven! Numbers like that you send to the EPA, the FDA, the FBI. The wives, send them to AA, because that's just about all that's getting anyone through this. Me, I don't drink much, never have. I am a doctor; I support my own small pediatric practice. Witold's paintings: brilliant. Some sold, more didn't. That's the way it goes.

"You should tell him," I told Garry. "You *could* tell him. If you wanted."

"Patrick?"

I nodded.

"Maybe he already knows?"

"Maybe it'd be nice to hear it from you anyhow?"

"Maybe . . ." he conceded. He walked away then, down to the water first, and then back up around the other side of the garden shed to the party, because we are not obvious. It doesn't matter so much if people know—would they blame us, really?—still, discretion seems in better taste, considering. I watched him, hidden where I was, as he returned to the party, to his guests and his wife, not yet in a wheelchair then but nearing it. I am often, it seems, watching Garry walk away, back to Calista, back to their children, to his outer life, to that preposterous iron foot on his lawn, and I cannot say I mind it so much. I am grateful for him. And I also don't mind being left again, to a spanakopita, say, or just to the view.

Garry called me at home later that night. He'd cornered Patrick in the kitchen when the last of the late-talkers had finally sobered enough for the drive and they'd gotten Calista to bed, laid her out, pillows propped under her legs, pillows wedged under her back. I've put her to bed myself on occasion, set her rear on the edge of the mattress and hoisted her legs up, swiveled her body into position. The stiffness is remarkable, as if the rigor mortis is already setting in. This disease is the slowest death, everything stiffening, slowing, lurching, dribbling, until it all finally stops for good, and I, of course, can't help but wonder what it would have been like to do this with Witold, what Garry does for Calista. So they'd put her to bed, and Garry'd had enough gin to give him the gumption, and he cornered Patrick and said, "What did you mean before, what you said about Lindy, Pat?" And Patrick seemed befuddled for a moment, then asked, "Wait, Dad, why?" and Garry realized he didn't know anything, and then he told him everything.

When Witold died it made sense that Garry was the one who was there, on hand, taking care of me. He was Witold's closest friend, of course, but we had ties beyond that already, both of us spouses of this disease. Calista was bad then, but every stage seems bad until the next creeps in and is inevitably and terribly worse and you wonder how you ever could have complained before. When Witold died, Calista understood what had happened, certainly, came to the funeral with Garry, dressed in black, was quiet and hunched but said appropriate things when asked and no one minded the mumbling, as it was somber, for a somber occasion. It'll be three years in August, and her decline in that time has been swift. She is a gouged-out version of the woman she was, and it's clear that soon there will be absolutely nothing left but a body pumped and coaxed into sustaining existence, for what purpose it's unclear. When Witold died, Garry kept saying to me the thing that everyone will one day say to him, which is what people said to his mother when his father passed away twenty years ago: *It's those who've had good marriages who are able to go on and love again.* Garry said it to me when it was too soon to say anything like that, and it made me angry and I told him so. And as the months after Witold, without Witold, passed, he said it again and again. He said he had friends, colleagues, widowers and divorced men who'd very much like to meet me, when I was ready, *whenever* I was ready. *I'm not ready*, I told him. *I have someone*, he'd say. *I'm still not ready*, I'd tell him. *You just let me know*, he'd say. *Okay Garry, enough already.* He'd say, *Lindy, you just let me know when.*

Which is where my preface, or my disclaimer, my plea for leniency comes in. I don't know why that matters so much to me, but for some reason it does: the forgiveness of strangers. Please try to understand the circumstances of the situation: my husband of thirty-eight years was dead, gone, not coming back. Witold was the one. There's no question anywhere, in anyone, about that. He was the man I was supposed to spend my life with. And I did. We did. Like his paintings, there was something about Witold that will seem forever unknowable, made him fascinating to me, every day, always one step out of reach. And then he died, and I was supposed to go on somehow, and I did. And with Garry it was the same: I wasn't the one he was supposed to be with, that was Calista, absolutely. And though Calista was not—is not—dead, *his* Calista *was*, shriveled away inside a wizened shell that bears her likeness. Somewhat. So when Garry asked, needled one more time about getting me back out and into the world again, which meant getting me out and attached to a man, I told him the thing that was really on my mind, and I said it without apology and—I hope you will believe me—without expectations. I said, "Garry, I think the only person I could ever imagine getting involved with is you." I don't think I even realized before I said it the way it might sound. All I think I meant to say was what I knew to be true: he really was the only person I could imagine being with. We were together so much already, and he knew Witold so well, knew that no one would ever replace him. And then there was Calista and the whole sick irony of our circumstance. This was true: I couldn't imagine another man, but I could imagine Garry. It was something he hadn't let himself imagine at all, but once it was said, once it was out there, we knew, of course, it was the thing we would do.

So he told Patrick everything that night after the graduation party. Or everything that Patrick would need or want to hear. He asked some questions—not prying into his dad's business, which is clearly what Pat saw this as, his dad's business—just trying to get some things straight, and then he left it, gave his blessing, as it were, *mazel tov* to you both. He said, and I am relaying here only what Garry told me, he said, *I'm glad you have each other. It seems like that would make things a little easier.*

A year after the graduation party, Patrick was home from his first year at school, the term just let out. Garry called me from his office downtown, as he often does in the afternoon. "It's me," he said.

"Hi me," I said.

"What're you doing?"

"Not much, puttering. You?"

"Getting ready to go," he said. It was nearing six o'clock. I leave my office most days by five. I am not a doctor the way other people are doctors. I do sore throats, chicken pox, tetanus shots, referrals to specialists. I have time for other things. "Mrs. Velasquez is with Calista until eight," he told me. "Want to have a drink or something?" He gets shy when he asks me to do something, as though we were dating, as though we were lovestruck.

"Come over," I told him.

"I'm coming," he said.

I fluffed the throw pillows on the couch and put a CD of Witold's in the stereo. I had gin and some tonic, slightly flat, and a not thoroughly desiccated lemon in the vegetable bin, which I sliced, thinly, so the browning rind wouldn't show. I thought to make dip: a can of chickpeas in the cabinet, some cilantro from the farmer's market. I threw things into the food processor. Too late I realized I had nothing to dip, then found tortillas in the freezer, cut them in fourths, and stuck them on cookie sheets in the oven to crisp. I was setting the basket of warmed chips on the coffee table when I heard Garry's feet on the stairs and the ring of the doorbell.

Our hug was long, then he turned, an arm around my waist, and guided me to the couch. "How was your day?" he asked, his hand kneading my knee. I cannot help but wonder how it feels for him to touch me. Is it the way he used to touch her? Is the touching an action that comes from him or a reaction to me?

"How was yours?" I asked.

Neither of us answered.

"Would you like a drink?"

He shook his head, looked at his watch, imagined, I assume, the traffic he'd hit on his way home. He shook his head again.

"There's a conference in Sacramento next week," he told me. "They asked me to go as an envoy for the practice. I think they think I need a vacation."

"In Sacramento!" We laughed.

"And with Patrick home . . ." he said.

"He feels okay, staying alone with her?"

"He thinks so," Garry said. At that point, for the most part, it was like taking care of a child.

"That's good, for you to get away," I told him. Good for Garry to have a few days filled with something other than decay, which is worse than death, if you ask me.

"It makes me nervous," he said.

"It'll be good for you," I said again.

We kissed on my living room sofa the way teenagers do, his hand still on my knee, both of us sitting upright as though we expect to hear the turn of our parents' keys in the door. He kissed the crown of my head, my eyelids, my mouth. I curled my legs underneath me and leaned into him. He stroked my hair. Every few minutes he checked his watch. At seven he got up to go, and I got up and wrapped the untouched dip and put it away in the refrigerator, feeling a little looser, twilit, as though I'd had a gin and tonic after all. I called my favorite Chinese place and ordered mu shu for delivery.

Garry flew to Sacramento on a Tuesday. Thursday, at 4:30 a.m., my phone rang.

"Lindy, this is Patrick."

"Patrick," I gasped, "what's wrong?" It is my great failing as a medical practitioner, this inability not to leap, immediately and with great alarm, to the worst-case scenario.

"I'm so sorry to call so early," he said. "I'm really sorry. You're the person I thought of. I just woke up to pee and found Mom in the hall. She was kind of sleeping in the hall on the floor, you know?" The poor kid sounded blurred in sleep himself, ripped out of it, some tenacious neurons still clinging to unconsciousness. "She woke right up, and she seems okay, really, but it's hard to tell. I mean you know how she is normally, and it's hard to tell what's okay. But she's got a cut on her head. It looked really scary at first—there was dried blood all clotted in her hair, but I got a washcloth and cleaned it off and it doesn't look so bad, not deep or anything, but there was a good amount of blood. I brought her back into the bedroom and everything, and I saw where she'd fallen, just gotten out of bed and tried to walk, which she really can't do anymore, and fell against the bookshelf. So there's blood on the edge of the bookcase and drops on the floor, and . . ."

"Okay, couple things," I said, "Can you go check her eyes? Check to see that the pupils are the same size."

"I'm on the cordless," he said. "I'm going in there." A pause. "Mom?" he said. "Hey Mama, hey let me get a look at your eyes, okay? I've got Lindy on the phone and we just want to make sure you're okay, so let me have a look at your eyes, please?" There was a moment of scuffle, of Calista's garbled murmurs, Pat's voice soft and cooing, and then he was back with me. "They look okay, her eyes. I don't see any difference. She really does seem totally okay, I just wanted to make sure, you know?"

"It was right to call me."

"Okay," he said.

I pressed my fingers to my eyes, thinking. "We just want to make sure she doesn't have a concussion, is the thing. She's not nauseated, is she? She's not throwing up or dizzy or anything?"

"No, I don't think so. It's hard to tell about dizzy, but she's sitting up okay. No, I don't think she's dizzy." He paused. "It looks like what's bothering her most is her finger."

"Her finger?"

"I think she fell on it or something. It looks pretty swollen. It's her ring finger. I tried to get the ring off, but it's too swelled up already. Do you think that's bad? Should I be worried about that? Is it going to cut off her circulation or something? It's really swelled up pretty big . . ."

"You can't get it off at all?"

"No," he said. "I can't budge it. It's really tight. It's a little purplish."

"Shit," I said.

"That's bad, isn't it? Shit." He was scared.

"Well, it's not good. But let's see . . ."

"Shit—Dad said something about this, I think. I think her fingers were getting really swollen already, from the medication I think, or something, and they couldn't get the ring off her finger and Dad was nervous about it. He wanted to go get it cut off, and I think Mom got totally upset, like she really didn't want to have it cut off . . ."

"It's okay, we're not getting it cut off yet. Let's see if we can get the swelling down on its own, get the ring off intact. Do you think you can get her to ice it? Make up a bowl of ice cubes with just a little bit of water and get her to keep her hand in it, really ice it down?"

"I can try . . ."

"Keep her awake, if you can? Keep looking for signs if she's feeling ill or acting strange or different from usual. And ice her finger down like that awhile and then maybe try some grease—butter, or cooking oil. Or something soapy—dish soap, maybe Windex, something like that—see if you can't get the ring off on your own?"

"Okay," he told me.

"I'll call you in an hour to check. But if you need anything before then, you call me, okay? I'm awake. You call."

"Okay."

And we hung up, I lay back in my bed, the bed I shared with Witold, our wedding band still round my own fourth finger. My husband and I were married thirty-eight years, from a wet spring in '59 when my heels sank into the country club turf on my way down that lily-lined aisle, until a rainy afternoon three summers ago when he gave up for good. Not on me. He didn't give up on me. And not on himself. You could say he gave up on life, though that wouldn't be quite accurate either. Really he gave up on a fight he knew he was going to lose, and though it hasn't been easy without him, it wouldn't have been any easier if he'd stuck around, and I will respect his decision until the day I die myself, and probably beyond. He did it when he felt it in the painting—when he felt it in his hands—and he did it as smoothly as he could: every pill in the medicine cabinet one afternoon I'd gone to the movies with Lorraine Fuchs looking for a little respite from the rain. The note he left me I can recite by heart, not because I'm morose, but because I loved him and couldn't help it, and I'll say this: anyone in my position would do the same. Not intentionally, but I memorized it the way I know every line, back and forth, of the telegram that arrived for me at a Miami hotel in 1956, three days after the man who sent it was supposed to have arrived. *Dear Lindy*, it said. *STOP. Stuck in Toledo. STOP. Can't get away. STOP. Sorry. STOP. Please don't call. STOP. Bob.* And what could I do then with the rest of my romantic week in Miami but walk the beach and feel those few abbreviated lines scroll through my head like stock tickers. *Please don't call.* It was clear right there—was it not?—that he was married. *Bob.* No love, no nothing. *Bob.* No promises, no futures. Just *Bob*, come clean, down to the barest bones of himself: *Bob.* And he's no one to me, *Bob.* He's a memory of disappointment, a path I thought my life might take forty-odd years ago but didn't. Still, his words are stored in the same part of my brain that takes care of the Valentine I received from Freddy Arthur, school champion track and field, in the seventh grade: *I'd trade my shot put for you . . .* The part that will forever remember what Jake Abernathy penned in my high school annual: *Lovely Lindy—why weren't you ever mine?* Why indeed? I asked. Why indeed? Peter Barkley's final scrawled goodbye, not the sweetest, but not by far the sorriest farewell bid me in my time. He fancied himself a poet. *L—Misconnections abound. Shouldn't we let what falls apart must? We DO have this . . . don't ask for any more. I'm not. P.* Witold's last note to me rests there among them, not the company I'd choose for it to take, but there it lies despite me. *Dearest Lin, please do not hate me for doing this. I think you'd never have let me if I'd asked, so I am not asking, just doing, and I'm hoping you will understand. I want to erode in the ground, where folks were meant to erode, not up here, before your eyes, before my own. I feel more sadness in leaving you than I ever knew a person could feel, but I also feel relief and I hope you will allow yourself to feel it too. Go on, my love, and live.* There is more, and I could tell it line for line, but this, I think, is enough.

At eleven, I dressed, got the car, and drove out to Marin. Pat was in the kitchen making lunch, and he greeted me with a handless hug, his fingers wet with tomato and mayonnaise. I hugged him back awkwardly, wondering how strange it must have been for him—*was* it strange?—to welcome the woman who is not his mother, who sleeps with his father. He was gracious and friendly and nice as he always has been, and I wondered if I could muster that, in his place, my mother dying slowly on the other side of the wall. He waved me toward Calista's bedroom. "She's belligerent today," he warned, and I thought how much he is like Garry, acknowledging and sad, but ever tolerant of their situation with Calista, talking matter-of-factly about the state of her degeneration, whatever it may be. Perhaps this is just what it's like: like watching children grow and monitoring their progress. *Today she made a fist. Today she said Mama. Today she forgot my name. Today she forgot her own.* I remember Calista when Patrick was just born, dress styles so short then that the ends of her long, long hair met the hem of her skirt, as she stood and swayed on the porch, the baby in her arms, and I watched her long thin legs, the muscles over her knees bunching up and releasing as she rocked, and I envied her those legs, nothing detracted from them through the ordeal of childbirth. She was a dancer in her youth. I am not an ungraceful human being, but Calista was something quite more than graceful.

That day she lay in bed, her yellow-gray hair matted in choppy chunks around her face, sheared off last winter when she got it caught in a door and they finally said to hell with vanity, against protestations from Calista so vehement they sent Garry crying to the phone to call me. When I came into the bedroom, Calista was involved in something that looked like exercises, and she seemed angry, muttering to herself as she moved her arms up and down, from her sides to her head, like a child making snow angels, trying to imprint some evidence of herself on the face of a world she'd already left behind. She showed me no recognition at all as I checked her eyes, found them clear, checked the finger that was worrying Pat. As near as I could figure, she seemed to be making something of a plea, an angry, adamant, I've-had-enough-of-this-crap sort of a plea. She seemed to be mad about the exercises: why was she being forced to perform them? Whose life was this anyway, goddamnit? Did we just expect she'd keep up this bullshit repetition forever? I asked Pat later in the kitchen, "Are the exercises part of some doctor's regime?"

"Exercises?" he asked. "What exercises?"

I called Garry from their house. Pat and I decided that to hear it from me would panic him less. I was worried about the ring; her finger was purple, and I thought something needed to be done. Patrick sat in a chair opposite the living room couch and watched me anxiously as I dialed, waiting to see the change in my face when Garry answered the phone.

"Garry, it's me."

"Lindy!" And I realized he thought this was a love call, a quick buzz in his absence to say, *I miss you darling*, which I would never do.

"I'm calling . . . Everything's okay, basically, but I wanted to call and let you—"

"What? What happened? Lindy. What's wrong? What?" I cursed myself for his anxiety.

"Everything's fine. Garry, shhh. We're all fine. But Calista took a fall last night, in the middle of the night. I'm at the house now, and she's fine: a bump on the head . . ."

"Oh Jesus."

"No, really she's fine." Such an absurd thing to say. *Fine? She's fine?* Could she have been any further from fine?

I told Garry about the ring, and he swore at himself, loudly, with such violence, alone in his hotel room. "Dammit! Goddammit!" he cried. "I knew it! I knew we should've . . . She got so angry. I couldn't fight her again . . . Goddammit to hell!"

"It's okay," I told him.

"It's not okay!" He sounded like me.

"I know."

He was silent a moment. "I'm coming home," he said. "I'll catch a flight tonight." His voice was at once imperative and resigned, as though he had done this sort of thing a thousand times before. I thought of him suddenly as a parent whose child has run away for the umpteenth time: does the panic feel any less acute the twenty-second go around?

"There's no reason for you to come home," I told him. "No reason. Stay. We're under control. Don't cut the trip short."

I could feel him slipping off an edge. "Well what am I supposed to *do*?" he wailed.

I started to say, *I don't know*, but that wasn't true; I knew exactly what I thought he should do. "I think we need to . . ." I stopped. I started again. "I have less right than none to order this . . ." And I had to stop again: this wasn't about right, it was my medical opinion, and that ought to prevail. "The ring should come off, Garry. It's her finger I'm worried about. I think the ring needs to come off." I waited, afraid of what he might say, realizing that I had never been afraid of Garry before. Across the room, Patrick waited, frozen. His face is Calista's face, and it was set as Calista's might be if she were over-hearing this conversation.

Suddenly Garry choked on the other end of the line—"No!"—as though someone had burst into his room, grabbed him in a headlock from behind and pulled. "I'll come home, I'll be there tonight, I can't . . ." and I could see then why this was so much more than irony, so much more than medicine and sense and logical decision-making. I asked myself: Could I have mashed up the pills in vanilla ice cream and fed them to Witold on a spoon I'd fetched myself from the kitchen drawer? Could I have done that? And the answer was no. It didn't take much hesitation for me to know that. No, I could not have done it. I was searching inside myself for the right thing to tell Garry, a compassionate way to say, *this is a decision that a person should not have to make*, but I couldn't find the words. All I could find was the stark and irrelevant idea that this was Calista's decision—not Garry's—to make, and I was suddenly and preposterously angry at this woman, this woman who should have been *insisting*, god-dammit, on her own, finding the language for it somewhere in the twisted circuits of her mind to tell me herself: *Saw off the ring, Lindy. What use do I have for it now?* She was cognizant enough at the time of Witold's death. Witold said goodbye, and it was hard to say and hard to hear and always would be, but it was right, and inevitable, and he is gone and we are left, and that is sad, but it is true, and that is that. Calista couldn't have wanted her life anymore, and I realized I was angry for every day that had already passed. Every day she had been left alone for an hour by herself and not attempted to swallow the arsenal of pills stocked in the kitchen cabinet like vitamins, to amass the Cognex, the Exelon, Reminyl, Aricept and wash it all down with the Draino they keep under the bathroom sink, so old it doesn't have a safety cap. Even if it didn't kill her . . . She hadn't tried. And I resented her for that, for not even trying.

"You shouldn't have to make this decision," I told Garry. Patrick's face had fallen in resignation. I could not help but imagine Garry's doing the same all those miles away.

There was only silence from Garry, and I was afraid again. When he spoke, his voice was hard and uncompromising. "Well who the hell's supposed to make it then?" he demanded.

There was nothing to say to that, so I didn't.

"Do you think," Garry spat, "Do you think that Witold was more valiant? That he loved you more? That not putting you through this meant he was a better person than she is? Is that really what you think, Lindy?" And he waited. He wanted a response.

"That's not what I mean . . ." I started, suddenly certain that Patrick could hear everything Garry was saying, everything I was thinking, too. I hated that I might become something new in Patrick's eyes, not *awesome*, not the person helping his father through that time, but something horrible, someone horrible: someone who wanted to see his mother dead.

By the time Garry said, "Don't pull that, Lindy," I was already in tears. Patrick stood and left the room, in deference to my privacy. Garry thought I should cry *more*, for god's sake. Because there's a part of Garry that hates Witold for leaving. Part of him that thinks I should hate him too, for taking it all into his own hands, for leaving the rest of us with nothing to do. "Witold was the selfish one," Garry said. "He never let us—goddamn it!—He didn't even let us mourn! *Go on*," Garry mimicked, "*go on and live your lives!*"

"Don't," I shrilled. "You have no right to . . ."

"*I* have no right?" he yelled. "Who has a right then? Who has a right then, Lindy, tell me that, okay?" And he was crying then, too, and I didn't know what we were yelling about anymore, and there was nothing more to say. I just kept holding the phone to my ear as if I could will him through it, will him close to me, so we could hold on. That is what we have done best for each other, what we have been: someone to hold onto.

When we hung up, I wanted to compose myself, blow my nose, splash some water on my face. The guest bathroom is past the kitchen and I didn't want to see Patrick yet, not like that. I walked down the hall to Garry and Calista's room, heading for their bathroom, hoping Calista would not be awake, knowing it wouldn't matter if she was. I could not stop crying, but what state was Calista in to even notice? I pushed open the door and there she was, on the bed, her arms still working, up and down, up and down, and I was too far gone for patience. "Calista," I scolded her, my voice condescending and mean, "what are you *doing*?"

Her arms stopped abruptly and dropped to her sides, and she looked down at them for a moment, bewildered, then turned her face back up to me. The look in her eyes was no longer blank. Her forehead furrowed in intelligent consternation and she spoke, her voice lucid and clear as it used to be. She said, "I have absolutely no idea."

For a moment I stood there just staring at Calista, Calista staring at me like she was back, snapped out of it, returned from her delirium, sobered and steeled and ready to get on with her life. For a moment she was Calista again, and I was me, and we were friends. And then the next moment she was gone, the light of recognition passing from her face the way the soul may seem to pass from the eyes of the dying, and I thought, this is what she does, day after day: she practices dying. Her eyes went blank, and with great effort she lifted her arms from the bed again, above her head and then back down, up and down, up and down. I don't even think she saw me when I turned away, into her bathroom, where I tried to put my face back on.

WIN'S GIRL

I'm not ever going to be Win Cryer's girl—still, I'm here at the Quarry Bar to hear him play every Friday night at ten, up front, watching him like I *am* the guitarist's girl. Like I *am* someone Win Cryer loves. I get off work at the slaughterhouse at five, and that's enough time to drive home, have a shower, heat something for dinner, open the mail, watch a little TV, and still make it to the Quarry before the crowd claims my table near the stage. By nine the bar's filling up, most folks not even changed from their work clothes—some guys from the cheese factory shooting pool in their coveralls, a young pimply drunk zipped into his Jiffy Lube jacket hunched over a tall glass of bourbon. Lonny Bondorf—*Officer* Bondorf—walks toward my table like he's ready to arrest me.

I take out a cigarette and go for my matches, but Lonny's there with a lighter so fast he nearly burns my nose off. "Here for Win's show?"

"Always," I say.

Lonny's quiet a minute. "Think he knows you? Win? Think he remembers you from every week?"

I shake my head. "I don't know."

"So how're things with you?" asks Lonny. Lonny is a thirty-eight-year-old bachelor who'd like not to be. I guess you could say nearly the same thing about me: past forty, not a lot of prospects.

"Going okay," I tell him. "My money from the accident just came through." Lonny was one of the first people on the scene that night when they pulled me from my truck, blood running out my knees like garden spigots. I'd been on my way home from work, stopped at a light waiting for it to go green when a drunk from Fairfield jumped the divider and plowed me head-on. He didn't die either, which I'm glad about.

"You should get something nice for yourself, Doreen," Lonny says.

"I'm thinking I'm going to have the house rewired," I tell him.

"Aw, that's no fun . . ." Lonny chides.

"Funner than frying in some electrical fire," I say. "You know how overdue that house is for an upgrade?"

"So you got someone to do it already?" Lonny asks.

"Rudy Hatch had a look at it a while back . . . since he moved I've been nervous about finding someone else, getting bids . . ."

"My sister-in-law had some work done on her fuse box couple months ago," Lonny says. "Some guy drives in from Solon. Said he did a good job, if I remember right."

"You remember the name?" I ask.

"Duane," he says, then pauses, thinking, "Duane . . . Miller maybe?"

"Duane Miller," I repeat. "I'll look him up."

On stage, Win turns to talk to his bassist, and then a drumbeat starts in and I'm recognizing one of my favorite songs. And for a second, as Win turns back around to the audience, I think that maybe he's playing it for me, because even if that smile tucked into his face in the shadow of his hat brim is for everyone out here, it's for me too.

Monday on my lunch break I call Duane Miller, who sounds like the nicest guy in the world, but he's over his head in work and doesn't foresee an end to it any time soon.

"Shoot," I tell him. "I really want to get this done . . ."

"Hey," he says, "I know someone who might be able to fit you in. He's union, so this'd be off the record. He's got a side business, totally legit tax-wise and all, but the union'd bust the hell out of him if they found him out. But it's totally cool," says Duane. "Only way some of these guys can make a go of it."

I'm thinking that Duane surely knows more than me about all this. Also, maybe it's not a bad idea to have something on the guy I hire, something that'd make him scared to do me wrong.

"Here, I got the number," says Duane. "His name's Rich. Rich Randall. Real good electrician. He'll do you what needs done."

Rich Randall's answering machine says, "Hey you've reached Rich at A-1 Electric. Can't catch you right now. Leave a message and I'll give y'a ring," and he sounds young and laid back and I don't feel stupid leaving my name and number, my little story.

He calls back that very afternoon, and the fact that I'm at a desk at work to answer the phone makes me grateful all over again in a weird way for my accident. I used to be on the floor, standing all day, sawing carcasses, but my legs can't take it now. Lots of people thought I shouldn't have been doing it in the first place—it's more men's work on the floor—but I'm no small girl and I had the strength for it.

"Hey Doreen," says Rich. "Thanks for your message. Love to come have a look at your wiring. When's good for you?" Rich agrees to come over after I get off work. "Look forward to meeting you," he says. I hang up relieved that this is going to be easier than I'd thought, taking care of my parents' house the way a grown person should. It's been mine since my dad passed. He was a house painter by trade, a handyman of all sorts at home, though since he's been gone, I've found out my dad didn't know quite all he *thought* he knew about house repair. Last year I started blowing fuses right and left—that's when I had Rudy Hatch in to see what the hell was going on. Rudy was hooting at some of the rig-ups Dad had going. Crazy wiring strung together like daisy chains, all the parts salvaged from junk and practically held together with duct tape. The bid he made to bring me up to code came in at just under four thousand dollars, which I didn't have at the time. Plus, it seemed sad to take apart all Dad's work.

Rich Randall arrives at my house a few minutes behind me, just enough time for me to clean out the cat box. He's younger than I am, maybe thirty, and the first thing I think is he looks like my ex-boyfriend Walter, but in a good way. The bad parts of Walter take over the good ones in my memory. Walter had told me he was a roofer. We'd been going out five months before I found out he was making methamphetamines in his bathtub. And I'm not the kind of person who dates a drug dealer, and a liar on top of it, but somehow, in the end, it was like I got dumped for not being cool enough to be the girlfriend of a big-time Iowa meth dealer. Same with the car accident: it was Lonny Bondorf who made me press charges, found me a lawyer, and made me go through with it. I'd never have done it on my own. I'd have found some way to think that sitting at a stoplight and getting head-onned by a drunk guy in a Blazer was something I was a hundred percent to blame for.

Rich removes his cap, holds out a hand. "Real good to meet you." He looks like a little bit of a brute, but sweet too, balding too early but owning up to the truth of the thing and shaving his whole head. His sweatshirt says, "Local #329, Union Yes!" which comforts me.

We go through the house together, him apologizing for every bureau and plant stand he has to push out of the way, me apologizing for it being in the way in the first place. Rich speaks with authority, explains his terms, talks me through what he's doing and lets me stop him when I don't understand something—"*Pigtail?*" I repeat—and then tucks his face under the bill of his cap while he backtracks, embarrassed by his own failure as my guide through the world of electricity. "It's just the word we use," he says, "for how you attach the new wire to the old wire?" He's making sure I'm with him every step.

"Got it," I say.

"You're great," he tells me. "Most people just want to keep *not* knowing what the hell's going on in their walls. They're just like, 'You do it and tell me when you're done.' And then you get done and show them the bill and suddenly they're all *real* interested in it all."

"My dad was a housepainter," I say. "He used to get so mad about the people who'd hire you to do a job and then sit watching over your shoulder every move you made. Or they'd change their mind five times about what color they wanted for the vestibule and then acted like it was your fault when the paint looked different on the wall than it did on the True Value Hardware card," I tell him. "I guess I also just hate feeling ignorant."

"And *that's* great." He's looking right at me. "I believe everyone should know as much as they can about stuff." Pausing at the top of the stairs, he leans on the banister. "Like take for instance: I play guitar . . ."

"You do?" I blurt.

"Yeah, got a band, kind of on the edge. Lot of computer technology, samples . . . ? So like I was saying: I need someone to work on my guitar, I want to know what he's doing. I want to know he's not saying like, oh you need new pickups and the action adjusted, which'll be like five hours of labor, and then really all he's done is solder one miniscule fucking wire and I'm paying through the nose. It's the same thing. I mean, here's this thing that you don't know jack about, and here I am and this is what I *know*, you know? I mean, I *know* electricity. And I could tell you anything and you'd have to be like *okay, sure, whatever you say.*"

"I did have a couple other people look at it . . ." I tell him.

"And *that's* why you're the best kind of customer," he says, "because you're *informed*. Because you're not just letting someone tell you what to do."

"I hope so." I want to trust Rich, but you do hear horror stories.

"Here's what should happen," Rich tells me. "You need to think about this. Make sure I'm the right person for this job. I can get you some references, if you want . . ."

I shake my head, embarrassed that he thinks I'd check up on him.

"Well, I can give 'em to you. I'm a good electrician. I'm an excellent electrician, really. You don't have to have any doubt about that."

Downstairs, Rich sits at my kitchen table doing some calculations while I make him a cup of coffee. Then I sit down and we go over them. He points to some numbers: "Here's materials," he says, "and projected labor." He points again: "And here's your total. Might be a little higher than the bids you got before, and I know that I do charge a little more for labor than some, but I stand behind the fact that my work's worth it. I lose some business probably—people not willing to pay for a job done right. People willing to cut corners. And I'm just not. Not with electricity. We're talking about *safety* here." His bid is not too far over Rudy's, given that he's talking about dealing with the grounding in the basement and the outdoor sockets that Rudy never even thought about. "Not to take anything away from your old electrician," Rich says, "but some people just don't think of everything, you know?"

I wait a day before I call Rich back to tell him yes, let's start, whenever he's ready. "I actually just had a cancellation on another job," he says. "Haven't wanted to take too much on, with the move and all . . ."

"Oh! You're moving?"

"Yeah, yeah, we've been out in Texas part-time for a while, back and forth, seeing how hard it's going to be to find work and stuff. My wife's there now, in fact, trying to find us a place, so I'm on kid-duty till she gets back. But I can start Monday, if that's good with you, Doreen?"

"You have kids?"

"Seven and three," he tells me, and for a second I think he's telling me he's got ten children from two different women.

"That's great," I say.

"Yeah, we'll see how great it is by the end of the week. They miss Mommy right now. Tell you the truth, I don't blame 'em. I miss Mommy, too."

I laugh a little.

"So I'll see you Monday, Doreen?"

"Great," I say, and it all seems way too easy. "Um, I work, but the door's unlocked. You can just come in . . ."

"That's okay with you?" he asks. "You're okay having me here while you're not home? Some people are funny about that—s'why I ask."

"Oh, it's fine," I say, the doubt washing over me, sudden as a sickness.

Rich hedges a moment. "I hate to bring money into this, but I guess that's what makes work go 'round. The way I usually do it is I have you give me half up front, for purchasing supplies and materials, and half on completion."

"That sounds fair," I agree. I try to think of what I'm supposed to ask. "Should . . . could I leave a check for you on Monday?"

"A check's just fine. Oh, oh, also," he says, "I just wanted to make sure—Duane told you about the union stuff right? We all do it—only way to hack it with the way everything works nowadays—I just wanted to make sure Duane let you know about that. That you were okay with that, and all."

"Yeah," I stammer, "yeah, he said about you doing stuff on the side . . ."

"That man is a fucking prince," Rich says. "When you said it was Duane sent you, I knew this was a job I'd take. He puts me in touch with the nicest people."

After the car accident, the doctor at the hospital assigned me to a lady at the Community Mental Health Center to go talk to if I wanted, if anything about the accident—or anything—was bothering me, keeping me awake at night, making it hard to go about my life, work, whatever. Honestly, I think it was my job the doctor was worried about. When he found out I worked on the slaughterhouse line he went a little white. Men worry like that, can't believe what I do—what I *did*—for my job. But he meant well, so I took the number, and then when I was feeling sort of blue afterward, working in the office, feeling washed-up and old, Sherry, who works next to me, said, "Why don't you go see that counselor, Doreen, see if she's got anything to say."

The therapist's name was Brianna, which she pronounced like she was royalty: Bree-*ahh*-nah. When I first went to see her, she pried a while into the accident but more into my job, like she was sure I had a whole world of rage under my skin she was dying to tap. She scheduled me for another appointment. I was too embarrassed to argue. Maybe there really was something smoldering in me that I didn't even know about? I go and see her every other week now. Mostly she tells me the sagas of her love life, which are always turbulent and interesting in a soap-opera kind of way.

The day after I meet Rich I'm scheduled with Brianna, and when she politely asks me how I am before she launches into her latest drama, I find myself talking about the electric job and about Rich Randall.

"Is this a man you're attracted to, Doreen?" she asks right away.

"No," I say too quick. "No, I mean, no, I mean, he's married."

Disappointed, Brianna switches tactics: "Is it . . . ? Are you . . . nervous about having this man in your house while you're not there? That can definitely feel very invasive, Doreen. Your home is a private place. It's your nest, you know, where you're most fully yourself. Maybe think about taking Monday off work? They can get along without you at the slaughterhouse for one day. *You* let yourself get worked too hard." Brianna is always suggesting this, and I've run out of ways to try to tell her that I'm fine. It seems like unless you're lower than low or happier than God, no one believes a thing you tell them when they ask how you are.

But when my alarm goes off Monday morning, I don't want to go to work. By seven-thirty I've convinced myself that it'd be irresponsible to just leave my parents' home in the hands of some stranger. For the first time in ten years at the slaughterhouse—not counting after the accident, when I couldn't even walk—I call in sick.

It's almost noon before Rich arrives. "Doreen! Didn't expect you here!"

"I got the day off," I say, but suddenly I'm scared he thinks that I'm mad he's getting started so late, and the thought of him—a grown man waiting to be scolded—makes me suddenly miss my father. Dad took care of things, and even if he didn't know exactly what he was doing all the time, he *felt* like he did, and I felt sure in his sureness. His absence hits me in the chest and it's like I can't breathe.

"Great," Rich says, "great to see you. I guess I'll just get to work then, if that's good with you." Rich hoists his tool belt on his hips and starts toward the nearest socket, aiming something that looks like a screwdriver with a crank to wind it like a music box. He unscrews the outlet cover, me feeling dumb just standing there watching.

"How are your kids?" I think to ask.

Rich laughs. "Surviving!" He pauses, leans against the wall like he needs a rest, shaking his head in near disbelief. "They're such a trip, you know?"

I shake my head. "I don't have any." I gesture around the house: no children hidden anywhere.

"Ha! It's a crazy thing . . ."

"Crazy?"

"God, you ever just listen to the things that kids'll say? I mean, just the shit that comes out of their mouth? It's such a trip! Kaylee, my daughter, she's three . . . ? She's got these really bad allergies and we have to pump her full of Benadryl before she goes to bed at night. And before she goes to sleep, she'll be totally wandering around the house all doped up saying the craziest, trippiest things. Last night some guys from the band were over and I swear I just followed Kaylee around with a mike, just picking up the crazy shit she was saying. It's going to be awesome when I get it looped onto a track."

I'm laughing, almost not believing what he's saying but laughing anyhow.

"God, you should totally have kids, Doreen. They're so damn

awesome." And he makes it sound like a good idea—like I should remember to pick up a couple kids next time I'm at the store. Rich turns back to the socket and pulls a wire from the wall, inspects it. "Okay," he says, "I see what we need here. Hey, so, Doreen, if you've got that check on you now, I'll go ahead, go get the supplies I need . . . ?"

"Oh, sure!" I say, way too chirpy. I get my purse and my checkbook and make out a check to Rich Randall for $2,500. "Don't spend it all in one place," I say, and Rich laughs like I'm actually funny, and I feel grateful for it. For the second time in ten minutes I feel the loss of my folks again so hard it could've been yesterday.

Rich is gone a couple hours, comes back carrying an old worn cardboard box full of stuff—tools and screws and nails and stuff—which he plunks down in the dining room and starts digging through. "Menards was all out of the wire I needed, but I hunted some down through my distributor," he holds up a spool, "so we're good to go." It's nearing three in the afternoon.

Rich works steadily through until four-thirty when he comes and finds me in the living room reading a magazine and tells me he's got to pick up his kids from his wife's mother's place. "Looking good," he says. "We'll have you all safe and up to code in no time."

"It'll really be a relief," I say. "I never had the money to do it. Until now. I was in a car accident and the settlement just came through, so I finally had some money . . . I mean, I don't *usually* have money. It was this crazy thing."

"It's weird, isn't it?" Rich says, "How you get a bunch of money all of a sudden and you think that it'll make everything easier, but it just gets super confusing. I mean, for instance: me and my wife, we came into a bunch of money kind of recently—like a good chunk of money, you know? And we thought, oh it'll all be so much easier now. But then there's all that shit about what do we spend it on, and her being like, *you are not using our money to buy that vintage guitar*, and me being like, *I sure as fuck am!*" Rich smiles. "And here you are doing the responsible thing, like my wife'd do, not like me. I'm bad. I mean, sometimes. I've been sober for five months now, but before that, you know, I used to get into some shit. In my youth, you know? And I know maybe it's not the most responsible thing, but you gotta live, you know? I mean, you ever do coke?"

I shake my head, no.

Rich's eyes are almost closed, like he's reliving a great pleasure. He breathes in deep. "Oh, boy," he says, letting his breath huff out of him in resignation. "Man, we used to do some incredible shit down in Mexico. You know how they make coke?" he asks. Again, I shake my head. "They do this whole process thing," he explains, "but the guys we knew down there, the guys who were making it, they'd have the purest kind, like the first, most pure stuff, and it'd be cut with peaches or coconuts. I mean, peach cocaine! You never had anything so incredible! But I got kids now. Family to think about. No more of that shit for me. No more heaven . . ." His head's beginning to wag back and forth as though he's watching it all slip away.

The next day I go to work, but I drive home on my lunch hour just to see how things are going. Rich isn't there, and it doesn't look like he has been. I make myself a sandwich. When the front door opens suddenly and it's him, I start, like I have something to hide.

"Doreen!"

"I'm sorry, I didn't mean to scare you. I just came home for some lunch." I hold up my dirty plate as evidence.

"I just didn't expect you is all. I'm just a little late getting started. It's been a hell of a morning. Jesus." He runs a hand over his head. "Jesus, it's been such a fucking morning. And I've got work to do. I've got a job to do here!" He looks around my house like it's the most important thing in the world to him, this old place. "I have been on the phone with lawyers all morning!" he blurts out. "They got my wife in jail. In Texas! Can you believe that bullshit? They want two thousand bucks' bail to get her out. So I'm down at the bank trying to get money fucking wired to Texas or some shit, and trying to get a lawyer out there for her. It's going to be a fucking fortune!"

"Wait," I say, "wait—what? Your wife's in *jail*?"

"Oh, it's total bullshit," Rich says. "Something about the place she's working out there. Or the place she worked at last year. Something. Like the company's being investigated for tax fraud or something and everyone who's working there during that time in question, they came and arrested them all. They say my wife knows something, which is bullshit; she doesn't know anything. And now I have to come up with two thousand bucks to get her out of jail. Which is such bullshit!"

"Wait," I say, trying to slow him down, trying to back this up to where I can understand it. "Wait, here, sit down." I pull him out a chair at the table. He looks about to bury his face in his hands and cry. I pull out the chair across from him. "Okay," I say, "go slow. Tell me what happened." I feel sort of like Brianna, if Brianna ever did her job right.

"Do they even understand the fact that she's got fucking *kids*? That there's two little kids at home saying 'Where's Mommy?' Jesus!" He hangs his head, and I'm afraid he really will cry.

"Okay," I say, "your wife worked for some company that's in trouble with the IRS and they arrested all the employees?! That can't be legal . . . They can't just . . ."

"Yeah, well, they did," he says. "And now I got to figure out how I'm going to get to Texas to go get her out of jail. And I've got this job to do for you, and . . ."

"Rich, you can finish here when you get back. It's okay."

He looks at me, then away, like he can't bear the kindness. "God, I'm glad it's you I'm working for right now. A union job and they'd say that's shit for luck, man, your wife's gonna have to find some other way out of prison, 'cause you ain't going nowhere!" Then there's resolve in his voice. "No," he says. "You know, my wife's mom's got the kids, and there's nothing I can do till the damn lawyer calls me back." He pats the cell phone in his pocket. "So I'm going to stay here, get as much done as I can so I can finish tomorrow maybe and have it off my mind. I tell you what, Doreen. I'll get to work, get a jump on this. Hey, and I'd really appreciate it if you didn't say anything about this, just for the kids' sake really. I just don't want everybody going around knowing Hailey Randall's in jail, you know? There's a lot of people who'll judge you without knowing anything about what it was about, you know?"

"It's no problem," I tell him. By my watch, it's ten past one and I'm about to be late back to work after lunch for the first time in my life.

Rich isn't there when I get home at 5:10 p.m. But at 8:30 p.m. there's a knock on the door. "Really sorry to bother you, Doreen," Rich begins. "I'm just trying to get all my business taken care of before I leave for Texas. I got a flight out, day after tomorrow. Kids're with my old partner, Butch, tonight. He's looking after them so I could buy some time, get things finished up. I got everything inside the house here done today. I've just got that stuff we talked about in the basement left. If I can get that taken care of tonight, I'll finish up tomorrow."

And now I'm feeling scared—wary, like this is too much, too irregular. But he's in such dire straits that I don't know how to figure out what's true. "How's your wife doing?" I ask.

"A mess," he says. "She's a total wreck. She's freaking out. It looks worse than she thought. I guess it's looking like she *did* know about what was going on in the office and all. Like she was aware and didn't do anything or just went along or something. I don't know what. She's just totally freaking out now." He stands there shaking his head a minute, then says, "Hell, might as well get some work done, keep my mind off it all." He starts fast toward the cellar door.

Late that night when I know Rich is gone, I go down to the basement. There's some sawdust on the floor beneath an outlet, which looks new, but I have no way of knowing what he's done—if he's done anything. In the morning I wake up panicked and take the day off work again. Rich arrives just past nine, looking like he hasn't slept. I have thought up a long story of why I am not at work today, but Rich doesn't even seem to notice I'm home when I shouldn't be.

"How you holding up?" I ask.

"To tell you the truth, it sucks," Rich says. "To tell you the god's honest truth, it's so much more messed up than I can even describe." He sinks down at the kitchen table. At a loss, I pour him a cup of coffee.

"What happened?"

"Well." He sips from his mug. "The truth is my wife *did* know about what was going on with her boss and the money and stuff. The thing is, I knew about it, too. It was, like, a totally low-key thing. Sort of a Robin Hood thing. The only people—and I mean *the only* ones—getting screwed were the fucking feds, and they're assholes. It was just this thing that had been going on forever at this company, just like a thing you went along with when you got hired, you know? So after all these years they finally get caught, and now it's *my wife* facing jail time! It's so fucking backwards!"

I don't even know what to say. I just want this all to be over.

"There's not much I got left to finish here," Rich says. "I'll be done today with pretty much everything."

"What *is* left?" I ask. Suddenly I wish I had an inventory, a plan, all written down in front of me. But it's way too late for that.

"Well, let's see . . . There's that fuse box," he remembers.

"And the outside switches," I remind him.

"Oh, yeah, right, forgot about those. The outside switches."

"And you did all the pigtailing already?" I say.

Rich smiles, slow and deep, like he's remembering a joy he'd thought was lost. "All pigtailed," he assures me. "Okay, so, I'll go out and get those switches now. Could I ask you, Doreen"—and he looks pained for a second—"could I ask if you could lay out that money? I left my check-book at home, and they put a fucking freeze on my credit cards while this shit gets sorted. Can you lay out for this material, and we'll subtract off what you'll still owe me?"

I feel frozen. "How much do you need?"

"Fifty'd do it. Or you could just make out the check to Menards and I'll fill in the amount. Whatever's good for you."

I panic. Everything in me's saying don't give this man any more money, but how do I not when he's acting like this is just how these things work? And maybe they do—what do I know? I try to tell myself about the union, that I can report him if I have to. I can't think: is it safer to give him a check or cash? I head for the stairs. "I think I have some money in the bedroom." *God, what a moron I am!*

Rich is gone for two and a half hours. I spend them practicing what to say when he comes back: *Rich, you can't just tell the person you're working for that you're part of criminal activity. You can't expect someone to trust you with their money when you tell them you've stolen money, even if it is from the IRS.* When he breezes back in the door, it's like he's been gone ten minutes. The pile of switches he drops on the kitchen table don't look like they came from any store at all. "Doreen? You think I could use your telephone for just a minute?" He looks like he's going to cry again, and I don't know what I can say but, "Sure."

He dials, leans against the wall, and waits. "Pumpkin," he says, "Pumpkin, it's Daddy . . ." And I think at least he wasn't lying about the kids. "Hey sweetheart, go get Uncle Butch and put him on the phone to talk to Daddy now, okay? Good girl."

"If she calls," Rich is saying into the phone, "you tell her keep her mouth shut. I'll be there tomorrow. I'll figure it out. Tell her *stay quiet,* okay?" He pauses a moment, listening. "Thanks, man, you're my hero." He hangs up the phone, then turns to me. "Oh, Doreen, what a fucking mess . . ." He sinks down at the table and lays his head on the switches and wires.

"Did something else happen?" I am a little kid: squeaky and dumb.

He lifts his head, wagging it back and forth remorsefully. "What a fucking disaster . . . This whole thing," he says. "It was supposed to be so easy. We were just going to do it and be done and that's it. It was so fucking easy . . ." He looks right at me, then back down, like he's ashamed. "I haven't told you the whole story," he says. "There's a lot more going on than . . . it was such an easy plan, and it worked so damn well. This guy, the one Hailey worked for—*works* for, I dunno—he got this RV, you know? One of those huge honking ones . . . ? And he got the whole inside hollowed out, and all Hailey has to do, for *two-thirds* the profit— *two-thirds!*—all she has to do is sit in the goddamn passenger seat and pretend the guy's her lover and she's going over to Mexico with him for the day—just going over with her little boyfriend for the day to have their little affair."

I don't want to know this. I don't want to be hearing this. And I know I don't want him to stop until I've heard it all.

"So they get pulled over on the way back into the States," he says. "Done it five, six times, no problem. *This* time they get pulled over. And you got to understand: the take was so good. How can you say no to money like that? We thought, we'll do it a few times, be able to get the kids some nice Christmas presents, just live comfortable. You know? We weren't trying to strike it rich or anything, just trying to make things nice for our kids . . ."

I'm nodding, I think. At least I mean to be nodding.

"So they get pulled over. And Hailey, Hailey's fucking intelligent. When they find the stash—the whole back of the RV's filled with pot now—marijuana, you know?—so when they find it Hailey starts doing a whole act like, 'What the fuck is going on, you bastard? You invite me to come over the border with you for a little fun and really you're running drugs? You fucking bastard!' She's making like she's got no idea beyond that she's having a little fling with a married guy, no idea about anything in the back of the RV. She's fucking brilliant. Only they bring her in anyway, with him, seize the whole fucking RV—we're talking five hundred grand in the back of that bus, sitting in some federal pen— five hundred grand of really fine marijuana, drying out in some government warehouse . . . it fucking kills me!"

"But she knew?" I manage to ask. "She knew the pot was there, right?"

"Yeah, yeah yeah yeah, I mean, we all knew. There was just Hailey and me and the guy driving the RV, really. Marshall. He's Butch's brother." Rich gestures toward the telephone.

I nod. I'm thinking: one-third Marshall's, and the rest—two-thirds— for Rich and Hailey. I'm thinking: I don't know how to live in this world.

When Rich leaves that night there is a pile of old electrical switches on my kitchen table. When I get home from work the next day, the pile is still there. When I call Rich's number, the machine picks up, same voice as before: "Hey you've reached Rich at A-1 Electric . . ." Of course, he's in Texas by now. If I can believe that much. I call and leave so many messages on his answering machine I'll be scared if he ever *does* call back. I try being nice, at first, but then I lose nice. I threaten to report him to the union. I threaten to sue him for the money he has taken from me, for the work he hasn't done. I threaten to report him to child welfare. It's easy to threaten an answering machine. The threat I do not make regards what I know of his drug smuggling operation. The thought of saying "drug smuggling operation" makes me feel like I'm playing Nancy Drew.

Maybe the drug story was a lie, too, like everything before it? Maybe Rich Randall hasn't gotten all the way to the end of his tale?

About a month after Rich's disappearance, I'm at the Quarry one Friday night, sitting at my table just before Win's second set, ready to light myself a cigarette, when the bar door opens and suddenly, standing there, shaking the snow from his wool cap and stamping his feet on the indoor-outdoor rug, is Rich Randall, and I'm so knocked over I can't even move. My stomach hollows inside me, my lighter shaking so hard in my hands I can't even raise it to my mouth. I just sit there, dumb and shaking and staring. I've had two beers already, and part of a third, and maybe that's what kicks in once the nausea passes, because what I'm left with then is a fury like no fury I have ever known. I stand up.

He recognizes me from a few feet away, but that first recognition is friendly, eyes lit up the way they do when you come back to a place you've been gone from and start spotting people you used to know. First you don't realize who they are, just that you know them. A split-second later they come into focus: a name, a context, a placement, history. I watch all of this happen in Rich Randall's face as I walk toward him. His expression, shifting: recognition, realization, fear. And then from fear—from that tiny little millisecond of fear I see in him, which I know he knows I see—from fear he crosses seamlessly into disdain: a clear, smirking, righteous grin. And then he tries to pretend he's never seen me before in his life.

"Did you just plan on never coming back, on never finishing what you started?"

Rich Randall just looks at me, his eyes gone deliberately blank. He blinks. "Scuse me?" He looks around, like maybe I'm talking to someone else.

"You fucking bastard," I say to him. "You fucking . . ."

"Whoa, lady . . ." He backs up a step. "Take it somewhere else, sister."

The words are choking in me. I'm so angry I feel like I'm spitting, only I realize what I'm actually doing is crying. I'm standing in the middle of the Quarry Bar while Win Cryer takes the stage, tears running down my face as I say to this man, this stupid, cowardly, criminal man: "Get out of here. Get out of here right now. You don't deserve to hear a note that man plays. You're a thief. Get out of here. Get out of here now!"

On stage Win starts strumming, and I can see Rich's body respond to the music, soften and find the beat, like he's relaxed as anything. He looks right at me then, tosses his head, and laughs. And then he turns back to the stage, grooving along to the music.

I spin away and run to the ladies' room where I splash my face, pull myself together. Without looking at Rich, I walk back to my table where Lonny Bondorf is sitting now, Miller Genuine Draft in hand, staring up at Win like he's in love with him, too. I fish a cigarette out of my purse and hold it up for Lonny to light. My hand is shaking, and Lonny sees something's wrong.

"Doreen," he says, "are you okay?"

I make a quick glance back at Rich, standing smug in his spot by the door, hands shoved in his pockets, his head nodding in time to the music. I say to Lonny, "I don't know. See that guy over there?" Lonny nods. I say, "I was waiting for the ladies' room and he started sort of hitting on me, and then he just started saying weird stuff . . ."

Lonny looks like he can't decide what kind of suspicious to be: suspicious like an older brother or like a policeman. "What kind of weird stuff?" he asks.

"Like sort of crazy stuff, like do I want to see the gun in his pocket, and do I know it's loaded. And that he's got all sorts of other stuff out in his car. And do I want some drugs, he's got pot if I want, or coke. He was trying to get me to come out to his car to smell his peach-flavored cocaine. I just said, 'no thank you.' Then he called me a bitch."

Lonny stands without a word and sets his beer down on the table. He pushes in his chair and starts walking toward Rich with the kind of purpose in his step that makes people afraid of the police. On stage, Win and the band play the final chord of a song, and it's like the whole place is holding its breath together. Win's mouth is moving, which makes me realize I'm staring right at him, but I can't even hear what he's saying, like it's just his mouth moving but the volume's gone mute, or I've gone deaf, and I'm frozen, staring, waiting for the world to start again, only it's like everyone else is staring too, and who they're staring at is me. The first thing I hear again, breaking through my ears like they're popping, is someone yelling from the back of the bar, some man yelling "Yo, lady, what the fuck song you want to hear? Let's get a move on, the man ain't got all night!" And I'm confused and disoriented, and then suddenly I'm afraid he's talking to me, and I don't know what I've missed, and I don't know what to do, and everyone seems to be waiting for something until finally it's Win who's talking again, and I can hear his voice this time, sounding like he doesn't understand what's going on either, looking at me like I'm crazy as they come, and then to the audience like he's saying *go figure*, only what he's saying is, "Well, I guess we'll just go and choose one ourself . . ." and then he shrugs and turns to confer with the band. From the back of the bar I hear someone say, "What the . . . ?" and I turn and see people clearing the way for Lonny, who's coming up on Rich Randall, and I can see down the path that's cleared for Lonny in the crowd, I can see Lonny say to Rich, "Would you please step outside with me a minute, sir?" And Rich is just looking at him, like, *no way, fuck off, dork*, so that's when Lonny gets to flash his badge and say, "Sir, I'm going to ask you to step outside, and I'm not going to ask you again."

THE CHURCH OF THE FELLOWSHIP
OF SOMETHING

Ginny Maakestad was in the middle stall of Our Lady of the Prairie's ladies room, struggling blindly to unwrap and insert a tampon without reducing her wedding dress to something out of *Carrie* when the tornado sirens commenced their purgatorial tugboat-wail. The dress had been sewn in its entirety by the groom's sister, Eula Yoder, on a new Singer 2662 that Eula had purchased at the Highway 1 Walmart with money she earned cleaning the Iowa City home of the bride's parents, Phillipa and Michael Maakestad. The Singer took up residence in Ginny's old bedroom at the Maakestads', as Eula still lived on her dead parents' farm and the Yoders had neither believed in, nor relied upon, electricity. It was Silas (Eula's brother, Ginny's betrothed) who ferried his sister those forty miles round trip (which was eighty miles for him, as he lived in town and had for some years now, in a condo, full amenities, rent-to-own) every other Wednesday and thus enabled her budding career as a housecleaner and matrimonial seamstress. During its creation, the dress had suffered at least two tulle-shredding attacks by what was suspected to be either a mouse or a vole, and one near-fatal encounter with a bottle of acetone nail polish remover that spilled across the front hem of the dress, prematurely aging the taffeta to a crisp fawn-colored paper that crumbled to the touch and had to be shorn off entirely, reducing Ginny's wedding dress to "tea-length," which was both odd-looking and unfortunate, for the bride's razor-scarred ankles were not her best, nor her favorite, feature. *Fortunately*, Ginny was heavily medicated.

The skirts of this wedding dress—tea-length, tiered, trained, and apparently somehow bustle-able—were at the moment being held up by the bride's mother (Phillipa Maakestad) on one side and Linda, the maid of honor, on the other. Phillipa and Linda were perched, respectively, on the toilet seats of the first and third bathroom stalls, heads and arms sticking up over the dividers like pranksters waiting to strike, clutching fistfuls of tulle like toilet paper bombs. The bride—in stall number two, eight pounds shy of a hundred, pantyhose at her knees—looked like she'd been caught by the blast of a subterranean volcano tunneled up through the plumbing from beneath the prairie. It was in this precarious configuration that the bridal trio was discovered by a heavily made-up soprano soloist from the choir who came crashing into the ladies' room and slammed the door behind her. "There's a twister!" she cried. "We've got to get to the bomb room!"

"The *bomb room*?" snapped the maid of honor from her stall number three toilet-seat pedestal. "Who are you, *Dr. Strangelove*?" Linda was a former junkie, well over two hundred pounds and known neither for her tact nor her gentility, though she'd been corralled, on this special day, into a dress made from a not-insubstantial quantity of satin yardage, and was bearing it stoically—among a host of other traditional wedding party indignities—like a hair shirt woven in Statue-of-Liberty green.

"What*ever* you *call* it," said the soloist.

"Who *are* you?" Linda said back.

"I don't matter," said the soloist, who then seemed so pleasantly shocked by this assertion that she was compelled to try it out again: "I don't matter!"

"Yes, you do," came a small, insistent voice from stall number two. "Of course you do."

Outside, the wind hurled something against the frosted bathroom window. It thudded, stuck there a moment, then whipped off again, like a swimmer flip-turning at the edge of a pool.

"Ginny, honey," said the bride's mother from her perch on toilet number one. "Have you got it?"

Linda was craning over to peer into Ginny's stall. "She's got it *in*," she announced. "Just don't *touch* anything, Gin. Your hands are a bloody mess."

"Jesus Christ," sighed the bride's mother. "You couldn't give in this once—your *wedding* day—and get the applicator ones?"

"It's unconscionably wasteful," Ginny said. "Besides all that *bleach*." She reached for the toilet paper, mounted on a SAV-U-MOR non-rotating dispenser, and pawed at the roll, her fingers sticky with blood.

"They don't make the organic ones with applicators?" her mother pressed. "That seems rather—" It was difficult to converse over the drone of the tornado siren.

"They *do*," Ginny whined. "They were *out*." She held her hands as far from her person as possible, picking at her fingers like a child covered in glue, or paint, or cookie dough.

"*Stop* that, Gin! Look at the mess you're—" Phillipa Maakestad lifted her attention from her daughter on the toilet seat below and addressed the soloist. "Could you—could you please wet down some paper towels for her?" She jerked her chin toward the bay of sinks on which two bouquets rested, and then to the towel dispenser. The singer didn't budge. "Could you please?" Phillipa said again, this time indicating with her chin toward her bloody-fingered daughter in the stall below, concurrently seeming to realize that the woman could not *see* Ginny inside the stall and had no idea what was going on behind door number two. "She's . . ." Phillipa lifted her own hands above the stall divider so the woman could see what she held. "Her *hands*," she explained. "She needs to clean her hands."

And though the soloist looked like she'd just been asked to *wipe* the girl, she strode obediently to the sink and moistened a wad of brown towels until they looked like grocery bags left out in the rain. Then she turned back toward the stall, only to be momentarily confounded by the fact of the door, as though it had just materialized between herself and the bloodied bride. She stood blankly as if awaiting direction.

"Gin," Phillipa said into the stall. "Can you . . . ?" but it was clear that Ginny could not reach the lock from where she sat. Phillipa turned back to the soloist. "Can you put them under, reach them under the door to her?"

"*Down* on my—?"

"Well come and hold *this* then," Linda interrupted. "And *I'll* hand her the fucking towels, for chrissake!" At which point the soloist, cowed, looked down to inspect the cleanliness of the church's bathroom floor, apparently found it not unacceptable, and lifted her choir robe with one hand as she sank slowly to one knee, like a lover in proposal. She steadied herself with a shoulder against the frame of the stall and reached the towel wad under the door. Ginny grabbed it—"Thanks"—and began to pinch at it ineffectually. When she was done, she held out the defiled lump as though she expected it to be removed via the same means it had arrived.

"Put it in the trash, Gin," said her mother from above. "Right there, on the wall, beside the paper."

Ginny located the bin, on whose aluminum lid someone had appropriately, if not particularly tastefully, scratched the words *BLESSED BE THE BLEEDING*. She peered inside as though checking for mail, then deposited the soiled towels and clapped the lid shut. The tornado siren moaned on.

In the mirror, the soloist swabbed a clot of mascara from beneath her right eye and wiped the smudge on her choir robe like it was a cooking apron. Then she spun toward the stalls, her tone bolstered with a new authority. "I've got to ask you all to come down to the bomb shelter immediately." The frosted-glass window shuddered in corroboration.

Phillipa adjusted her hold on Ginny's skirts. "Can you stand and get your hose up?"

The bride hitched up her stockings as directed, Linda and Phillipa swaying above her like puppeteers. Then, Ginny undid the door lock expectantly, as though it were her beloved awaiting, and not just some lady from the choir, but as she moved to cross the stall's threshold Phillipa cried, "Ginny—Stop!" and they froze, as it seemed to dawn on all four of them at once that if Ginny took one more step Linda and Phillipa would be forced to either let go of the skirts or fall off their toilet perches or both.

There was a moment of relative silence, the tornado siren white noise in the air. No one seemed to know how to proceed. It was finally the soloist who sprang to action. "I'll come in," she cried, "I'll get behind, hold the dress from behind!" She looked up to Phillipa, then to Linda. "I'll take it from you. Below." She turned to face the mirrors to demonstrate, lifting her arms over her head like she was making to land an airplane right there in the ladies' room. Then she doubled back, shimmying sideways past Ginny and into the stall. Pausing, she seemed to consider the advisability of flushing the toilet, decided against it, and moved to part the tulle, like a canopy of mosquito netting, and duck beneath Ginny's bridal trains, lifting her hands above her to catch the skirts as they settled.

She was able to follow Ginny out of the stall, the dress tented safely over her, like the back half of the inevitable two-man sheep costume in Our Lady of the Prairie's Christmas pageant.

The sky had gone the color of split pea soup. Outside the ladies' room the siren's drone was a physical presence. Phillipa held the door as the procession filed through, the soloist holding Ginny's skirts, Linda bringing up the rear, both bouquets clutched to her satin stomach. As she let the bathroom door swing closed, Phillipa stood suddenly task-less, and for a moment it seemed she might well bend down and lift the hem of the singer's robe so they could travel as a great train of billowing white.

At the far end of the hall—beneath an EXIT sign onto which someone had snaked a Magic-Marker *S* between the *I* and the *T*—a junior pastor in a black robe several sizes too large held open the stairwell door, his robe flapping around him as though billowed by a pair of enormous hidden wings. This junior pastor was a sylph of a man, elfin in stature, with attached earlobes, very blue eyes, and a chin so pointy it almost looked like Plasticine, all of which lent him an air of great mischief, as though he might be ready to throw off his cloak and reveal some extravagant peacock-blue Mardi Gras costume, all spangles, plumes and glam. Behind him, to the right of the door frame, a pinwheel of sinister triangles, yellow on black, marked the route to the relative safety of a World War II era fallout shelter, although the exuberant flair with which the junior pastor beckoned the bridal party (and their ad hoc, soprano fourth) toward the stairs created the impression that what actually lay at the foot of those stairs was more like the entrance to a very hip, underground, S&M club.

The bridal party, Linda now in the lead, made their way into the stairwell, and the black-flapping junior pastor followed, closing the door behind himself. At the bottom of the flight was a tiny vestibule that Linda nearly filled entirely. A door on the left opened to the outside, where a wheelchair ramp spouted off like a toboggan run. Lightning flashed through a porthole window; the sky turned the color of roasting eggplant.

A second door opened onto a dark, down-sloping ramp. "We call it the *Catacombs*!" the junior pastor called enthusiastically, still only halfway down the stairs behind the bride's mother, the soloist, and the rear half of the bride and her train. His voice echoed out like a funhouse ghoul.

From the vestibule below, Linda peered down the fallout shelter ramp. "Fuck," she said, and then paused as though waiting to hear what kind of echo might resound. "We're going to fuck the shit out of these dresses in there," she said, turning back to her compatriots, which was when she seemed to realize the utter inappropriateness of her language, which she acknowledged with a further, "Oh fuck," then silently vowed to try not to speak another word until Ginny was done and married.

"We *all need* to get to the shelter," the soloist lobbied. She still held Ginny's train, which she lifted in both hands for emphasis, her fingers clenched as though she might begin to wring the tulle in desperation.

Ginny said, as a matter of fact, "This dress can't take any more ruining."

"I refuse," said the mother of the bride, "to die as an Iowa tornado casualty." Then added, "In a church!"

"Well," said the junior pastor, who, if he was insulted, gave no such indication. "Then let's get ourselves to the shelter."

Down in the vestibule Linda turned her back to Ginny, gesturing something with her bouquet that Ginny did not clearly understand. "Un*button* me," Linda snapped. Ginny obliged and helped Linda step free of the dress. Ginny's maid of honor was not an immodest woman, but she'd already shrugged off the entire confection of the wedding as patently absurd and numbed herself down with a few strong shots before she'd boarded the ship that was her dress and prepared to walk down the aisle in support of the ninety-two-pound bride whom she credited as her personal savior, which was on account of Ginny's unflagging devotion as much as it was out of gratitude for the not one but *two* occasions on which Ginny found Linda, called 911, and performed the CPR she'd learned in high school until EMTs arrived with a defibrillator. For Linda, *wearing* that dress and *removing* the dress were equally ridiculous propositions, and she stripped down to her slip with no more than a second's deliberation, stepped out of that oxidized-green refrigerator box, and began bunching it up so she might pass it most efficiently up the stairs. "Hang it on the banister," she called to Phillipa. Then she took Ginny by the shoulders and spun her around as far as she'd go, her skirts and train twisting around her like a stowed umbrella. The soloist, still tenaciously keeping the train from the floor, tripped down a few steps, tugged by that leash of ivory veiling.

With incongruously nimble fingers and an almost magical dexterity, Linda unfastened thirty-six pea-sized satin-covered buttons from their looping as if they were so many snaps, then helped the bride step from her tempest of tulle, which the increasingly fastidious soloist swooped fervently up, her estimation of the bridal gown seeming to have inexplicably risen to par with the American flag. The dress was passed up the stairs and hung delicately on the railing beside Linda's, their bouquets set down on a step like a pair of extravagant bedroom slippers or elaborately coifed lap dogs. Then, led by the maid of honor, in a full slip befitting a geriatric nun, the party resumed its descent.

Our Lady's bomb shelter was long as a bowling lane and only a few times as wide. It was lined with wooden benches, which did not provide enough seating for the forty-odd people now assembled therein. At the far end of the bunker sat a child's playpen gone blue-gray and ochre with mildew, so thickly draped in cobwebs it had become a silvered angora nest in which a tenement of small creatures, some now deceased, had assumed habitation. Beside the playpen stood a three-foot-tall Fisher-Price kitchen, a slab of plastic sirloin thawing on the alert-orange counter beside a play sink that seemed now to serve dually as a grave and outhouse for resident mice.

Wedding guests, clergy, and choir filled the shelter. Elderly sat along the benches; the spryer crowded the center aisle like rush hour subway riders, their stances wide and sturdy as though they expected the ground beneath them to shift at any moment. A cheer rose as the bridal party entered, and it echoed through the underground chamber.

The expectant groom cut a path to his bride-to-be as if drawn by magnet, and no one tried to stop him, collectively forgetting, in the hubbub, that bride and groom were to be kept from such prenuptial consort. The only person who had not forgotten was, in fact, the groom himself, but the prohibition had been explained to him as a taboo against glimpsing the bride's gown before she came down the aisle, and since it was readily apparent that Ginny was wearing no gown, nor any dress at all, Silas saw no conflict in rushing to her scantily clad side. Silas Yoder was a small man by most standards, yet stood confidently taller than Ginny, who had managed to ingest little more than blue Trident and Diet Sunkist between 1986 and 1994, so silencing her pubescence and stunting her growth that she had, even upon reintegration to the living and eating population, never crested the five-foot mark nor tipped the doctor's scale far enough to require even a hundred-pound poise on the coarse-adjustment beam. Silas shed his tuxedo jacket and eased it over Ginny's frame, thereby completing a look that had gone from bridal to *Desperately Seeking Susan* in a matter of minutes. She wore a white satin bustier and a long tutu of crinoline, and in the oversized topcoat with its wilting pink boutonniere, Ginny Maakestad might well have been dressed for a Madonna concert twenty years earlier, dancing among the pre-teens in precocious paeans of renewal to a virginity they hadn't yet lost.

"I'd about die for an Advil," Ginny said, kneading at her cramping abdomen like she was wishing for the first time in her life that there was something more there to grab onto.

Silas thought a moment, then clamped a work-worn hand to the back of Ginny's knobby neck and steered her through the bustling bomb shelter toward Linda, who'd made it to the far end near the mossy playpen where she was hovering in her pumps—a girdled vision in white—over her friend and NA sponsor, Randall, who squatted on the ground by a filthy Sit 'n Spin.

"It's always the junkies they come to for drugs!" Randall said. "Hey, by the way, you know, I got whaddya call it . . . Online, some Church of the Brotherhood of something."

"Ordained," Linda said.

"Yeah, by the Church of the Fellowship of something or other."

"Your grandma's got my purse," Linda said, and they craned to search down the length of the benches for Bernadette Maakestad.

"I could marry you two right down here underground," Randall said. "Legal as a priest, swear to god." He held up three fingers. "Virginia Maakestad and Silas Yoder, by the power vested in me by the state of cyberspace, I now pronounce you . . ."

Bernadette Maakestad sat in the church-owned wheelchair she'd requested for the trip down to the shelter, though she was not actually physically infirm save for a measure of deafness that was, arguably, more practically useful than it was medically diagnosable. Upon her lap, buffered by the arms of the wheelchair, Grandma Maakestad had amassed an impressive collection of handbags, evening bags, and dress clutches in everything from scarlet patent leather to something that looked like the pelt of a marsupial. She'd either been designated the unofficial bag check of the underground party or was in the process of carrying out a strangely overt purse-snatching scheme. It took some minutes to figure out which bag was Linda's, and then to convince Grandma Maakestad to release it into Silas's custody, and for Linda to unearth from it a cache of Advil she had complicatedly interred in a swaddle of plastic sacks and rubber bands that lent the over-the-counter anti-inflammatory a darker contraband mystique. Though Linda stood just a few feet from Ginny, she handed the tiny Saran Wrapped bundle to Silas, who presented the nest of miniature mauve-colored eggs to his bride like an offering of delicate hors d'oeuvres.

Ginny peered into his hand, her own poised above like she couldn't decide which pill to choose. Silas remained like a little butler until at last she pinched one up and popped it into her mouth, then snatched up another few and crammed them in as if to stow them away in her cheeks for leaner times. Then she held up a hand to receive the glass of water she seemed to assume would appear by the way. When, unsurprisingly, it did not, Silas and Linda both began to cast their glances about in search of a remedy. But it was Randall—who was now improbably seated *on* the ancient Sit 'n Spin—who reached a stealthy hand into the front panel of his jacket and removed a sizable tin-colored flask.

Ginny removed the cap thoughtfully and took a whiff of its contents before swigging. She shuddered, swallowed hard, and shuddered again, clearing the burn from her throat with the dry phlegmy hack of a cat with a hairball. Silas gave her back a thump, gentle but not without potency. Silas's uncannily intuitive sense of Ginny's needs was a subject of great interest, particularly to Phillipa, who had never felt herself to be as adept a nursemaid to her daughter and could not decide whether Silas's proficiency stemmed purely from love, or from some innate, healing Amish-ness, the notion of which both mystified and repelled her.

"Keep off the junk." Randall's voice was a TV announcer's. "Embrace your inner alcoholic." He accepted the return of his flask and took a swig himself before stowing it back inside his coat. "Sure you don't want me to marry you all right now?" he asked again, earnestly hunched into the Sit 'n Spin.

Silas looked mildly alarmed, but Ginny just smiled her chipmunk smile, head swaying lazily as if in time to some sultry song piped in from outside to her ears, and hers alone.

The unquestionably ingenious Eula Yoder appeared to have fashioned herself a sort of a jumpsuit of industrial-strength trash bags: a neck slit and armholes in one made a smock, legholes turned another into a pair of plastic bloomers, the whole ensemble cinched at the waist with a Hefty sash. She'd become a walking garment bag for the bridesmaid's dress she wore. Eula had been shunned by her own Amish community for such deviant indulgences as her sewing machine, her Yahoo account, her mild obsession with *Witness* (and not-so-mild obsession with Kelly McGillis), and for the cruise she'd taken the previous winter, which had, in fact, been some sort of a Mennonite historical cruise, and though Mennonite wasn't Amish, it wasn't like she'd sailed away on the *Love Boat*, and if it had been a love boat, it was a *Mennonite* love boat, the exact nature of which was still a matter of some speculation, though there was only so far such speculation could go before one's thoughts turned decidedly unorthodox and patently unchristian. Eula had not been exiled or ostracized, but she was actively ignored in the marketplace and excluded from the marriageable pool. Presently though, she was finding herself wholeheartedly embraced by the bomb shelter congregation, for with typical foresight she had brought the roll of trash bags down to the fallout shelter and was now distributing them among the wedding guests and clergy as makeshift seat covers, picnic blankets, and protective garb. Two girls had opened the seams on one bag and sat cross-legged facing each other singing, "*Oh little playmate, come out and play with me . . .*" clapping and snapping and slapping their palms together in choreographed ritual. One mother had simply stuck her young son into a trash bag feet first and held him on her lap, his head and arms poking out the top like carrot greens too tall for the grocery bag.

A small crowd had gathered beneath one of the kerosene camping lanterns that had conceded to ignite, straining like seedlings toward a taxi-yellow shower radio blackening with mold like an overripe banana, struggling to hear the emergency weather broadcast.

The flutist—a music major from the university who'd been hired to play a rendition of "Let Hope and Sorrow Now Unite" for the recessional—turned to the man next to her. "Is it the whole state?" she asked.

The man (who was actually the father of the bride) faced the young musician, his eyes clouded with far more sadness and confusion than a stint in the storm cellar seemed to warrant, and said, "Sounds like it touched down over in Story City, so they've had us all on watch—Story County, Marshall County, Tama, Poweshiek, Johnson. And now it's touched in the Amanas, so they've upped it to a warning as far east as Illinois."

"Until when, did they say?" The flutist, who also played jazz clarinet, had another gig that evening with her quintet on one of the riverboat casinos up near Dubuque.

"Five forty-five?" he answered. He sounded like a soldier who'd seen enough bloodshed to know things could always be far worse than one imagined. He eyed Eula's roll of Hefty bags, then panned the shelter as though plotting where he might lay a few down and close his eyes.

"What time is it now?" asked the flutist.

The bride's father checked his watch again, as though it might have changed dramatically in the seconds since he'd last looked. "Five-fifteen."

It was unclear whether the flutist recognized Michael Maakestad as the father of the bride. He'd had a haircut, a shave, and approximately eighteen minutes of sleep since the rehearsal the previous afternoon. He looked unwell, as though an unshakable shame had crept over him in the night, burgled its way in during those few defenseless minutes when he'd abandoned his insomniac vigil and fatefully allowed himself to doze. To marry off one's troubled only child to a lapsed-Amish carpenter seven years her junior was not proving to carry the relief he'd anticipated. That his own thirty-two-year marriage to Phillipa was on the verge of collapse did not inspire confidence, and the treaty they'd managed to broker between them to make it through the wedding as the to-all-appearances-happy parents of the bride (which had involved, the night before, a variety of spanking that he thought would help diffuse his cuckolded hurt and anger but so far had not) was proving to feel less like the Geneva Convention and more like a crooked arms deal. It was all Michael Maakestad could do to follow the weather reports, for which, if he'd been able to think more clearly, he might have realized he was quite grateful.

The bride lifted one foot and then the other, inspecting the soles for dirt, then checked again once she was done, as though she expected their state of cleanliness to change spontaneously or fearful that she might have missed something on last glance. "What are we *doing* here?" she said.

Silas spoke patiently. "It's a tornado warning, Gin. We have to."

And then, as though Silas had said something else entirely, Ginny shook her head and spoke in the voice an adult might use to calm a crying child. She took Silas's hand in hers and rested her head on his thin shoulder. "It'd've meant a great deal to your parents," she recited drowsily. "May they rest . . ." Silas affectionately patted the salon tendrils that cascaded from Ginny's updo. His bride closed her eyes.

And then, as if on cue, from the far end of the shelter rose the dusky call of the flute in a melody only the children seemed to recognize. The little-playmate girls leapt from their garbage bag shrieking "Ariel! Ariel!" in breathless ecstasy and followed the piper's infectious mermaid-movie song.

The mildewed-yellow waterproof radio hiccupped loud burps of static until it lost its station entirely and someone thought to turn the volume down. A crack of lightning and thunder exploded with such violence that it seemed to come from the very earth under which they'd sought protection. There were gasps, then a hush, then the muffled cries of a child trying to bury its head into the illusory safety of a parent's body. And then the flutist resumed her song.

The power of the wind was surely tremendous aboveground, as even from beneath the congregants could hear the slam and barrage, feel the relentless death-bent pummel whip around and through the church above them as if to rip it from the ground and send it sailing off to Oz. It seemed impossible that the shelter would protect them from the determined ferocity bearing down, and no one would have been particularly surprised if even the earth below and around them began to tremble and quake, sending the white-robed soloist tumbling over, feet in the air like a slapstick cartoon, lifting from the sole of her crepe-soled shoe a tiny whorl of bloodied toilet tissue, sending it swirling into the air, caught in the twister of the Sit 'n Spin, knocking Randall to the floor, shedding its dust and cobwebs to reveal the blue and yellow spirals stickered crookedly on its seat twenty years before, the dust and cobwebs catching up in their whirl a hundred Hefty bags, a dervish-dance of black plastic joined by the billowing black robes of the junior pastor, flapping, and lifting from the wheelchair lap of Bernadette Maakestad a great sandstorm of pocketbooks, airborne and determined, it might seem, to fly back to their rightful owners like homing pigeons. Up the ramp the wind would rush, up through the stairwell, ripping the bride's gown from the banister where it hung to send it dancing up the steps, followed in quick pursuit by the enormous green ghost of the maid of honor bent on saving the wedding, the two of them trailed by their bouquets, breaking apart in the wind, a spray of petals tossed by invisible flower girls. Up through the church hall they'd fly, past the bomb shelter sign threatening to pinwheel right off the wall like a sinister boomerang. In the ladies' room, three bowls of toilet water—two clear, one pink—would eddy into whirlpools, and in the chapel the bride's veil might alight from the pew on which it lay, catch briefly on the *T* of Jesus's cross, sweep across the altar, and hover a moment in respect by the memorial bouquet for Obadiah and Orah Yoder, killed just a year before—in a horrific whorl of horsehair and collard greens and blood and steel because the SUV driver never even saw their buggy as he crested the hill by the Yoders' farm—and as the veil lurched upward, lightning flashing prisms through the stained glass cupola of the nave, and outside the new spring tulips in the parishioners' garden would be stripped to their skinny new-green stems, petals of orange and purple and yellow and red quivering through the air like firecracker flares and tails and star shells, until they slapped and stuck, wet, against the broken windows and mangled sliding door of Randall's old Chevy Caravan, crushed beneath the willow that had earlier offered plentiful shade, its split, splintered trunk now pointed accusingly into the premature night saying *you did this*, its other half torn and felled to the ground, splayed and gasping to ask *why*, the sky clearing, wind dying, debris settling, the day's second dawn brightening to say *because*.

WE SHALL GO TO HER, BUT SHE WILL NOT RETURN TO US

Nearly four years ago a born-again folk duo came through Pulverdale to gig at the fall harvest festival and stayed just long enough to knock up Cici Carver's older sister, Dane, a sixteen-year-old atheist with a weakness for men who sang harmony. Dane wouldn't tell which one of the duo it was, and no one else could remember well enough what they'd looked like to figure it out on their own once Trevor was born. Cici always suspected that Dane was never entirely sure herself which one of the Christian folkies had fathered her child. It's just one more answer Trevor will have to track down on his own someday if he decides that he wants or needs to know whose sperm was involved in his conception.

Rona Carver bore her teenage daughter's pregnancy with a cultivated stoicism she'd been honing since she'd divorced Dane and Cici's father years before. Kit came and went and came and went, and though there was always a spot at the table for him and no one Rona'd rather welcome into her bed, she made it clear that she'd take what he could give her, when and if he had it to give, but she was long since naive enough to *expect* anything from the man.

But this was about Dane.

Dane: seventeen when Trevor was born. Dane, who'd been testing Rona's patience since just about the moment of her own conception. Dane managed to graduate from Pulverdale High with Rona taking care of Trevor during the school day, so in love with him—her first grandchild!— she'd have nursed him herself if it were possible. To care for Trevor was a way to care for Dane without having to actually care for Dane, and thus, a situation that might have torn their family apart served instead to broker just about the only peace Rona and Dane Carver had ever known between them. And then, one afternoon the July after she graduated, Dane left. With the baby. Without a word.

Three years later—nearly to the day—Rona's house was abuzz and abang with preparations for Cici's wedding when an unfamiliar car came up the driveway. Cici, eighteen and a new high school graduate herself, had been out back helping her father and Bear build the dance floor and a little stage for the band. But working in the afternoon sun was making Cici queasy, and she'd started toward the house for something to drink. She was almost to the porch steps when she heard the protests of a car's engine and looked to see a great big rusting-white Mercedes lumbering like a tank through the mangled hairpins of the rutty dirt drive. The car advanced with prodigious slowness, and Cici stood watching its unpromising progress. For all the drilling and hammering, no one else appeared to hear the heaving engine.

Time seemed to pass according to principles unrelated to time. The car was a thing of the distance, and then it was so close Cici could feel the heat coming off its hood like fever. And then a person who was her sister was flying out from behind the steering wheel and Cici was engulfed by Dane, submerged in Dane. Dane was the air she breathed, some cheap and buttery shampoo, and beneath that was just the smell of Dane: rich, ripe, and somehow feral. Cici knew Dane's smell was connected to Dane's pull on people, which was more than just attraction. It wasn't just men, and it wasn't just sexual, either. It was men and women, prepubescent boys and adolescent girls, it was family, and it was people who didn't know Dane from a Mormon missionary. People wanted Dane. They wanted to be near her, and they wanted to touch her. And, Cici had always thought, whether they knew it or not, people acted as though they wanted to breathe her sister in like air.

Cici felt like she was being watched, but struggling up from Dane's embrace was like swimming for the water's surface long after you've run out of breath. Cici broke through to the air—the real world's air, the air people *actually* breathed—still clinging to Dane, the sisters grabbing at each other's skin. Dane pulled the flesh at Cici's upper arm; Cici palpated the meat at the side of Dane's ribcage. They pawed like they each had to make sure they were holding a real body, not a specter, and they both held fast as Cici turned them toward the car, whose wide rear passenger door stood ajar, big and white as an airplane wing. And there beside the door, standing on the ground where the driveway dirt turned to scrappy, mossy lawn, was a small person in a grimy yellow T-shirt, long red shorts, and a pair of high-top Velcro sneakers that were so dirty you almost couldn't tell they were girls' sneakers: pink, with stars that might have once been puffy or sparkly or both. Standing there was Cici's nephew, Trevor Winston Carver, who'd been a tottering Weeble of baby fat and was now a solid, upright, freestanding child.

Cici pulled away from her sister. Dane never let go easy, which had always made breaking from her feel wrenching and impossible. But that July afternoon at the edge of the driveway so soon before her wedding day, Cici peeled her body from the humid stick of Dane's embrace on Trevor's account, partly because he was standing there looking like he needed direction, and partly because she couldn't help it: she wanted to seize Trevor up the way Dane had seized her. She wanted to hold his little body and try to understand how it was the same body she'd once known, a body she'd washed and fed and probably held closer than she'd ever held another body at that time.

She went toward him with an instinct as blind as it was urgent, and he didn't flinch, just stood there, bobble-headed and glassy-eyed, his strawy blond hair stuck up in spots from sleep. She stopped herself just short of tackling him in a hug and sank to her knees in the dirt before him, looked into his soft, drool-marked face, the crusty corners of his lips and eyes, the sweaty mat of dirty yellow hair, the dark brown Carver eyes that had won out over whichever folksinger's genes he had. Cici looked into Trevor's eyes as if to tell him she'd trade every prayer she might have left in the world if he still knew his Aunt Cici.

He stayed there, just looking back at her, not scared or confused, just concentrating, opening himself up to the memory. Finally, he moved his gaze over Cici's shoulder toward his mom, and when Dane spoke, Cici realized it had been three years since she'd heard her sister's voice.

"She doesn't look so different, does she T?" Dane said. "You know Cici, don't you?"

Trevor looked back to his aunt, and relief seemed to spread through his body. He smiled, mostly with his eyes, and just a tiny bit with the edges of his lips, as though it was important to keep them closed over his teeth. But then they broke through and his face opened in glee. He said, "Soccer!"

Dane grinned at Cici. "He's kind of a genius," she said.

As it turned out, the photo Dane and Trevor had of Cici was a color clipping from the *Pulverdale Post*'s sports coverage of her JV season in ninth grade, and if Trevor—genius or not—recognized his aunt from that newsprint action shot it wasn't because Cici hadn't changed in four years but because that clipping was the only photo Dane had of anyone in the family.

Cici didn't notice the hammering had stopped until she heard her father's voice cry from behind her, "Well, fuck me!" as he rounded the back of the house. And then Dane was running at him like she was going to fling herself into his arms and wrap her legs around his middle the way, as a kid, she'd welcomed him home whenever he'd land on their doorstep. Dane was their father's girl; Cici was their mom's. That's how it had always been.

Bear was close behind Kit and nearly got dominoed over when Dane flew into her father's arms. Cici watched Bear, afraid for just a second that he might simply turn back around to snub Dane the way he felt she'd snubbed her family. But he didn't. He just waited near Kit like a foot-man and hugged Dane good-naturedly, if with reserve, when she and Kit released each other. Bear said, "Long time no see, girl," and this seemed to satisfy his desire to admonish her. Bear and Dane had dated, briefly, one summer a long time before, when he was a just-graduated senior and she was about to be a freshman at Pulverdale High, which was a small enough school in a small enough town that to have dated *all* the boys in your own class—or even most of the rest of the high school—didn't necessarily mean you were slutty, depending on what you'd let them do.

Time seemed to expand again, like algae in mitosis, and Cici was still on the ground beside Trevor, but suddenly Kit was there too, saying hello to the little boy he'd never even known that well as an infant. He hadn't been around much that year. No one really knew why or where he'd been that time. Bear was almost upon Cici too, coming toward her as though she might have been hurt there on the ground, struck down by Dane, mowed down by Dane's enormous car. And then Kit was up again, unsure how to handle Trevor and so returning to Dane, though that was awkward too. Kit Carver was a man of entrances and exits, not too strong on the murky stuff of life that came in between. He asked Dane if she knew about Bear and Cici's wedding and how she'd heard. They were the questions everyone would want to ask, but it looked for a second as if Dane might actually answer her father straightaway, saying, "I couldn't miss my baby sister's wedding, could I?" But then she just started singing a little, *"Heard it through the grapevine, honey honey, yeah . . ."* to tease Kit some, tease the man who'd taught her those coy, flirtatious ways. Dane's gaze went to the house and her chorus petered out. Then the screen door banged and everyone turned to see Rona, who'd emerged from the depths, wiping her hands on a dishtowel like in a scene from a Western where women of a certain age were counted on to come through screen doors onto porches to wipe their hands on dishtowels and see what kind of trouble might be afoot.

Rona shifted the towel back and forth in her hands with motions so slow and deliberate it felt as though the rest of the world was simply going to hold still until Rona Carver's hands were dry. The hand-wiping slowed and slowed until there was no more movement and the rag was clamped to one of Rona's hips beneath her hand and everyone remained still, waiting.

Dane turned to her small son, his soft smudgy face, those Carver eyes gone squinty with confusion. "You remember your Nana Ro, don't you, T?"

Cici's nausea rose. Trevor looked back to Rona on the porch; everything hung on him. A dog barked in the distance—probably Deanne Mooney's poor horrible collie—and horseflies circled the compost pile like planes in a holding pattern. Trevor's face seized in an expression that—if you were looking for it, or had a vested interest—certainly could have passed for recognition, and seemed to be all it took for Rona's girdled regard to go soft. She was steeled to many things—and probably more people—in this life, but not her grandson. Her arms fell to her sides and she dropped the dishtowel like a prop she no longer had use for. "Trevor Winston Carver," she said, "you can't possibly recognize your ancient old Nana Ro." And it's anyone's guess whether Trevor actually recognized her or merely sensed he was supposed to, or that he'd make that lady up on the porch happy if he pretended to know who she was. She'd been named for him twice in as many minutes. But people will see what they need to see, and when for the third time that afternoon the name "Nana Ro" came bounding out of someone's mouth and that mouth was Trevor's, for the time being the Carver family decided to see that Trevor was home, finally, and he knew it.

The afternoon continued in that same stilted, heady, awkward rush, everyone talking at once, then no one knowing what to say, then someone getting an idea—"We should show Dane the new well!" or "Let's re-hang the old tire swing for Trevor!"—and they'd all go hurtling off with the charge of destination and purpose until it was done and someone had to think up something else. Kit and Bear drifted back to the construction in the yard. Rona had been in the middle of making cheese sticks for the reception and suggested the girls could help. She scooped up her grandson, and three generations of Carvers started inside toward the kitchen.

Rona, who billed herself as ancient, was actually only forty and didn't even color her hair yet, though Cici'd lately begun suggesting that maybe it was time. She was strong and able, lifted Trevor with no trouble at all, though he had to be at least forty pounds. She moved him from one hip to the other before they climbed the porch steps. "You got a diaper under there, Trevor Winston?" she asked.

Trevor nodded absently. He was looking over Rona's shoulder into the stand of redwoods between the house and the Pulverdale Cemetery.

"You got a wet diaper or a dry diaper, Mister?"

Trevor nodded, this time with more interest.

"Wet?" Rona pressed him.

He kept nodding. "I pee-peed."

Dane had paused at the flower beds beside the porch steps, squatting to sniff at the roses and reaching in to deadhead the spent buds, flicking them down like cigarette butts.

"Dane," Cici called. She was on the stairs, between her mother on the porch and her sister in the dirt below. "You got extra diapers in the car?"

"He need one?" Dane kept pruning. She didn't sound like she meant it as a question. Her voice had a tone of resigned disapproval, as though she were disappointed that no one had been taking proper care of the flowers in her absence, which wasn't true at all. "There's some in the trunk, I think. Key's in the car."

Cici started back down the steps, and Dane paused and stood as Cici passed, seeming to consider the situation: Rona, with Trevor in her arms, edging the toe of her tennis shoe under the screen door to open it; Cici aimed toward the car. Then Dane said, "I'll come," wiped her hands on her back pockets, and rushed Cici in a little gallop. She rag-dolled her skinny arms, and then flopped them around her sister and herded her off toward the Mercedes, singing, "*I will follow Ceece, wherever Ceece may go. There isn't an ocean too deep, a mountain so high it can keep, keep me from Ceece . . .*" Sometimes, *Ceece* seemed to rhyme with *peace*; other times—depending on who said it and how—Cici couldn't help but think it rhymed with *grease*.

Dane reached into the car and pulled the keys from the ignition, then made to toss them to Cici. But she let go awkwardly, as though she hadn't fully committed to their release, and Cici had to dive a little to grab them. There were two—a car key, and one slightly smaller than a house key, for a padlock, or a garage—attached to a temporary valet tag from *Gino's Casino, Las Vegas, NV.*

Rona and Trevor had gone inside; the screen door slammed, and the shadows closed in behind them. Cici went to open the trunk of Dane's car. It smelled of spoiled milk and Clorox, and Cici stepped back and lowered her head. When the nausea passed, she lifted her eyes tentatively, but Dane hadn't seen: she was stretched, belly down, across the back seat, feet sticking out the open door. Her chunky mules slid off her feet into the dirt. She was digging for something under the front seat. Dane's trunk contained the largest package of diapers Cici had ever seen, squashed into the corner like a bag of marshmallows crammed at the bottom of a grocery sack. The trunk was mostly full of a collection of plastic bags from Aldi and Walmart. Some held clothes; some spilled toys: teething rings, Lincoln Logs, Legos probably too small for Trevor to be playing with yet. A miniature plastic arm poked through a Publix sack as though its owner had died trying to escape. Cici started to wrestle out the diaper package, then stopped herself, removed one diaper—misshapen as a slice of well-traveled Wonder Bread—and shut the trunk again. They could come back for the rest, if Dane suggested it. It was better not to assume anything about how long she planned to stay.

Cici rounded the car just as Dane was struggling to pull her arm out from under the seat, a deformed, drool-matted, dirty-gray stuffed animal in her hand. She poked it out the open window to Cici, then heaved herself up and scooted back out the door. Cici tried to mush the beast back into some recognizable form—it turned out to be an elephant—while Dane held herself steady on the roof of the car and slipped back into her shoes below.

"It's a good fucking thing," Dane was saying. "He cried half the way here saying Mr. Yucky was gone. I knew the fucking thing was back there somewhere."

Halfway from where? Cici wanted to ask. Instead she said, "Mr. Yucky?"

"Look," Dane said, winking at Cici over the car roof, "if the name fits . . ."

Cici stared pitifully at the creature in her hand. "Come on, Mr. Yucky—you like cheese sticks?"

Dane laughed, and it was still a laugh that lent Cici a reflexive relief. Not all of Dane's laughs did—many did quite the opposite—but this one was approving, and easy. Dane had started around the front of the car toward Cici when she paused. "Hey, you see, like, a blue blanket in there?"

Cici poked her head and one arm in through the open window. An old sleeping bag had been unzipped and mashed into the back crevice of the seat to hold it in place. A laundry bag and a pillow with a pink floral case were wedged against the door. Cici pulled out a scrap of a pilled, mouse-blue rag with a tattered blue ribbon of blanket-binding hanging off it like a tail. She held it up to Dane.

"Yeah. Just guess what *its* name is," Dane said.

Cici grimaced. "Mr. Grody?" She felt uncertain saying it, a little afraid. "Doe-doe."

"Doe-doe?" Cici repeated. She glanced into the car, to the bed in which Trevor'd slept while they drove from wherever they'd driven from.

"Doe-doe," Dane confirmed, and when Cici looked up Dane was rolling her eyes to say *don't ask me.*

"Doe-doe," Cici said again. They started up to the house, arms wrapped around each other's waists, Dane leaning to rest her head—girlishly, affectionately—on Cici's shoulder, Cici trying not to let on that she was trying to figure out if Dane didn't *know* you had to have a car seat for a child or just didn't care. But Cici knew Dane knew; she'd had a car seat in her old car when she'd left with Trevor. That old Ford was gone, it seemed. This Mercedes she was driving—Trevor'd be lucky if it had seatbelts. And with that, cars, car travel, and car safety joined the lists of things not to bring up around Dane. Cici wondered—not for the first time—when there simply wouldn't be anything left on the safe list, when nothing at all would be safe with Dane.

Rona said it was all walking on eggshells around Dane. They had to take Dane on Dane's terms or not at all. But it was worse than eggshells, Cici thought. It was a minefield: never any knowing what would set Dane off, so you had to avoid everything, stepping only on ground she'd cleared for you and marked herself. You wanted to please Dane, because to displease Dane was to lose her so fast you usually didn't even know what you'd done. Or when she might forgive you. When she'd first left with Trevor, people outside the family said she'd be back when she got in trouble or needed something—money, help, anything—and surely that wouldn't take long. They thought they were talking about days or weeks. Cici and Rona might have been the only ones who knew that home was the last place she'd turn. Which might mean that after three years she'd finally managed to run out of options. Rona used to have a framed little saying by somebody famous next to the coat rack in the entrance hall that said something like, "Home is the place where, when you have to go there, they have to take you in," but she'd taken it down when Dane was eleven or twelve and started running away on a semi-regular basis. Or maybe she'd taken it down after the divorce, because Kit did keep coming home, and Rona did keep taking him in, and that was a fine arrangement between the two of them, but she didn't need it hung up on the wall for everyone to see spelled out any plainer than it already was.

Rona changed Trevor's diaper—it was as though she and Dane knew how to maintain the physical space between them, handed off Trevor like a relay baton—and Rona even managed not to comment that she hadn't realized they *made* diapers for children as old as Trevor, managed not to say, *I might still have some Depends up in the attic.* Kit's father had lived with Rona and the girls while he was dying ten years before. Advanced, willfully untreated prostate cancer.

They got Trevor set up on a chair at the kitchen table rolling cheese sticks with Rona, all of which Rona would have to roll again, as if she minded in the slightest. Rona had loved her own daughters, certainly, but Cici had a really hard time imagining her mother deriving such pure pleasure—such joy!—from making Play-Doh and coloring Easter eggs with the two of them.

Dane needed a cigarette, so Cici went with her to the porch, and Dane smoked and asked questions, which was how Dane had conversations. She rested her butt in the crook of the porch rail and a column, then slipped off one shoe and hitched her bent leg onto the rail in front of her so she could look out over the land. You couldn't see the ocean from Rona's, but it was there, not a mile west, beyond the redwoods. The property was stuck between the cemetery and ocean, buffered only by some thousand-foot cliffs and the cragged boulders below, and Dane liked to say, in high school, that it would have made the perfect setting for an Agatha Christie: *Death On Every Side.*

The yard abutted a section of the Pulverdale Cemetery that was marked off from the other graves by a waterproof baby-blue banner staked into the earth on two white Little Bo-Peep crooks, announcing—in white stenciling, between bunches of pink and yellow balloons trailing their strings behind as they floated toward heaven—the entrance to BABYLAND. It was there, among the perfect rows of tiny graves lined up like cradles in a nursery, that Dane and Cici had passed a great deal of playtime as children. *In a graveyard in Pulverdale where nobody goes live lots of dead babies in very straight rows,* they chanted. They thought of those babies as their wards and tended the graves like nursemaids, as though their occupants needed the same things as a real baby: naps, burps, bottles. They brought their dolls out from the house to lay to sleep on the BABYLAND graves, headstones as pillows, and they were dirt-smeared to a one, their coarse doll-hair stuck with dead leaves and twigs. Dane and Cici read the epitaphs and made up lives for the little people who hadn't gotten to live their own: *Gracie Cora*

Geller, May 9–May 11, 1912, We Would Miss You More, Did We Not Know That We Shall See You Soon. Little Gracie, they imagined, would've been a hellion. Driven her poor mother to distraction. And drink! *Flora Linnea Burne, infant daughter of Mary Louise and Carl Anger, Sept. 15, 1933,* was a prodigy, they said: sweet and shy and bright as sunrise. *Oh What Glory To See A Rainbow From Above!* But their favorite was *Trevor Winston, Jan. 27–Feb. 3, 1964 If Love Could Have Kept You Here, You Never Would Have Gone.* He'd have been as old as Cici, this golden boy, the angel of their dead-baby nursery. When, years later, Dane had christened her illegitimate, born-again-fathered child Trevor Winston Carver, no one else knew where she'd gotten the name. Rona had no idea where "Trevor" came from, but there'd been a barn cat—one of trillions—once upon a time when the girls were little, which they called Winston, and Rona thought Dane had given her son the middle name for that long-dead mangy calico, which she said was just a stupid thing to do. Cici could only imagine her mother's thoughts on naming him after a dead infant in BABYLAND. But to Cici, at the time, it had seemed like a hopeful gesture on Dane's part, a chance to do something right, at least for one Trevor Winston in the world.

Dane perched on the porch rail and sucked her cigarette, gazing bitterly into the distance. She exhaled as though performing a yogic relaxation technique. "Cici Carver and Bear Winewski," she marveled. "Who would've thought?" She sounded like Kit, who delivered such canned phrases as though he'd coined them himself. "How long've you two been together?" There was a remove to her voice, as if she were ready to pull rank and dispense some advice.

Cici sat on the porch rail by Dane's foot and faced the house. "The real answer or the official one?"

Dane waved her cigarette, shook her head, demanding eye contact. "Duh?"

"Nearly three years." Cici took both shame and pride in this fact and expected Dane could hear both in her voice.

"Fuckin' A, Ceece—what were you, like fifteen?"

"Yeah."

Dane softened. "Three years. That's a long time."

"Yeah."

After a minute, Dane asked, "So what's everyone else think?"

Cici arched her back, stretching, then let go. "I don't even know. I think they think whatever they can deal with thinking."

Dane pulled the cigarette from her lips, aborting a drag, and regarded her little sister with a cocked head and a proud, glinting eye. "You're a smart cookie, Cici Carver."

Everyone in Pulverdale knew Bear, knew his folks, his family, had watched him play Little League, varsity, cheered him all along the way. Straight out of Humboldt State, he'd landed a phys ed position back at Pulverdale High coaching wrestling, track, spirit squad, and, among other things, girls' soccer. He was twenty-three when he and Cici had fallen in love. No one had known anything officially until long after, until Cici'd graduated and turned eighteen and they were legal at last and announced their plans to marry that summer. Of course, it was coming out gradually and wouldn't stay a secret for long. That stretch was in the past now, and no one wanted to dredge up trouble. People had no beef with Bear and Cici, wished them only happiness. They were just two kids, really, good kids, the both of them.

"How long'd Mom know?"

"Officially? She didn't."

Dane waited.

"I think she always knew," Cici said.

"You think?"

Cici caved. With Dane she always caved. "She knew."

Dane waved her cigarette again. "And it probably never even crossed her mind to object!" She laughed, and Cici thought suddenly that Dane seemed drunk, just letting fly with whatever she actually thought.

Cici shrugged.

Dane noodled her in the side with a bare toe. When Cici turned to look, Dane was all kindness and smiles again. "My baby sister's going to be a bride!" she said, and Cici smiled back, and they sat there on the porch like *Hallmark Hall of Fame* versions of themselves.

Finally it was late enough to justify mixing up some gin and tonics, and that helped them get through dinner, which was just steaks and corn from the grill and some supplementary spaghetti with tomato sauce from a jar, because Rona'd planned a meal for four, not six. In dinner's aftermath they sat around on the back deck looking over the frame of the small, unfinished dance floor.

"We still have three days," Kit said.

"The chairs and tables and everything else comes Saturday," Rona added.

"We'll get it done," Kit said.

Then Dane asked questions about the wedding—the plans, details of food and dress, flowers and favors and rings and music. She didn't ask about people, which could've meant she was steering clear of any *whatever happened to?* questions, lest one get turned back on her. She seemed excited about the wedding, though, drawling that she hadn't "a stitch to wear!" to which Rona and Cici both offered—too quickly, and at the same time—to loan her something before pulling back, embarrassed. Dane said she'd figure out something, and Rona joked that she'd be keeping an eye on the window curtains, so she better not get any Scarlett O'Hara ideas while she was home, which was when Dane, without responding, decided it was time to clear the table.

They cleaned up, and then Bear took the opportunity to escape to the basement to take care of some imaginary stuff he had to take care of. He left the Carvers—Kit, Rona, Cici, Dane, and Trevor—to sit around their living room imitating the family they'd never been. Rona found an old plastic truck in the shed, and Trevor entertained himself running it over the treacherous terrain of the ill-piled coffee-table magazines until he started to get yawny and impatient, pulling at Dane's legs on the couch and clinging to her arm so she couldn't drink her wine. Rona suggested maybe it was time for B-E-D and left to make up the guest room for him and Dane to share. When she returned, Dane hefted Trevor up from the floor, humped him onto her hip, and instructed him to wave goodnight before they disappeared up the stairs to enact a bedtime ritual that the Carvers left in the living room would have been curious to witness. Instead, they could only overhear Trevor crying in plaintive, overtired-child sobs, and then Dane calling down the stairs, "Don't pay attention to him, okay? He's just got to learn!" Then a door closed and the shower went on in the upstairs bathroom, and they sat and listened as water ran noisily through the old pipes and the water heater clanked and moaned and Trevor cried and called for his mother until Rona finally got up and turned on the TV, for which everyone was quite grateful.

Half an hour later, when Trevor had cried himself to sleep and *Law and Order* had moved into its courtroom drama phase, Dane came back downstairs, her hair washed and blown out long and straight. She stood beside the couch, laid an uncharacteristically tender hand on her mother's shoulder, and said, "You okay to watch T awhile?"

Everyone just sat there, not saying yes or no, just watching Dane to see what she'd do next, until finally she said, "I'm just going to go down to Geo-Jo's, see if anyone's there—I haven't seen people in ages," and the only thing to do then was to shrug and nod, *sure, okay.* It was nothing new: Dane was going out and they were babysitting. "He usually sleeps through the night. He's a good kid," Dane said. And then, in a tone so uninviting and obligatory it was almost embarrassing to be on the other end of its ostensible offering, she said, "Anyone want to come?"

Rona and Kit demurred in the style of old folks who haven't been to a bar in decades, even though they'd both been not only drinking but working in bars for much of their adult lives. Cici was underage, though so was Dane, but the idea of Dane *not* being served in a bar was ludicrous, and not because she looked so old (there was a hardness to Dane's beauty that would age her fast and, whatever her lifestyle was, it had already begun to show its wear) but because it was hard to imagine a bartender in the world, male or female, refusing to sell Dane a drink, especially in Pulverdale, where having a baby seemed to up your status to twenty-one, whether your driver's license corroborated it or not.

"Hey, Ceece," Dane called back from the doorway. "Come help me carry some stuff from the car?"

Cici rose from the couch, and Kit started to get up too, but Dane said, "That's okay, Dad, there's not much," and Kit obliged and sat back down.

"'Night, baby," he said.

"'Night, Dad," Dane called, and she wrapped her arm around Cici's waist and herded her sister out the door. "Oh, Ceece," she said. "I missed you." They took the stairs slowly, like lovers lingering in each other's every movement.

"We missed you, too."

"You surviving here with Mom?"

"It's just till Bear can get the house done."

"He's building it himself?"

"Mostly. He's got some guys helping. It's straw bale; they go up pretty quick."

"Just don't let anyone huff and puff and blow it down."

"Lots of people are doing them here now. It's pretty sustainable, you know? Anyway, we should be able to live in it by when school starts, even if it's not totally *done* done."

"School for Bear?"

"I might try Humboldt State for a term," Cici said tentatively. "See how it goes."

"Sometimes I think about doing massage school, you know? Good money, and there's lots of demand. In Vegas there's always customers."

Cici didn't know if massage school actually meant massage school. She stayed quiet.

When they got to the Mercedes, Dane turned Cici around to look back where they'd come. "That fucking house!" Dane said. "It's like being back in high school!" And Cici could have reminded Dane that a month ago she *had* been in high school and that she'd never lived anyplace else, but it didn't seem worth it. It was as though Dane imagined Cici'd left when she had, that no one could have stayed this long.

"It's okay," Cici said. "It's not too much longer. We've got the basement, so it's sort of private."

"Okay, I lived in that room how many years, Ceece? That is *not* private." Dane paused. "My waterbed still down there?"

Cici nodded, then laughed.

Dane let herself laugh too. "That fucking thing!" She was shaking her head ruefully, exaggerated. "How many summers did I work at fucking Dairee Freez and Safeway? And I blew it all, practically, on that fucking thing. And you *cannot* fuck in a waterbed." She was still shaking her head, smiling. "That's my lesson I learned from that one. Waterbeds are not made for fucking."

It had taken a long while for Bear to convince Cici that he'd never slept in that waterbed until Cici brought him there for the first time. It took even longer until she really, honestly believed him. "No kidding," she said, forcing brightness in her tone. "Whose bed do you think it's been the last three years!?" As the words came out, she felt instant regret, a flush of fear that there might be some way to take that wrong, and if there were, that's how Dane would take it. But she was still laughing and pulled Cici to her in a hug, one hand petting her sister's head in sympathy. "Oh baby," Dane cooed, "baby, baby . . ." They stayed like that a minute, the moon glaring off Dane's white car.

Dane pulled away first, swept around to the trunk, and popped it open. "You grab the diapers, Ceece? I got the rest of these, my be-yoot-i-ful luggage . . ."

"Think you got enough diapers here?" Cici joked, struggling dramatically under the package's awkward bulk.

Dane was gathering plastic bag straps onto her wrists. "Well, if T doesn't use them up, we'll save them for when you have yours." She winked over the trunk's raised hood. Dane was all play, but Cici choked and lurched awkwardly before she could get herself back, solid, in the world again. Dane's face curled from that mercurial tease to something graver, a shifting of comprehensions, a question. "I didn't . . ." she began. "You're not . . . ?" Dane's eyes gleamed, and she lifted her hands slightly, weighted down by the bags as they were, as if to demonstrate how powerless she was to hide the smile breaking across her face.

Cici peered at her sister over the top of the enormous diaper package that separated them. "I bought the test," she said. "I haven't done it yet."

Dane's smile dimmed as she got her advice-granting look on. "Don't do it till after the wedding. They can't blame you for what you do before you know, and the last thing you need is Mom telling you you can't have champagne at your own fucking wedding, okay?" She was looking into Cici's face seriously now, intently, like it was very important that Cici promise to drink the wedding champagne that was her due. Cici nodded, her chin grazing the plastic diaper wrapping.

Dane managed to lever up an elbow to slam the trunk shut, and they headed back up the moonlit path to the porch. Cici set the diapers down by the door to take some of the bags from Dane, but Dane shook her head, setting both arms down on the wooden porch floorboards to wriggle her wrists free. She rubbed at them with either hand. "Can you . . . ?" She indicated the bags, then motioned into the house. "So I don't have to *deal* again tonight?"

Cici nodded.

Dane stayed for a second more rubbing her wrists, cocking her head to look up at Cici. "You're going to be such a good mom," she whispered.

Cici bit her lips and tried not to cry. And then, with a hummingbird's flurry, Dane popped up, pecked Cici on the cheek, and fled back down the steps. She sprang into the Mercedes, its lumbering engine turning over with the rumble of a rockslide. It took about a twelve-point turn to get the car headed in the right direction, and then Dane eased it back down the mountain drive she'd climbed not many hours before.

Don't Sweat the Petty

They dispatched Georgia to fetch the best man. The midwestern humidity was relentless; she fiddled futilely with the car's nonfunctional AC controls. Best man John Smith had flown in from California to Iowa on the same flight as the groom's father, stepmother, and half sisters—über-blonde seventeen-year-old triplets, each more gorgeous than the last—and Georgia had to wait in Will and Carolina's old Subaru with the blinkers on while John lingered outside the baggage claim flirting shamelessly. The girls were only a few years younger than Georgia but made her feel particularly spinsterly as she watched them chitchatting in the rearview mirror.

Finally, John bid them all an obsequious farewell and made his way toward the Subaru. He tossed in both his backpack and himself with exaggerated desperation. "They're still driving this piece of shit?"

"Guess so," Georgia said.

"I'm John." He flashed a quick, toothy smile, his eyes still on the blondes being herded into the back seat of a rental car by their impatient and overheated mother. "Groom's best friend, best man, best all around."

Georgia shook his hot hand. "Georgia," she said. "Baby sister of the bride."

"Ah!" John sighed. "Caro . . . a bride!" He fluttered a palm dramatically to his heart. "How long do I still have to steal her away from this Will guy?" He stared out at the landscape in dismay.

Georgia glanced at the dashboard clock. "About twenty-seven hours." Will and Carolina had been together since boarding school, eleventh grade.

"Well, let's get going . . ." John's voice was mournfully resigned. He made no move to put on his seatbelt. "There is truly *nothing here* . . . That's fucking incredible. Nothing."

Georgia started up the engine. John still made no motion to strap him-self in. She waited another moment, then finally reached over, grabbed the buckle of his safety belt, and secured it herself. He succumbed without resistance.

They pulled out of the airport turnaround and onto the two-lane highway. "That's not true anyhow," Georgia said. She'd arrived the day before, surprised to find herself quite taken with the endless rolling green, and now directed John's gaze to one side of the car and then the other. "The tall stuff is corn, the short stuff is soybeans, anything else is a cow."

"Man, I don't know how they're making it . . ."

They drove in silence.

"*No,*" John said suddenly, emphatically. "*Now* I'm in love with Will's *sister.*"

Georgia shook her head. "You mean the triplets? Walter and Regina's girls? They're Will's *half* sisters," she told him. John was Will's best friend; that he did not know Will's relation to the triplets was virtually inconceivable.

"Whatever," said John.

"Which one?" asked Georgia.

"The gorgeous one."

"Justine." *The gorgeous one* was what Will and Carolina called her too.

"Justine . . ."

A school bus stopped on the road ahead of them, its lights flashing, and Georgia braked cautiously. A child jumped from the steps and scam-pered down a dirt road of rust-eaten mailboxes. The bus door slid closed and the driver continued on. Georgia could never remember the exact rule about passing school busses. She followed at a respectable distance.

In the passenger seat, John bounced his legs like a hyperactive teen-ager. And then suddenly, like he was under attack, he flung his arms in front of his face for protection. "Holy fucking shit!"

Georgia concentrated on not driving off the road. She tried not to panic. "What?" she demanded.

"Look." John pointed desperately at the bus's back window, pointing and punching the air with his finger.

Georgia craned to see. "What? I can't . . . what are you seeing?"

"Someone just passed a machine gun across the aisle of that school bus! There's a fucking AK-47 in there—*this* is where it happens. Out here in the middle of nowhere, on a goddamn *school bus!*"

"*Je*-sus," Georgia said. "Paranoid much?"

John looked sheepish. "Maybe it was an umbrella . . ." He shook his head. "Man, this is going to be more than I can handle."

"You haven't been here before, I take it?"

John shook his head again. He and Will had been college roommates in California, an odd couple but fiercely devoted to one another. Will was the hippie, the intellectual: mild-mannered and bitterly funny when he got a few beers in him. John was the playboy, the showman who'd gone on to Hollywood, "The Industry." He waited tables for a living and had landed, in the two years since college, a walk-on bit on *Friends* and the lead in someone's undergrad thesis at USC—a ten-minute film about date rape, Jesus, and goldfish. John was good-looking, irresponsible and neurotic, a guy who showed up at college parties not with the usual six-pack of Rolling Rock, but bearing whatever he appeared to have found in the house: unshelled peanuts he'd dumped into an empty marshmallow bag and secured with a twist tie, half a block of cheddar cheese Will had bought to make nachos the week before, an open liter of Coke. But Will spoke of John with the greatest affection, and Georgia felt inadequately prepared for the mess of nerves she was now chauffeuring through the Iowa farmland.

John gazed out the window at the passing cornfields. "That's cool," he conceded. "The way the wind makes the corn look like waves, like water . . ."

Georgia turned off the paved road and a cloud of dust bloomed in the car's wake. They passed a dilapidated farmhouse, its old stone silo looming like a lighthouse.

"It's fucking *In Cold Blood* wherever you look," John said.

"Don't say that around my mother," Georgia advised. "She gets upset."

"Fucking *Children of the Corn* . . ."

Rocks banged the car's underbelly, then rolled off into the ditch. A bullet-pocked sign for FUNK'S Fertilizer bent backward as if pummeled by a heavy wind. Snagged in the cornstalks, a white plastic bag shivered as they passed. John said it looked like a bride's veil, lost as she fled the altar and disappeared into the corn.

The weekend forecast—"Thank god for *small* favors," said the bride's mother—was not for rain. It was, in fact, for sun. Lots of it. "Lows in the eighties," said the weatherman. "Highs in the upper nineties, humidity bringing the heat indices up to a hundred and five." It was an amazing thing about the Midwest, Georgia thought: they had real people on the news. The anchor was overweight, in a flowered dress and big, round purple-framed eyeglasses. The sports guy looked like he'd set his beer down backstage and slipped into his suit as an afterthought. The weatherman smiled a gap-toothed smile and wiped the back of his hand across his forehead as though he too, in that air-conditioned studio in Cedar Rapids, were subject to the dramatic heat.

"Join us for our wedding"—Carolina laughed—"in *hell*."

They held the ceremony and reception in an 1883 octagonal barn that felt more like a cathedral than a hay loft, shards of colored light filtering in through a stained glass cupola at the peak of its great arching dome. The buffet was nestled in beds of melting ice that dripped from old horse troughs and streamed across the sawdusty stable floor. It was six in the evening and the temperature hadn't dropped below ninety-five. In an attempt to compensate, the bride's parents, Jake and Genevieve Osterman, had gone and rented four enormous fans from an industrial supply company in Cedar Rapids.

"My wife wants me playing god," Jake boomed. "I'm supposed to regulate the *outdoor* temperature." From a table by the corncrib he kept up the hollering even as Carolina's Grandpa Harry stood to make a toast. "He's going to make the same damn speech he gave at my wedding thirty years ago!" Jake shouted.

"Thirty-one," his wife corrected.

"You betcha I am." Grandpa Harry was a fiscally conservative son of a bitch, with eyebrows like great clumps of alfalfa sprouts that small children were often unable to refrain from grabbing onto and yanking gleefully. He cleared his throat. "When I married my beautiful wife"—he gestured to Grandma Maxine, who waved away the attention, batting her eyelashes modestly—"my own father, rest his soul, had a few pieces of advice for me. He said there are two things you need to check before you go and pledge the rest of your life to this woman: her teeth and her brassiere straps. Now, we've already taken care of the orthodontia—look at that beautiful smile!" He stuck a hand in Carolina's direction. She and Will were curled on a hay bale, grinning and sweating. "And just in case your old ones are getting ratty"—Grandpa Harry reached into the inner pocket of his suit coat, which he'd only put back on to make the toast and which was already soaked through with sweat, pulled out a damp envelope, and handed it to Carolina—"there's a little something to get yourself some new skivvies."

"It's the same goddamn speech he made at our wedding," Jake kept saying.

And Grandma Maxine said, "His father really told him those things, you know. A real bastard, my father-in-law, god rest . . . And now, who's the one with dentures, Harry? Who's the one without a real tooth left in his head?"

The barn smelled of hay and sweat and sweet hydrangea. By sundown everyone had shed shoes, socks, ties, even shirts. The temperature dropped a few blessed degrees. Cake was cut and served. John took a slice and a fork and strode to the table one over from Georgia's where two of the triplets picked at the same pink bakery rose.

"May I?" John asked, sitting.

One of them nodded; the other gestured disinterestedly toward the chair.

"So which ones are you?" John filled his mouth with buttercream.

"Justine," said Justine.

"Jade," said the other. "Aren't you *hot*?" she asked John, who was still clad in the dark wool suit he'd insisted on wearing despite its profound inappropriateness to both the season and the occasion.

He shook his head noncommittally, as though the heat had not crossed his mind. "So, I have a question," he said, swallowing. "This might sound kind of silly, you know, but I was wondering: when you wake up in the morning, how do you know that it's *you* waking up and not one of your sisters?"

Jade rolled her eyes, pushed back her seat, muttered an insincere excuse, and stalked away. Justine rolled her own eyes in turn. "Don't mind her, she's having a selfish time."

"A selfish time?" John asked.

"Oh, you know." Justine waved her hand vaguely. "She's into proving her individuality or whatever."

"Do you all go through that sort of thing?"

Justine looked bored. "Jade more than me and Jos."

John pulled his seat closer to hers. "How come?"

"We always thought it's because she was the last one to get boobs . . . but who knows?" Justine shrugged.

John choked on his drink. "Who was first?" he ventured.

"Me," she said, unfazed.

"Hm," said John.

"It's really annoying," Justine said.

"What is?"

"Everything."

John's face lit with an idea: "I'll go get us some drinks!" And he stood and got sucked into the dancing crowd, party guests swimming in a fog of their own humidity.

Justine sat alone, her face a plain of utter disinterest. Then Tex ambled over. Tex: brother of the bride. His real name was Austin, though no one ever called him by it. Like Georgia, Tex had not brought a date to the wedding, and economy of housing space had forced them to share a room for the weekend at the old converted orphanage across from the barn. Georgia thought her brother to be an insufferable prick, and as if to prove her right, Tex had characteristically rented a car for the weekend but then refused to help shuttle guests from the airport or even to lend the car for the job. It was his name on the rental contract, he argued. The rest of the family generally agreed that Tex was his mother's fault. Willfully oblivious to Tex's egocentrism, Genevieve Osterman appeared to think her son shat sunlight. Yet it had surprised even Genevieve that he'd bothered to make the trip to Iowa for the wedding. Something had happened to him, at least since Georgia'd last seen her brother. There was a new air of desperation. Once a strapping football player, cocky and loud and mean, Tex had morphed into a thirty-year-old bachelor with thinning hair who was weathering poorly the effects of twelve years of steady binge drinking.

Tex stood awkwardly by Justine's table for a minute. Was he thinking about tipping it over and running away? Instead, he asked her to dance, and Georgia thought—or rather hoped—that maybe she'd underestimated her brother. Maybe he'd grow up one day after all. She watched as he took Justine's hand with princely attention and led her to the dance floor.

A few minutes later John reappeared with two shot glasses, limes clamped to their lips like little green Pac-Men. He held a saltshaker tucked under his arm. "Your brother stole my triplet!" he cried.

"Two more where she came from," Georgia suggested.

John cocked his head: *very funny*. "But that one was mine," he whined.

"Isn't it a little soon to get possessive?"

John held a shot glass toward her.

"That was awfully nice of you."

"It was for Justine," he admitted.

"You poor thing," Georgia said. She plucked the saltshaker from him, dashed herself out a lick, and drank her shot down.

Suddenly John brightened. "*You're* not available by any chance, are you?"

She pulled the lime from her teeth and winced.

John left to smoke a cigarette, making room for Grandma Maxine to lean provocatively over from the next table. "Georgie," she said. "How's my Georgie these days? There's a *man* in your life, my beauty?" She nudged her head toward John as he headed out the barn door.

"Not exactly, Grandma."

Maxine's eyes lit at the intimation of intrigue. "Oh there *is* someone, now, isn't there? Come on, Georgie, make an old woman's day. Who's your fella?"

"No fella, Gram. Sorry."

"No? A beautiful girl like you should have a *companion*. Now, I know someone, maybe you'd like him . . . ? A man from the synagogue, very clean . . . You'd like me to introduce you, maybe . . . ?"

Georgia was exhausted. She felt like a boiled turnip. "Actually I already have a *companion*."

Maxine's mouth opened in an *O* of joy. "You're holding out on me, Georgie! Come, tell me about your friend . . ."

Georgia sighed. "Maybe when you get a little more liberal, Grandma . . ."

"What's not liberal? I voted for Gore . . ."

Georgia chuckled again. "A little more open-minded then . . ."

Maxine's face froze. She leaned closer, laid a hand on Georgia's arm, and spoke as though wary of spies. She said, "He's not a Jew?"

"Not a Jew," Georgia repeated. "Not even a *he*, Gram."

Maxine's brow furrowed in confusion. "A girl?" she said, and then her eyes widened in surprise.

Georgia nodded. So this was how it felt to come out to your grand-mother. She'd gone too far to backtrack now. "She's British. I met her when I studied in London last spring. She's in med school there."

Maxine's eyebrows shot up, her chin drew back into the folds of her neck, and her face spread in pleasure. "Oh," she said. "A doctor!"

On his way back into the barn, John passed Will's father and his wife, Regina, who were pressing a set of car keys into the hands of Joslin, the third triplet. "Not too late, young lady, okay?" said Regina. They were not staying at the orphanage with almost everyone else. Reggie had insisted on booking what passed for a suite at the Well-Come-Inn a few miles down I-80, with an adjoining room for the girls.

"Yes, Mommy Dearest," said Joslin.

"Don't call me that," Reggie said. Joslin snickered.

"*You* drive, Jos," Walter instructed. He looked to Justine thumping on the dance floor with Carolina's hulking brother. "Keep a watch on your sisters, okay?"

Joslin rolled her eyes dramatically.

"Watch it, miss," said Reggie. She kissed her daughter quickly and took Walter's arm to make an exit.

From their table, Georgia and John watched them go. "Why *do* people have children?" Georgia said.

"So they can look like *that*," John said, his eyes on the dancing Justine.

Tex hustled Georgia outside the barn, away from the celebrants, and demanded her full attention. "Listen to me. And you have to tell me honestly, okay."

Georgia nodded reluctantly.

Tex was sweating profusely and fidgeting, kicking out his legs like he was trying to get the circulation going. He made a few false starts, then sputtered, "Would Mom and Dad . . . do you think they'd kill me if I tried to get with one of those triplets?"

Georgia burst out laughing.

"Don't be such a *bitch*," Tex whined. "Come on, shut up, really, would they kill me?"

The barn seemed to heave in the heat, then sigh and settle back down. Georgia looked at her red-nosed brother. "*I'd* kill you," she said. "One of those orphanage beds is *mine*, if you haven't forgotten."

"Aw, fuck," Tex said, kicking dirt. "You're no help." He turned away and left her.

Georgia shook her head, then shut her eyes. "Un-fucking-believable," she said aloud. When she opened her eyes again, she saw Will's Grandma Elsie being herded toward the parking lot by Will's mom. Elsie was eighty-seven and riddled with Alzheimer's, but when she noticed Georgia there in the shadows of the barn, a look of recognition crossed her face and she raised a gnarled hand to wave, as if in awe at finding a long-lost relative. Georgia waved back, and Elsie flashed her a grin like a watermelon wedge. And then, grandly, she winked. It was such a sober gesture, such a knowing and portent look on Elsie's face, that for a moment it seemed plainly clear to Georgia that the woman had been getting the better of her family with this Alzheimer's ruse for a good long time.

Following a lengthy diatribe from Grandpa Harry on the importance of retirement funds and an unfortunate run-in with a friend of her mother's who apparently had very strong feelings about the trajectory of Georgia's college career, Georgia finally bid her good nights to Will and Carolina and found her way back to the orphanage. She climbed the steps to her room. Tex's tie—a terrible pig-pink foulard—was draped over the knob. Georgia had the vague notion this was some sort of a fraternity signal. She knocked loudly.

"Go *away*," Tex hollered.

"What?"

"*A-way!*" he called again.

A good and benevolent person, Georgia knew, would storm in there and save that poor girl from a night she'd probably regret the rest of her blonde-borne life. Georgia slammed her fist into the door, which gave half an inch—there were no locks at the orphanage. She grabbed the knob and pushed, but the door wouldn't budge any further. "What—do you have her *captive*? You are *not* seriously barricaded in there with a fucking seventeen-year-old?"

From inside, a high-pitched giggle, then Tex booming, "Go away!"

"You are fucking unbelievable!" Georgia yelled.

Down the hall, a door opened. John appeared in the corridor. He was still wearing his wool suit, a bottle of Jim Beam in one hand, a glass in the other. He held his arms out to her, offering either the liquor or a bear hug, it wasn't clear which. "Need a place to stay?" he asked.

Georgia was beyond tired. And somewhat drunk.

John stepped aside and held the door for her.

He wiped off the neck of the whiskey bottle with the end of his tie (still knotted at the neck, though it hung down his shirtfront like soggy crepe paper), poured Georgia a glass, then refilled his own.

John raised his glass. "To . . . the happy couple."

"Will and Caro?" Georgia asked. "Or the fuckbunnies down the hall?"

"To happy couples and fuckbunnies everywhere!" He paused. "Should we maybe join them?" he said carefully. "This being a wedding and all . . . ?"

Georgia laughed. "Join them?! That's a little incestuous, don't you think? Tex being my brother and all . . ."

John looked dismayed. "No, no, not join *them*," he stammered. "Join in the whole *thing* of it, you know?" He couldn't seem to find the right words for what he wanted to say and was growing increasingly pained with the sad, futile effort.

"No, I"—and it was Georgia stammering now—"It's not . . ."

"I'm not your type." John nodded solemnly. "I understand. I understand that . . ." He seemed to drift away, then partially return. "Do you mind . . . could I . . . ? Can I ask what your type *is*, just, you know, out of curiosity . . . ?"

"Well," Georgia said, "mostly just a little more on the not-male side I guess you'd say . . ."

John's face twitched like he'd been suddenly awakened. "Oh! Ohhhhhh . . ." He drew it out, as if to meditate on the syllable, delve deep inside its koan of meaning. "Ohhhhhh, wow. Wow." He wagged his head, shaking off the disbelief. "Wow. Sorry," he said finally. "I totally didn't realize."

"That's okay," she said. The magnitude of his reaction was actually a little bit charming. "It's not really a big deal."

"That's cool," he said, and then he began to rock himself back and forth on the floor, knees curled tight to his chest. "That's totally cool . . ."

When Georgia started yawning uncontrollably, John stopped rocking and gestured grandly to the single mattress on which she sat. "My bed es su bed," he told her.

"I'm happy to take the floor," she argued, but he just wrapped his arms protectively around his knees again, near-empty glass in hand. He looked confused or curious, like maybe he was stoned as well as drunk, his brow wrinkled like he was watching a wild animal to determine whether it was dead or just sleeping. He took his eyes from Georgia, looked deep into his drink like he was going to give it one more chance to save him, then downed the last of it, set his glass on the window sill, and took a deep breath. He reached an arm over his head and flicked off the light switch. And then he literally tipped himself over sideways to a fetal position on the floor.

Georgia sat dumb for another moment. "At least take the pillow," she said finally.

Georgia woke early. Still in her maid-of-honor dress—a rayon spaghetti strap number that had doubled nicely as a nightgown, not even too wrinkled—she sneaked past the sleeping John and made her way downstairs to the orphanage porch. Her hangover loomed like a vague and nonspecific regret. She had some memory of leaving her shoes near a silo. A heavy dew had fallen, and Georgia laid a stray towel over a boxy wooden rocker that heaved under her weight as she sat. Steam seemed to rise off the cornfields. The morning air wasn't stifling, yet, and the sun felt nice on her face, though in another hour she'd undoubtedly be ready to sell her liver for a dark room with air-conditioning.

The screen door creaked open. John looked like he hadn't slept at all. His wool suit looked like he'd gone over Niagara Falls in it and baked himself dry on a rock at the bottom. His shoes were old, the black leather deeply creased with brown-bleeding cracks. His face was heavily shadowed, though Georgia could remember him being freshly shaved—nicked, even—for the ceremony. On the porch, John tried to light a cigarette from the crumpled pack in his jacket pocket, but the matches were limp and waterlogged. He patted himself down for a lighter, but, finding none, pitched the cigarette over the railing, took a glance at his surroundings, steamy dew rising off the green-green fields, shuddered, and began to pace the creaking floorboards.

"You're probably not a smoker, huh?" he said.

Georgia shook her head. "Tex might have a lighter upstairs . . ."

John crushed the pack vigorously to show her it was empty. He pitched it off the balcony and into the grass, then rested his head against a peeling white column, his eyes cast out. It was the stillest Georgia'd seen him. She felt sad for John. But then he was back to pacing, which made Georgia want to shove him down and inject him with a sedative.

"You want to go into town?" she asked him suddenly. "We could get some breakfast. You could get some cigarettes. And a lighter."

John stopped pacing and turned to her, his face awash with sheer relief, and he looked younger then, and kinder. "You are my angel," he said. "You are an angel from God."

"I'll steal Tex's keys," Georgia said.

She was able to push the door open just wide enough to slide through before it hit the oak dresser that Tex had hauled in front of it. The girl was gone, the twin beds pushed clumsily together, Tex across them, belly down, passed out, breathing hard, his red face smushed sideways, skinny white legs poking out from his thick middle like two sticks in a candy apple, his little white ass pointed up like it was seeking sunshine. Georgia slipped on some tennis shoes, fumbled through Tex's pockets until she hit on the car keys, and didn't look back.

They found a diner. John bought cigarettes at the counter. By the register, a drowned-looking man in a sweat suit was picking up cookie packages and inspecting ingredients. John and Georgia got a table and coffee, and he smoked, something he said you couldn't do in California anymore. It was the first appreciative thing he'd said about the Midwest since his arrival. They ordered breakfast and sipped their coffee, weak and too white with tubs of nondairy creamer, and Georgia felt the sun warm her shoulder through the window. The front door heaved open and a small, prim woman entered, dressed in neat pastels with sturdy shoes. The cookie-package man turned to look at her, and she greeted him with curt, churchly politeness, then strode to the counter, sat, and ordered coffee and a poached egg, white toast. The man followed and seated himself on the stool beside hers.

Georgia excused herself. She splashed her face at the restroom sink, then blotted her cheeks with a wad of coarse brown paper towels. The air-conditioning in the bathroom was delightfully frigid, and Georgia sat for a time in the toilet stall reading graffiti.

I want your pussy.

Women don't sweat the petty things, just pet their sweaty things.

Here's to the guy who wears red boots. He drives your truck and drinks your booze. He took your cherry, but 'twas no sin. He left you with a cigarette and a big ol' grin.

When Georgia returned to the table their food had arrived, but John was waiting for her before beginning.

"You didn't have to," Georgia said.

"That's okay." He shrugged. He was smoking another cigarette and didn't seem to have much interest in his breakfast.

The food made Georgia feel good, and chatty, and as she ate, she told John about the graffiti in the bathroom. He laughed, but like it reminded him of something he didn't want to think about.

John took a few bites of omelet, then flattened his hash browns with the back of his fork. "You ever hook up with someone at a wedding?" he asked.

Georgia nodded, her mouth full. She took a sip of coffee and swallowed. "Lost my virginity at a wedding, in fact."

"No way!" John's face lit up, then crumpled in confusion. "To a girl?"

Georgia shook her head. "Noah Schnackenberg."

John smiled, as though relieved.

Georgia laughed. "I was so scared I kept forgetting to breathe, and my head went pins and needles—literally from lack of oxygen. He tried to convince me I was having an orgasm."

John was smiling, nodding his head like he'd caught a good groove and wanted to ride it. He lit another cigarette. At the counter, the sweat-suited man was talking to the woman beside him, who seemed clearly too Christian to turn him away. He spoke loudly and fast, hardly pausing to breathe.

"I'm a real extrovert," the man was saying, "but I don't have the good looks to go with it. Sometimes I'll be around people and I'll be talking and I forget that I'm not physically attractive. I'm forty, but I'm told I look young. It's the lack of a fat stomach and facial wrinkles. I don't eat cheese. People that don't smoke eat more than people who do. I get a lot out of smoking. It's an appetite suppressant. Someday I'll quit. I did good with Nicorette back in '93, but you need a doctor. I'd be in better shape if I didn't smoke."

John raised his eyebrows at Georgia. She shrugged back.

"I'm totally in love with your sister," John said with a sudden, mournful honesty.

"Will's sister," she corrected him. "Half sister."

John shook his head. "No, *your* sister."

"Carolina?"

He nodded, clearly pained.

Of course he was! Why not? *Will* was in love with Caro—plenty of people probably had been. But why would *John* be in love with her? Carolina was low-key, not flashy at all, certainly pretty, but nothing like Justine. Georgia spoke her first thought. "Why?"

John shook his head: *why not?* "She's so *good*, you know? She's like the perfect *girl*. The perfect *woman*. She's like the epitome." He paused. "Will seems so happy with her. Always has. She just seems to make him so happy . . ."

Georgia squinted at John until she could feel the crease between her eyebrows.

John nodded. "It'd be nice to be Will," he said dreamily. "Don't you think it'd be nice to be Will?"

Georgia shrugged. The fold in her forehead deepened. But John looked so miserable she felt a kind of piteous affection for him. She reached across the table and riffled his hair encouragingly. "Buck up there, young friend," she said.

The waitress passed by with coffee and stopped to offer some. She smiled down on Georgia and John like they were her own kids. "You two married?" she asked. "You make a nice-looking couple, you know."

Georgia snorted. John smiled up at the woman. "Five years next week," he said, nodding with irrepressible pride.

"Well, congratulations," said the waitress, her grin unwavering. "That's just great. You just keep on." She smiled off to peddle her coffee at the counter, where the man's monologue was still in full swing, the church lady beside him, resigned.

"I was in peak condition back in '90, '91. Fast walking keeps you in good shape. I bundle up and jog—not really jog, but . . . around the block two times a day. I've got a big appetite. I only eat before I do physical activity. I don't eat after eight at night ever. But if you were a night person . . ."

John turned to Georgia, fear in his eyes. His voice was phlegmy. "Do you think Carolina finds me attractive at *all?*"

"Caro?" Georgia balked.

John nodded, embarrassed but desperate.

Georgia was caught somewhere between compassion and disdain. "*I* don't know . . ."

An idea seemed to seize John. "Do *you?*" he asked. "At *all?*"

He looked so pathetic Georgia couldn't deny him. "I can say," she said evenly, "that for a little while I did honestly contemplate sleeping with you last night."

"Oh!" It was too loud a cry of surprise. "I wish you'd said something . . ."

"It probably wouldn't have been a very good idea."

"Why?" he asked, though he didn't really seem to expect an answer. He looked like he was drifting back in his mind to someplace distant and dreamy, remembering something pleasant from long, long ago. "I don't know. It might've been nice . . ."

Georgia was at a loss, John far off in reverie. A few booths down, the waitress began her coffee rounds again, smiling her diligent, unwavering smile, as though she benefited personally from each cup she managed to refill. She held the pot at ear level and listened to an animated couple talking at her, then tried them once more, forcing the woman to cover her cup with her hands, shake her head solemnly, *no, no more*, before the waitress, defeated, moved on. Her smile pressed wider; she approached the next booth, a true salesperson, a woman unprepared to take no for an answer. Georgia almost couldn't bear to witness such determination. She turned away, back toward the counter where the sweat-suited jogger's monologue continued, no end in sight.

"I don't have good enough running shoes," he was saying. "You got to have really good running shoes, else you'll blow out your ankles. Mine crack when I get up in the morning. When you turn forty your whole metabolism changes. I've been in this town since '81. I'm single, and as long as I live here, I probably won't meet the right woman. Women don't like beards. Tall and clean they want. If I want to meet the right woman I'll probably have to move. Or shave. But I like this town. It's a pretty good town. But to meet the right woman I'll have to move away. I've studied the occult and physics. This town looks down on Christian people who try to live in a certain way. It's not a real Christian town. Cedar Rapids is a Christian town, but they've got more violent crime."

HOME IS WHERE THE HEART GIVES OUT AND WE AROUSE THE GRASS

Finally, the Good-Nite Inn had a vacancy. "Big dog show," the desk clerk explained. His name tag said BOGDAN. His efficiency was disarming, the way he snapped up her license and Mastercard and pivoted to the copy machine. Spinning back around, he clapped the charge slip and pen to the counter and held the papers down while she signed, her hands shaking from exhaustion and caffeine. Swiping the pen up from the final stroke of her name, she caught him across the back of the hand and yelped, startled by the brush of resistance—flesh—where she hadn't expected it, like a car traveling fast on solid asphalt until it hits a patch of something else.

"God, I'm sorry," she said.

He didn't flinch, just lifted her signature and regarded it sternly. His hand—now cut by a blue-inked line—was otherwise pink and terribly chapped, as though scrubbed and scrubbed and scalded. She had known a girl in college with hands like that. OCD. When Bogdan looked up, small eyes dark against the sick-blue pallor of his skin, his face opened kindly. "Katya is Russian name."

She nodded, too vigorously. "Katy," she said. "But, yeah, my grandparents were." She gestured behind her, as though the pair of aging immigrants were waiting in the vestibule.

"I am from Ukraine," Bogdan enunciated so beautifully it was as though words had a new, higher purpose.

"Oh!" She kept nodding, grinning at him, as though she too had been raised in the Communist Bloc, overwhelmed to meet a comrade.

Bogdan smiled then, with his cheeks and eyes, not his mouth—a chastely maternal expression. "Room number one-five-nine," he said, placing the keycard in its protective envelope onto the counter and sliding it toward Katy like something illicit, speaking slowly, as though she might be hard of hearing, or slow. "Is just around . . ." He leaned and pointed.

She lingered uncertainly by the desk. "So there's a dog show going on?"

"Tomorrow. In Omaha." Bogdan gestured vaguely to the east.

The lobby door chimed open then, and a dozen Chihuahuas came tumbling in, climbing and crawling over each other like drowning ants. Their owner was a rather pretty woman, in her forties probably, whose spray-set hair and loafers seemed incongruous to the maroon sweat-pants spilling out from below the hem of a dark wool dress coat. She held twelve individual leashes, apparently unconcerned by their inextricable tangle.

Bogdan lifted his hands helplessly, then touched his fingers to the gelled spikes of his prematurely thin hair and turned to help the Chihuahua lady.

It took Katy three tries to pull into the parking spot for room #159. She almost felt guilty leaving her little Honda there in a phalanx of backloading vans and animal trailers, like a shrimpy new kid at school among the bullies. A gigantic, anachronistically mustached man in leather chaps stood in a patch of grass beside four delicately squatting white poodles. In the window of #158, a tiny pack of dachshunds barked the glass into a fog, nosing desperately against it as if they were for sale. Behind the pups, a grandma in quilted slippers reclined on the bed, a copy of *Sports Illustrated* splayed across her lap.

Across from the Good-Nite Inn on the far side of a shallow, trash-strewn ravine was a steakhouse whose sign read *Bubbas*. Katy pushed into a perkily lit, overheated foyer, then through a pair of saloon doors and into the dining room. It was ten-thirty and Bubbas was sparsely populated. A few people were staggered around the narrow wooden U of the bar at respectful intervals. A teenager in a ski cap lay back in a booth reading a garage-sale pulp novel called *Love Is a Gentle Whip*. A couple, tucked in the corner booth, looked like they'd been there a long time, drawing a dinner date as far into the night as it might go before they had to make any decisions about what would happen next.

Katy took a seat at the bar. She ordered a lager and asked for a menu. The bartender asked for ID, then took Katy's license offhand-edly, as though she *hadn't* requested it but was pleasantly surprised by its offer. "Wyoming," she said, peering up at Katy, then back down at the card. "You're a ways from home, huh?" Her voice was husky. Her hair—a little bit greasy or maybe just wet—was dyed black, and she was tall, broad-shouldered, large-breasted, in a black mock turtleneck gone gray-green with wear and stretched out like a smock. She had a strong jaw and was alarmingly sexy: the sort of woman who forced everyone she met to instantly imagine themselves in bed with her.

Katy shrugged as though shy to admit that, yes, she'd left Wyoming far behind. In truth, it had only been that morning, but she'd covered a lot of miles.

The bartender smiled knowingly, set the license on the bar, and tapped Katy's beer into a glass at least a foot and a half tall. From an angle, Katy thought the bartender looked a little pregnant, but then she moved and the impression vanished as the woman lifted a lit cigarette from an ashtray on the bar and inhaled. She set the butt back down in its cradle and released the smoke slowly through one twisted-up corner of her mouth. "What can I get you to eat?" she asked, squinting against the smoke.

"Cheeseburger?" Katy said tentatively, like it might be too much to ask.

"Fries?"

Katy nodded eagerly. The bartender nodded once, took the length of the bar in three long strides, and burst away through the swinging doors at the far end.

"I was in Wyoming once," piped the man three seats to Katy's left. He was white-haired and red-faced, with the cloudy, unfocused eyes of someone who's been drunk a long time. "Flew in," he said. "One of those puddle jumpers." He lifted a hand from the bar, palm down, and then let it fall back, slapping the surface a few inches closer to Katy. Then he lifted the hand again, gesturing back and forth between himself and the kitchen door. "Only 'bout as long as the bar here." As he waved, the bartender reemerged from the kitchen, doors swinging, with a small dinner salad balanced on her palm.

"You need something there, Burt?"

"Nah, just telling a story." He turned back to Katy. "Melissa takes good care of me." Melissa placed her large hand over his and squeezed reassuringly. She set the salad in front of Katy, who was confused.

"Oh, does that come with . . . ?"

Melissa jerked her chin toward the salad. "It's good for you." She reached below the bar and hauled up a rack that held three covered aluminum pots of salad dressing, a notch in each lid for the spoon to poke through. Beside this she set down a pepper grinder that was even taller than the beer glass. Katy took a sip. The glass was heavy. Her hands still shook.

"One of those tiny little planes you can't barely stand in, yeah?" Burt continued. "And I was on it there with the whole friggin' football team from I-don't-know-where. Some football team. And we get our cocktail service and some weather—there's some snow and we're up circling round and round over the airport"—he began to swivel his head and torso to indicate a circling plane—"Round and round for I-don't-know-how long. And these guys, they got to *piss*, but they're so big and that lavatory's so small they can't fit inside. No kidding! And the waitr—the waddya call, the stewardess—big girl, real pretty, almost pretty as Melissa." He winked at her, washing glasses at the bar sink, and she made a *poot* of retort with her lips. "And she was"—Burt tapped the side of his head, *brainy*—"that girl. Pulls the curtain closed, you know, between where the seats are and the restroom, up by the pilot, yeah? She tells 'em, 'Leave the door open, stand in the aisle, and aim yourself good. I don't want my airplane smelling like a damn urinal!'" Burt laughed, stamped a fist on the bar. The peppermill jumped. It startled him, and he picked it up, turned the wooden totem over in his hands. "Now what do you suppose . . . ?" he started to say. "Hey Meliss," he called, "what do you suppose . . . ? You got any idea what that's meant to be?" He tried to shake it by his ear and nearly fell from the stool.

Melissa rescued the peppermill. "Pepper grinder, Burt." She poised it demonstratively over Katy's salad.

"Ah, yeah," Burt said thoughtfully. "I thought that's what that might be, but then I didn't see holes."

Melissa turned to Katy. "So, in town for the show?"

"The dog show?" Katy started, like she'd been caught in a lie. "No . . . No, just passing through, I guess. Just stopped for the night, really."

"Headed where?"

"I don't . . . I guess away from where I was . . . Just to, you know, get away . . ."

"*I hear you,*" said Melissa, each word a stress of its own.

"We *all* run away," Burt said, and he swept out an arm for emphasis—that infinite span of *away*—and caught Katy's beer with a karate chop that sent its entire contents flooding directly into Katy's lap. She leapt from the barstool and stumbled backward, avoiding none of the cascading drink. The bar was silent and staring.

Burt's face reddened further; his scalp flushed magenta. Katy's jeans were soaked from zipper to knee, her underwear as drenched as if she'd wet herself. And then the sense that she *had* wet herself felt so dreadfully, viscerally familiar it filled her with nausea and the fear that something was about to turn terribly wrong.

The man to Katy's other side at the bar had also jumped up at the crash of the beer and was now handing Katy a wad of cocktail napkins. She touched them to her jeans; the paper soaked instantly through. Katy stood, dumb, felt a trickle down her calf, and felt her eyes and throat welling.

"Hey," Melissa said, lifting aside a drop leaf section of the bar. She held it open like a drawbridge. "I've got a pair of sweats you can put on." Katy knew she'd cry if she opened her mouth, so she just nodded and followed Melissa under the bar and back up its U to the kitchen.

From a coat rack on the cement-block wall, Melissa grabbed a small nylon gym duffel. She tossed Katy a pair of navy-blue sweats that felt warm and spongy.

Melissa crossed the kitchen, reached out a hand, and covered the eyes of the cook—a tall young man with fuzz for a beard—who stood, docile, arms obediently at his sides.

Katy might have liked a bit more privacy for the clothes-change, but she had the sense that this kind of modesty would disappoint Melissa somehow. And so, in the middle of Bubbas' kitchen, Katy slid off her jeans, along with her sopping underwear, grateful for the hanging shirt-tails of her oversized flannel.

"There's a hand dryer in the restroom," Melissa was saying. "You could dry your pants on it."

Katy heard herself say "cool," but she wasn't thinking about drying her pants, because the thought of wearing Melissa's sweatpants without underwear had forced her into the sudden awareness that the underwear she'd just shed was the same pair she'd put back on at four that morning at the foot of Abe's futon before she sneaked away with promises to call him later, once she'd talked to Scott, told Scott, and dealt with the immediate aftermath. The thing that had freaked her—the image stuck in her head all day as she drove—was the condom lying in the metal trash bin beside Abe's bed where he'd dropped it when he took it off. The light in the room was shadowy, yes. And she'd had a lot to drink. But she could almost swear that there wasn't anything inside that condom, and she could not—no matter how she spun it in her brain—*could not* figure out if the condom had broken (and at just about the perfect time in her cycle, of course) or if he hadn't actually come.

From Melissa, across the room: a sharp, long intake of air, like a vicarious experience of pain, a whistle escaping the purse of her lips. "Man, those are some scars . . ."

Katy looked down at herself. They were faded from what they'd once been but were still shocking, she supposed, to someone who didn't know. "Car accident," she said, and she'd learned in eight years how to say it very flatly and a little too loud so whoever was asking stopped. Because even now, when she thought of the accident, what hit her first—even before the pit of the void where Abe—the first Abe—should have been—what hit her first was the mortification of the ambulance ride. Or, really, it was the mortification of the embarrassment of the ambulance ride. Because inside the scream of the sirens it hadn't been Abe she was thinking of. Fear, she knew, had the capacity to get pathetically misplaced, and in the ambulance she'd been utterly consumed with the fear that she'd pissed her pants in the wreck, only remembering Abe on the heels of that, and then not to wonder if he was alive or dead but to wonder whether he'd lost control of his bladder too. It wasn't until days after the accident that she'd realized no one could have told one bodily fluid from another amid all that blood. Anyway, the EMTs had cut off her jeans when they pulled her from the car.

Katy tugged Melissa's enormous sweatpants onto her otherwise naked lower body. She slid back into her clogs and rolled her jeans into a tight ball, underwear trapped inside.

Melissa gave in to the cook's silent protestations that the fries needed to come out of the fryer. Then she slid off the counter where she'd perched and went to hold the swinging door so Katy might pass back into the bar, clutching her ball of wet clothing like a dirty diaper.

Katy's barstool, and the floor at her seat, had been neatly mopped, and another improbably tall glass of beer sat by her place at the bar. Both men—Burt and the guy from the other side—were gone. Katy reclaimed her seat. When she was up next to it, the beer glass seemed to loom even taller. She jammed her wet jeans behind the brass footrest bar, kicking at them every few moments to make sure they didn't go anywhere.

The saloon doors swung open behind her and the not-Burt man returned to the bar. He was sort of middle-aged, part cowboy, part biker, somewhat imposing but for a weak iguana chin. He nodded at Katy's outfit. "Good look for you there."

She gave a little snort of a laugh, smiling stupidly, mute again until her smile broke and twisted into a contortion of both guilt and pity. "Did Burt *leave* because of . . . ? I feel . . . the poor guy . . ."

When he smiled, the man's face flattened into his neck like a ping-pong paddle. "Nah, he's just in the can."

And then the kitchen doors swung open, and there was Melissa with a burger platter, the aroma of dark golden fries enveloping the bar. The fries had been salted, lightly, and the crystals glimmered, iridescent as fake snow.

Katy's mouth was full when the bar doors swung open again and Burt lunged back to his seat at the U, nodding to everyone as though he'd just pulled up in the parking lot, hadn't seen Melissa since the night before. "Melissa, my love," he said, holding his voice as steady as he could, "the usual, if you don't mind?" He regarded her curiously as she tapped his beer, her weight rocked back on one hip, waiting for the head to settle, then pumping in a little more. "My love!" Burt said, his voice suddenly merry, a mischievous twitter of anticipation. "You're going to have a baby, aren't you?"

Melissa turned slowly, cocked her chin into her neck and looked at him as though she were peering over a pair of bifocals. "You calling me fat, there, Mister Burt?"

Burt shook his head vehemently. He lifted his glass to her. "You are the crazy gypsy in my soul," he said. Melissa busied herself at the bar. Katy ate her burger. The iguana-chin man sat on his barstool grinning delightedly like any old happy drunk.

"I'll just go across to the motel and change," Katy told Melissa, "and bring these back to you, if that's okay?" She had no spare clothes but balked at the idea of standing in the ladies' room holding her pants up to the hand dryer.

Crossing the ravine, hands thrust deep into the pockets of her pea coat, the lump of her wet jeans under one arm, Katy passed the Chihuahua-woman from the lobby. She was dogless now, struggling to erect what appeared to be a sort of a fence, or playpen, on one of the grassy islands in the floodlit parking lot. Katy nodded in greeting as she passed, then ducked her head back down as though the specifics of her shame were obvious. She fished the keycard from her coat pocket and stepped out of the wind into room #159 with a measure of relief.

She got the electric heater going under the window and closed the drapes—heavy and plastic-backed, like the leaden smocks in an x-ray lab. The short, cold walk from Bubbas had frozen her jeans, and they were stiff as she unrolled them across the heater. It wasn't until she slid off Melissa's sweatpants that she remembered the underwear, which were not, it seemed, stuffed in the leg of her thawing jeans, nor fallen to the motel room carpet. In her mind Katy saw them—pale blue bikinis with thin orange striping, some white crusting in the crotch—lying on the sidewalk outside her door, object of extraordinary interest to a passing poodle, or left on Bubbas' floor beneath her barstool like a calling card. Or in the middle of Bubbas' kitchen, the young cook staring them down from behind the stove.

Katy yanked the sweatpants from her ankles inside out and carried them back to the sink vanity to examine them under the light for traces she'd be embarrassed to leave behind. They were clean. She walked back to the heater, catching sight of herself in a full-length mirror on the back of the bathroom door: navy pea coat, skinny stubbled legs, wool socks that had begun to feel gummy inside. She bent to sit on the edge of the bed to wait for her jeans to dry, but then remembering what people said about motel bedspreads, pulled it back, and sat on the sheet, which smelled reassuringly of Clorox. On the night table sat an overturned ashtray, its bottom stamped with the ubiquitous red circle slashing out a smoking cigarette. She righted it: a perfectly functional ashtray.

She tended her jeans on the heater, flipping them impatiently like a novice chef, and it was, of course, impossible not to look at those jeans and think about, as she had for many years now, what *had* happened to the jeans she'd been wearing in the accident. They'd belonged to her boyfriend at the time, a perfect pair of Levi's, irreplaceable. And though, clearly, she wouldn't have *wanted* them—or what was left of them—it bothered her—intensely sometimes—that she did not and would never know exactly what had become of them. It was the sort of thing that made her worry about herself, this concern over the fate of those Levi's. Brian had never asked about them, never asked for them back, and she wondered if he'd somehow known that she'd been wearing them in the car that day, or if he'd simply forgotten about them—one of many such pairs of old Levi's in his life—forgotten that she'd ever borrowed them at all. It had crossed her mind a few times to tell him, but she'd forget when they talked on the phone or when he visited her in the hospital. There was too much else to worry about saying or *not* saying, and by the time she went back to school they'd already been broken up for months and simply avoided one another in the library, ate in different dining halls, steered clear of the places they'd once frequented together, as though in the end they'd split on account of some malicious wrongdoing or cataclysmic betrayal, not simply parted in the aftermath of the accident, one more thing crushed beyond salvation. "Your relationship died of complications," her friend Betsy had once said, and it was true.

The motel room smelled like burnt sugar, cloudy with heat, and Katy leaned to reach under the drapes and press one wrist against the cold front window. She imagined what it might look like from outside: a Halloween novelty, one hand reaching up from the grave.

She folded Melissa's sweats neatly and held them again under one arm as she recrossed the parking lot, the damp heater-warmth of her jeans stiffening against her body as she moved. She walked with her head down. Her missing underwear did not make itself known.

In the light of Bubbas' entryway, a tiny young woman in a fur-trimmed jacket and an enormous man in shirtsleeves, jangling car keys in his pillowy hand, appeared to be saying goodnight, and it took a minute for Katy to recognize them as the couple from Bubbas' corner booth. From the shoulders up the man was a regular-looking guy—quite attractive, really, with dark blue eyes, heavy lashes, and an expertly trimmed goatee. But moving down from the top of his chest, his body seemed to flood outward; Katy thought of a pyramid of bulging lava. He wasn't just heavy but obese. Morbidly, mesmerizingly obese. And then here was this tiny woman, lingering with him in the awning light, a pretty blonde with pale, intelligent eyes and smartly tailored clothes—a professional sort of a woman, Katy supposed. She slowed her stride, imagined she might see a kiss, and the image of that kiss led to the image of this man and this woman in bed, making love.

"Get dried out there?" said the man as Katy entered their spotlight.

Katy beamed at them stupidly, nodding, practically bowing her way through the vestibule doors.

The bar was empty: Burt was gone, the reading teenager gone, the iguana-chin man wringing out a rag and wiping down the booths. He looked up as Katy entered.

"Is, um, Melissa around?" she asked.

"I can take 'em," he said. "She went up." He gave a flick of his head toward the ceiling.

Katy felt herself fizzle with disappointment. She handed over the pants, looking around again with a rush of panic, like she might spot Melissa hiding somewhere in the bar, avoiding her.

"I'm Melissa's husband," the man said.

"Oh," Katy said. It took more energy than it should have. "So this place is *yours*?"

"*Hers*," he corrected. "I'm just the love slave." He shrugged toward the wash bucket.

"Bubba?"

He laughed, chin accordioning back like a bellows, as though she'd just told a great old joke they both knew well. "Joe," he said, and they shook hands.

"So who's Bubba?"

"A bunch of years back Mel hitched a ride to some swimming hole she'd heard about outside Austin, Texas. She got picked up by two guys in a truck." He paused, forestalling the punch line. "They were both named Bubba."

"Both of them?"

Joe nodded, and his smile carried them through a silence. He seemed to be regarding her with mild, curious concern, but said nothing more, just hung Melissa's sweatpants over a barstool and retrieved his rag to swab down the bar.

Finally, Katy managed to say, "Thanks."

"You take good care," Joe said.

She'd made it only as far out as the vestibule when she heard him yell, "Caught ya!" and she froze, remembering the underwear. She could practically see him coming toward her with his arm extended, her blue-striped panties pinched between his thumb and forefinger like something soiled and rank. And then there he was, reaching toward her, but it wasn't her underwear in his hand; it was her driver's license. "Katya," he said again. "That's pretty—I have to tell that one to Mel."

Katy's clogged voice gushed out of her. "Thank you so much. God, I'm such a . . . I don't even know . . . I'm just not . . ."

Joe looked again at the ID in his hand, then back at Katy. "You're young for the gray," he observed, nodding at her hair.

"Yeah, thanks," she said. "You too."

Joe looked puzzled. He pressed the ID into her hand. "You get some sleep," he said, and then he pushed back inside calling, "G'night!" as the doors swung behind him, slowing and slowing until they were still.

The light outside was falsely bright and hazy, like a movie set. In their fenced pen on the parking lot knoll, a dozen Chihuahuas yipped. Katy nodded again to their owner as she passed. The woman was smoking, and her bare hand had gone bluish from the cold. "They'll quiet down," she said. Katy stopped, turned back. "Don't worry," the woman assured, "they'll quiet down."

"Oh," said Katy. "I mean, I wasn't—"

"They're real good once I get 'em inside. Some other people's might keep you up." The woman leered suggestively toward another bank of motel rooms. "Won't be mine though. Won't be mine." She turned her cigarette, faced it down like a gun barrel, and knelt to stub it in the grass.

"Do you show them *all*? When you come to a show, like this?" It seemed like a reasonable question. "Do you have more? Like back home?"

The woman lifted an elbow like a hen and pointed it at a nearby RV. "*That's* home," she said. "I don't show 'em all. 'Specially . . ." She withdrew her hand from her pocket and directed Katy's gaze to the pen. "I mean, like, Princess Boo's set to whelp any day now, so she's for sure not showing. And you can't show the pups till they're six months."

Katy found she could in fact see that one was more barrel-bodied than the others, like a Chihuahua who'd swallowed a buoy.

"You ain't with the show then," said the woman. She wore a navy-blue knitted hat that almost looked like a beret, but the weave was too loose to be warm, the yarn too shiny to be wool. It sprouted tiny frayed tendrils that glowed in the floodlights like electric eels or the tentacles of a luminous sea anemone.

Katy shook her head. "I just needed a place to stay the night. I came from Wyoming. All the way. I just couldn't drive anymore. This is where I got to. I had no idea all *this* was going on." She swept a hand toward all the big silent vehicles packed into the lot like animals at a state fair, sleeping beneath the hypnotic neon sputter of the strip, the faint aroma of Burger King forever hovering in the air.

"I never was to Wyoming," said the woman. She thought a moment. "What do folks do for work out there?"

Katy felt as if the cold had slowed their brains. "I guess there's ranching, you know?" Her mouth seemed sluggish as well. "Most people I know work in the outdoor industry, I guess you'd call it. Around the national parks and stuff. I lead river trips in the summer. You work for the mountain in the winter, skiing stuff." She gave a kind of a bitter snort.

"Oh, yeah?" said the woman. "There's good money in that then? *Skiing?*" It was a foreign term the way she said it.

Katy snorted again. "Only if there's snow. This winter there's been *nothing.*"

"Oof"—the woman shuddered—"that's rough." She shook her head sadly. "You looking for work here?"

Katy breathed into the air, stamped her clogs on the ground with a clap that seemed to still the dogs—one instant of pure quiet—and then the racket yapped on. She shook her head. "I wasn't really *coming here,*" she said. "I just, I guess I just, well . . ." And then it seemed the jig was up. "I just cheated on my husband last night with this guy I know and freaked out and got in the car at like four-thirty in the morning and left his house and just drove . . ."

"And here you are?" said the woman.

Katy nodded. The dogs yipped. Somehow it was easier, she thought, to talk with the dogs clamoring on, like in a club where the music's too loud to hear people talk so you have to shout into their ears, short and clear, so what would be some long, drawn-out flirtation turns, by necessity, into *DO YOU WANT TO FUCK?*

"Aw, girl," sighed the woman. She clapped one cold, raw hand on Katy's shoulder and jostled her companionably, dropping her head, shaking out her hair like she was hearing some great old song she hadn't heard for years. She held the shoulder of Katy's coat, wagging her head like a soul queen. "Man, could *I* tell *you* stories . . ."

"You want to hear something totally crazy?" Katy said, and the woman straightened, and—to Katy's relief—removed her hand. It seemed a sign to continue. "The guy, the one I cheated with, he has the same name—the exact same name, first *and* last, exactly the same name as a person I was in love with a long time ago, who I *didn't* ever sleep with—because I had another boyfriend at the time, and he had a girlfriend too, and even though we knew we were pretty much in love with each other we didn't want to have it be a thing where we cheated. We wanted to do it right, you know? Break off the other relationships and then be together honestly, you know?"

And the woman was nodding, serious, chewing her chapped lower lip with a look like she was watching her own stories play out on a private projector in her head.

"And then he died," Katy said. She shook her head briskly, waved a hand to show the way he'd simply vanished, *poof*, gone.

"Wait, wait," said the woman. "Which one?"

"The one I . . . the one I *didn't* sleep with," Katy said. "The first one with the name. The one I thought I loved." And she hated the way that sounded when she said it, finally, flighty and melodramatic.

"Oh, god . . ." said the woman. She put her hands to her ears, pulling down the beret as if to protect herself from hearing any more sadness. Her hair was an unnatural, dark blonde—brittle, as though it had been ironed and then torqued to give the impression of waviness. It poked out from beneath her hat like it was trying to escape, to break free and set off for someplace where it might be treated with a little more kindness.

Katy sort of smiled then—a bewildered smile, skeptical, but open, too—like she was so lost she might be willing to accept some forms of aid or consolation she'd never before imagined. "And then someone shows up, years later, someone shows up, and you've already spotted him, you know, had an eye on him already by the time you actually meet . . ."

The woman nodded slowly, her gaze rising to the neon horizon like she'd remembered to miss something she'd taught herself to stop missing long ago. She almost looked as though she might cry, and Katie blundered on in fear of exactly that.

"And then you meet him, and then the name, and then everything is weird and kind of amazing and terrifying, but there's the husband too, who you love, really, who's been there through so much—*seven years*—but now there's *this*, and what do you *do* with it? And then finally what you do is get drunk enough that you can't *not* do anything anymore, so you do, and it's . . ." She ran out of words, just ran utterly out of words to describe how she felt about anything. "And then you get in your car and start driving. And then you're at a dog show in the middle of somewhere, and you're bawling at a stranger in the middle of a parking lot in the middle of the night, and *then* what are you supposed to do?"

Katy was wiping her nose on the rough wool sleeve of her pea coat when the woman produced a folded brown wad of industrial paper towels from her pocket and peeled one off. She looked quickly to the dog pen, as if to make sure she wasn't going to need that particular towel for poop-scooping, then pressed it into Katy's hand the way a magician stuffs his fist with a rainbow of handkerchiefs, then—*abracadabra*—opens his palm and—*what do you know?*—they're gone! The woman wrapped Katy's hand with both her own and held it firmly, as though she were handing over something sacred and irreplaceable—a secret key, a silver locket, a medallion of Saint Christopher, patron saint of motorists, porters, and travelers, of sudden and holy death—and stood there squeezing Katy's hand up and down. She began to speak then, slowly and resonantly, like she knew she had something big to impart. "A man loved me once," she said, "likely before you were born. *Married* man. And I knew that was wrong, the way people know right from wrong, and I left, because it was wrong, you know? And it wasn't for a long time till I saw that wasn't what it was about at all, when I could see that there wasn't *right* and *wrong*, and that everything was just something what happened." The woman took a deep breath, as though steeling herself for what was to come. She shook her head, fast, and the loose flesh at her jowls shimmied like love handles on a belly dancer. "I didn't have no idea when I left that man that no body'd ever do again what his body and my body did, no body on this earth in this lifetime. I fucked a hundred bodies in the back of that RV before I even saw that maybe I wasn't gonna get that chance again in this life, on this earth. Those times with him, when coming wasn't a question of 'Did you?' It was him saying, 'Sweet Jesus, Marnie, did you just piss the bed?' Because how often does *that* happen? Well, then, with *him*, answer was it happened a *lot*. It's what makes me get to think that if you're fucking the right person, it might happen a lot. But then you're back to right and wrong, and right and wrong got that way of pinballing against each other so hard you can spend your life working the goddamn flippers, you know? Or you can take things into your own hands and you find a life for yourself that doesn't count on some man who can make you come like a racehorse or *can't* make you come like a fucking racehorse 'cause whose business is that besides your own anyways? Nobody's." She broke off, stopped like she was out of breath or out of story. She dropped Katy's hand. "You got a cigarette, honey?" And when Katy shook her head *no*, the woman dug a hand into her own coat pocket and pulled out a pack, got one lit, and seemed to calm under its care. *Come like a racehorse?* Katy thought. She envisioned a thin, foam-mattress in the back of the RV, a stain spreading wetly across pale blue sheets, stained no matter how far away you drove that RV or how loud the dogs yapped and the highway droned and people in parking lots in bitter cold told you stories of their own scarred and patched and piece-meal lives.

"Sometimes," the woman said, squinting from behind her cigarette like it was a long telescope she had to look through just to see who Katy was. "Sometimes," she said again, and then it was like she was standing there in a lone spotlight on a dark stage. "Sometimes, least when you want it to, your body's got a way of reminding you what it felt like once, when everything let go and what came pouring out was something you had no idea was in there in the first place. Bill'd tease me, say, 'Marnie, I hope you washed those sheets!' And sometimes I did, but sometimes I didn't, you know, because the thing with that whatever-the-hell-it-*is* that comes out of you then, it's *not* piss. It doesn't stink. Not at all. It dries like water, like nothing. You don't even have to do the laundry."

Katy flushed with shame and horror. "I don't think . . ." she started.

"Oh you *will*. Honey, you *will*. Don't you worry about *that*." She fixed Katy with a look that was hard, and her voice slowed down, like someone giving instructions in an emergency. "What you need to worry about is getting yourself some *sleep*."

Katy agreed as though hypnotized.

"You need to get yourself into your warm room there"—the woman jerked an elbow toward #159—"and you lock the door—they're not so safe, these places—you lock the door and you make a phone call to some-one back home who can call both those two boys of yours and anyone else who's likely losing their shit over where in hell you are, and let them know you're alive."

Unity Brought Them Together

One early December weekend, three months before Catherine Fjord and Jeremy Bunn were to be married, Catherine flew by herself to California to attend the wedding of her former sorority sister Ariella Barnstable. That Sunday, Jeremy took two subways from the Brooklyn apartment he and Catherine shared to a Chelsea coffee shop where he planned to finish writing their Christmas cards. Before Catherine left on Friday, Jeremy had already been imagining himself spending Sunday at the one Javaroma table by the window, but when he got there it was already occupied. A guy with a ponytail had entrenched himself with books, his papers stacked around him as if to fortify the position. Jeremy had to take the next table over. The ponytailed guy looked up as Jeremy sat, nodded, then went back to his work grading handwritten papers scrawled on cheap, institutional loose-leaf. As he read, he lifted both hands to stroke back his hair, running one hand again and again down the length of his ponytail like he was milking an udder. Jeremy began to unpack his own work.

He was behind on the Christmas cards—or, rather, *they* were behind—due to what he and Catherine had agreed to call a "miscommunication" regarding a few boxes of cards he'd bought on sale at the Strand. They weren't holiday-y per se but wintry and New Yorky and classic—a Steichen photo of the Flatiron Building from 1904 with a lone, top-hatted, Dickensian figure in silhouette—and they seemed, to Jeremy, to capture a subtly beautiful Christmas melancholy. He'd inscribed a good dozen before Catherine got home, peered over his shoulder, and got a look. "What's it say inside?" she asked. "*Have yourself a dreary little Christmas?*"

Jeremy was surprised, and defensive. "It's a quintessential snowy New York scene!"

"That is not snow, Jeremy." She pointed accusingly at the photograph—so beautiful, it almost looked like a painting—she pointed at it and said, "Rain. Look. The ground is wet. That's not snow; it's rain." And then it had turned out that Catherine had issues with more than just the cards: those black and white Flatirons were emblematic of what she feared for their impending marriage. "I know you try hard, Jeremy," she explained, "but sometimes you're so utterly clueless that your attempts at taking responsibility only make more work for me." She would, she went on, have to clean up his mess before she could even get to the task at hand and then do the whole thing herself so that it got done right. She was so exhausted by him that she didn't have the energy to be angry, she said, only hurt and sad. That meant that if he got mad it would only prove what an asshole he was. The quote, unquote, *inappropriate* Christmas cards occasioned the enumeration of other similar examples of Jeremy's ineptitude, which were harsh and cutting, and for which, admittedly, Catherine had since apologized many times, trying with arguable success to clarify her position. Her insistence that Jeremy was *well-intentioned* only made him feel worse. Their fight lasted so late into the night that delirium began to waft through the argument like a scent. Jeremy found himself in the middle of sentences he didn't remember starting, articulating thoughts whose origin he could no longer recall. The next day while Catherine was at work, he exchanged the cards for some pleasantly benign, tastefully nonsectarian, peace-connoting, blue and white, Matisse-y-looking doves.

When Catherine had gotten home that evening, she returned to a different conversation-slash-argument they'd been having the week before. This was about Ariella's upcoming wedding. That night, Catherine raised the topic with apology and in the spirit of compromise. "You're anxious about Christmas," she said, which was true, a point Jeremy had stressed the night before in his own Flatiron defense. "And about *our* wedding," she added tentatively. "And you don't even *really know* Ariella and Bill." A lawyer in every synapse-leaping neurotransmitter in her body, Catherine had already convinced herself with this very line of argument. "There's no reason for you to be subjected to the toll of their wedding just because I have to be. Would you rather stay home and use the time to get a handle on things here?"

He almost wept with relief. It wasn't Ariella's wedding, specifically, that he dreaded; he just couldn't bear another one. Catherine's particular Gamma Ramma Lamma clan was comprised of fifteen core members; Catherine and Jeremy's wedding was slated to be number thirteen. Catherine had already logged so many hours of wedding-party duty that Jeremy thought she probably had enough credit to graduate to marriage without even donning the bridle of bridehood. And he'd done more than any man's fair share of waiting around in bars and hotels with the other boyfriends and husbands, handshaking and small-talking and nice-making. Fifteen was a lot of best friends, even Catherine would admit. (Jeremy steadfastly refused to have groomsmen, but even if he'd had his every male relative and friend in the world stand up beside him, they'd still be outnumbered by Rama Llamas—as Jeremy liked to call them—practically two-to-one.) But certain brands of tragedy bond people in ways necessitating continued acknowledgment, and the Rama Llama story was just such a tragedy. During their sophomore year, Llamas were allowed—or maybe even required—Jeremy had trouble keeping all the details straight—to live in the sorority house. It was only a few weeks into fall semester when, after a normal Friday night of serious partying, Vicky Hrksta passed out in the upper berth of the bunk bed she shared, and while the other three girls in the room lay wasted and unconscious and unaware, Vicky vomited, and because she had passed out on her back, vomit filled her airway, and she choked to death in her drunken sleep.

Vicky Hrksta's death had far-reaching consequences for the Llamas. A number of the girls hadn't had a drink since that night, Catherine included. And, when they graduated college and began to marry off, it seemed an unspoken understanding that when each girl stood up in white to say "I do," she'd be flanked by the other fourteen girls who'd woken in the Rama Llama house that fateful morning feeling sexy and hungover and collegiate, only to discover the death that would thenceforth guide their waking lives.

The agreement Catherine and Jeremy came to in the wake of the Flatiron debacle seemed to be that reprieve from Ariella's nuptials would be granted Jeremy if by the time Catherine returned on the red-eye Monday morning from California he could manage to finish the Christmas cards. Neither thought this an unreasonable trade-off.

Dear Jen and McNeil, Jeremy began, *So great to see you both at Ashley and Don's wedding . . .* When someone passed by outside the plate glass window it was difficult for Jeremy not to look up and away from his task. Just a reflex. But, of course, every time Jeremy'd glance up, the guy at the window table did too. At first he pretended that his looking up had nothing to do with Jeremy's looking up, but then it got absurd and they wound up exchanging a little smile of understanding—like strangers approaching each other on a sidewalk who get trapped in a deadlock of sidestepping, each trying to make way for the other, but always stepping in the same direction and continuing to block each other's path until they finally break form, laugh, freeze, and one gestures to the other: *after you.* The window guy and Jeremy shared an unspoken acknowledgment of the inevitability of their situation at the tightly packed Javaroma, and somehow, silently, tacitly agreed that when someone passed by, Jeremy would look up, and the ponytailed guy would look up, and then they'd go about their business without enacting a ruse of coincidence and oblivion. The way the guy's eyes flicked around when he looked up made Jeremy think him to be a self-conscious person. Jeremy didn't find the guy exceptionally good-looking, but he seemed to be aware of himself in the manner of someone who *is* that handsome or suspects himself of that kind of beauty. To Jeremy, he looked like an actor on stage before the first line: just him, alone, pantomiming Teacher Grading Papers. He sipped his coffee as if to convince someone he lived on the stuff, but his flushed, unblemished complexion made it impossible to imagine his inner organs as anything but pink and plump as newborn guinea pigs. Jeremy could picture the guy ordering a glass of milk with his dinner in a restaurant. Midwestern as a county fair Pork Princess. And Jeremy would know: two of his sisters had worn the very crown.

Before the sun went behind the buildings, such a glare developed for a stretch of the afternoon that it was hard to distinguish the features of passersby. At one point someone came past who Jeremy thought for a second could have been Catherine—the sleek, dark outline of her head, hair pulled back low in a ponytail. But Catherine was in California; she was not, Jeremy reminded himself, following him around New York to make sure he finished the Christmas cards. Besides, the body was too big, too tall, too lumpy for Catherine, who'd been a dancer in her youth and still walked with the rigid carriage of a frightened animal. As he studied the figure in the Javaroma window, meting out its not-Catherineness, Jeremy realized that the ponytailed paper-grader was having his own reaction to the Catherine-ish person standing just on the other side of the glass. He kept glancing up, then poked his head closer, squinted, craned, and finally began to rap on the window. The person outside turned at the noise and was proven, instantly, to be so not-Catherine as to be a man.

A flurry of movement ensued as the outside man tried to see and place the inside man, and when he did, there followed a clownish pantomime of surprise and reunion: the inside man beckoning grandly, the outside man nodding, pointing toward the door through which he'd enter and effect their reunion. Rising, the paper-grader seemed to step backward over his own chair, a move of the sort of macho grace he might have practiced in the mirror at home, like a greaser training to jump in and out of his car through the window so as to eschew the bourgeois affectation of opening and closing the door.

"Rudy Masters," cried the paper-grader from the depths of the backclapping bear hug in which the two men had grabbed one another.

"Jug jug, Juggie, Jug jug jug!" howled Rudy, and they were, for a moment, the center of the Javaroma and the universe.

"Sit down, sit down!" Jug cried. "Can you?" He stroked his ponytail like a rabbit's foot.

Rudy looked at his watch, as if he had someplace to be. "Yeah, yeah." He hesitated. "No, yeah, I can sit a minute, sure." Still cocooned in coat and scarf, Rudy sat. Jeremy busied back to his cards.

"Dude," Jug was saying. "It's been what? Shit? Years!"

"And you know what's crazy?" Rudy said. "You know what I'm in town for? Emily and Russell's wedding!"

"No shit!"

"They got married yesterday," Rudy spoke as though the words were beyond his own comprehension. "Totally. I just saw all of them, everyone—Rob, Goatie, Gina, Susannah, Phil . . ."

With Rudy's every utterance Jug's face broke into a deeper, more dramatic, more astounded display of shock, each name sending him into such a whirlwind of memories he looked whiplashed by the end of the catalogue. "Wow," he kept saying, "wow, so you're all still in touch. Phenomenal."

"They're my best friends," Rudy agreed.

"Wow, all of you best friends, still. Phenomenal."

Suddenly, with a desperate fling of his arms, Rudy whipped off his scarf like he'd been overcome by a hot flash. Rudy had a ponytail too, about the same length as Jug's, which made Jeremy think there must be some agreed-upon professional-person code that a grown man can have hair of a certain length and still be taken seriously *if* he pulled it back into a low, tight ponytail. That was when it crossed Jeremy's mind that he had no idea if either of these guys were people other people took seriously. Jeremy thought everyone looked more like someone who'd be taken seriously than he did.

Jug's stacks of papers fluttered in the wake of Rudy's scarf. As Rudy recovered himself, he seemed to notice the contents of the table and swooshed a coat-sleeved arm to take it all in. "So what's all this? What're *you* up to?"

Jug inhaled deeply, eyes rolling up in conveyance of some implied shared understanding. "Teaching high school." He sighed.

"Get out of here! Good for you. Good. For. You." Rudy was nodding with his whole body like he'd caught a sweet groove of some jam band they'd loved in their youth—Dave Matthews, the Dead—but the effort seemed to overheat him again and he reached to unbutton his coat. He wore a navy pea jacket that had an air of affectation to it, as though he were trying to pass himself off as a longshoreman or clammer. But Rudy also had a slightly effeminate look, and Jeremy thought the coat might have been his way of telling the world: *I'm not gay.* "So you live here then?" Rudy asked Jug.

"Yeah, yeah." Jug caught Rudy's imaginary groove and rode it. "You?"

"Portland." Rudy paused. "Oregon." He pronounced *Oregon* as if to make it clear he'd never dream of giving it three syllables. He sounded like a pretentious Yankee saying he was headed down to *Nawlins* for Mardi Gras.

"No kidding? What do you do out there?"

Rudy tilted back his head and cocked an ear toward his shoulder. "Environmental law?" He seemed to be gauging whether Jug might have heard of such a thing.

"No kidding? That's super. That's great, great."

Rudy waved both hands around his head like he was trying to keep the compliment from penetrating. "Teaching *high school* is *great.*"

"Yeah," Jug agreed. "I mean, it's just a one-year thing. *Could* be more. If I went back to school, got a certificate. Now it's just like: *we're so desperate for teachers we'll hire anyone with a master's in anything.*"

Rudy grew serious. "So they bring you in for a year and then . . ."

"Try to ensnare you for life! Hope you won't be able to give up the glory of it!"

"So, you're not exactly digging it, then?"

"Oh no, no no no no," Jug crooned, "no, it's great. I mean, I just, being there, doing this, it's so *relevant*. It's amazing sometimes, you know, how, like, how just *thankful* these kids are . . ."

"Oh? Yeah?" Rudy eyed the espresso counter longingly.

"Hey," Jug said, "so, wow, so Russell and Emily, married. Wow."

"Yeah."

"They've been together a *long* time."

"On and off," Rudy conceded.

"But I guess they decided they were *it* in the end, huh?"

Rudy ticktocked his head back and forth like he was weighing options. "Let's just say I think Russ might've been about ready to back the fuck out in about the middle of the friggin' ceremony, tell you the truth. The priest, or whatever, said, 'let's bow our heads for a moment of silence,' or whatever, and everyone's head goes down except Emily's—well, and mine, I guess . . . Ha!" He barked a laugh. "And she reaches over and adjusts Russ's bowtie before she bows her head."

Jug waited for more. When it didn't come, he asked earnestly, "And Russ was . . . pissed?"

"*I'd've* been."

Jug's smile seemed forced. He grabbed at his ponytail.

"I'm going to get some coffee," Rudy announced. "You need anything? Hey, am I—you let me know if I'm interrupting you, okay? You need to get back to work?"

Jug brushed off the thought, waving at the reams of un-graded papers like they were nothing, odds and ends, busywork.

Rudy went to the counter, Jug returned to his grading, and Jeremy opened a dove card and wrote: *Dear Cassandra and Willie, HAPPY HOLIDAYS! So great to see you both at Ashley and Don's* . . . The only other thing he could think to write was to thank them for snagging, for *their* wedding date, the only potentially decent-weathered weekend left in the Llama wedding calendar. Unless they wanted to wait another year, Catherine and Jeremy were stuck with the inhospitable month of March. It *would* keep costs down, Catherine had argued, trying to appeal to Jeremy's financial anxieties, and to be fair, it wasn't entirely Willie and Cassandra's fault: between Catherine's sorority sisters (for there were many others in addition to the core fifteen), Jeremy's actual siblings (seven full, four half, two step—and his parents weren't even Mormon or Catholic), and their combined friends and family, there wasn't a lot of flexibility. And when you were dealing with groups of interrelated guests you had to leave some leeway in between nuptials so no one was expected to spend their own honeymoon going to someone else's wedding. The Llamas had gone so far as to hire a scheduling consultant—a development they found hysterically funny, and which they staunchly defended as a simple matter of practicality. When Jeremy suggested it might be an expense that they, as a couple, could ill-afford, Catherine looked at him as though he'd called her annual pap smear a feminine frivolity.

Jeremy heard a laugh and looked up to see Jug chuckling over the paper he was reading. Rudy approached the table, coffee in hand. "Oh, dude, you're working. Look, I'll get a newspaper." He swept out a magnanimous hand as if to suggest that somewhere out there in the great infinite world beyond the Javaroma, he, Rudy Masters, Esq., would be up to the task of locating a *Times*.

But Jug shook his head vehemently. He waggled the paper he held, scrunching up his face like he was watching something adorably pathetic, absurdly pitiable, at which he knew he shouldn't laugh but couldn't stop. Once, when Catherine and Jeremy had split up for a while—the first time he quit law school, soon after he and Catherine had moved to New York—Jeremy wound up staying in Des Moines with his mom and stepdad for an excruciating, interminable, "extended" Christmas vacation. He'd been on the couch one day when one of his mom's cats had walked smack into a sliding glass door and, staggering and dazed, kept stumbling back into it again and again until his stepdad came into the room, saw what was happening, and saved the poor creature from itself. Jeremy was laughing so hard he couldn't talk, and his stepdad glared at him with such hatred you'd have thought he'd caught Jeremy butt-fucking the cat with the takeout Chinese food chopsticks in his hand. In the Des Moines suburb where they lived, and where Jeremy'd grown up, you had to append "food" to "Chinese" lest it be mistaken for something else entirely.

Rudy sat, expectant. Jug steadied the sheet of paper, scanned down, and read aloud. *"The necessities they receive are very essential and needed for survival if they are going to make it out alive."* He shook his head the way adults do when some cute child says something precociously off-color and they have to catch the eye of the nearest adult to say, *Out of the mouths of babes.*

"Wait, this one's even better," Jug said. He pulled out a different paper: *"It is very important for a person to fit into a group that is important to them."* Bemused, he held the report away from himself as if to regard it through bifocals he did not have on. Then he laid the sheet down on the table and turned to Rudy with the superhuman placidity of a psychoanalyst. "So Russell and Emily are married."

"That they are." Rudy seemed to remember something. "Hey whatever happened to that girl you went out with, that really short girl—what was her name?"

"Marilyn."

"Marilyn! Marilyn. Any idea what happened to her?"

There was a catch of pain in Jug's voice. "We split up just over seven years ago."

"Yeah?"

Jug nodded solemnly. Seven years ago might have been last week, so unflagging was his anguish. The long-ago breakup with Marilyn seemed to him no less tragic than a death. Jeremy kind of felt for the guy. Jug!

"Oh," Rudy tried again. "Yeah? I'm . . . sorry. That's rough."

"Yeah," Jug said. "Yeah, you know, I mean . . . It was one of those things where . . . I mean, the fact of the matter is I could have, I could have scared her back into it. Done the 'asshole guy' thing." Jug's air quotes were bitter, terse. "But I didn't . . ." He trailed off.

Rudy tried: "So I guess you're not, like, in touch, anymore then, or anything?"

"We're not. But, you know, the fact of the matter is, we may not be lovers or husband and wife or even friends, but I feel like, you know . . . she was young, and scared, and I helped her. I helped her get an apartment. I helped her move. Helped her box all her things until five o'clock in the morning." The weariness on his face seemed to suggest he was talking about five a.m. that very morning, not five a.m. one morning seven years before. "All that shit. And she'd call me, totally miserable, crying, and I could have pulled some shit and got her back, done the 'abusive male' thing. But I didn't, and now she's married, has a kid, and I'm happy as hell for her, you know? I mean, the fact is she's about the sweetest, kindest person in the world. Someone you just know this world is going to just *use* to its advantage, you know?"

Rudy was nodding hesitantly, looking a little frantic. He took a sip of coffee, and the sip seemed to have a lot of steps to it, and he had to concentrate hard to remember them all, to get the sip done right. When he was done he said, "Hey, you remember Sarah Ellis from school? Beautiful, gorgeous, incredible Sarah Ellis?"

Jug said, "Sarah Ellis . . ." like he was trying to find a face for her in his mind.

"You can't *not remember* Sarah Ellis! No man who's laid eyes on Sarah Ellis has ever forgotten Sarah Ellis . . ."

"From school, yeah?" Jug said, eyes betraying his anxiety.

"Dude, she's about the most gorgeous woman alive. Okay, picture this." Rudy wasn't going to wait for Jug's memory to catch up.

"Picture Sarah Ellis eight and a half months pregnant in a red stretch-velvet bridesmaid's dress!"

"Wow," Jug managed.

"It was, like, the total most *indecorous fecundity* imaginable." This was obviously something he'd heard said the night before.

Jug let out a big puff of air in a sort of pained appreciation. Then suddenly he looked at his watch and half stood at the same time. "Shit," he said. "Shit, I have a haircut." He surveyed his papers. "Hey, were you going to hang out? I'm only going to be fifteen minutes—just around the corner—"

"Yeah, yeah," Rudy said, "no problem."

"Dude, thank you." And without even grabbing his coat, Jug fled the café, leaving Rudy alone, a little shell-shocked amid Jug's stuff. He glanced around and caught Jeremy watching him. Jeremy looked away, but then made himself look back and try to smile, and Rudy gave a little nod of acknowledgment. Then Jeremy went back to the Christmas cards, glancing up every so often when someone passed, then pausing to see what Rudy was doing before he turned back to the cards. Rudy painstakingly sipped his coffee, then leaned over to examine one of Jug's student's papers. He picked it up and began to read, and soon he, like Jug, was grunting out snorts of laughter. After a bit, his cell phone rang; he checked the number before answering.

"Dude, you will never guess who I ran into." There was a pause while Rudy listened. "Close, very close. You ready? Judge—what the hell was his last name? Yeah! Judge . . . Some coffee shop by Rob's . . . My flight's not till late. Totally. Get this: he's a high school teacher! No, no, he went to go get a haircut or something, I'm just here with his stuff . . . I don't even know." He picked up a few more papers from a pile and peered at them. "I don't know, English, maybe? I don't know, somewhere shitty. Listen to this. All his papers are here on the table. He's got some, some kid writing about god knows what, has a line in his paper: *Telling details tell us things.* How awesome is—" Rudy listened a moment, then hooted in laughter. "Totally!" he cried. "Wait, wait. Ready? Okay: *I know I will understand it when it becomes clear to me.*" He laughed loudly, drawing attention in the café. When he spoke again, Rudy lowered his voice, and though he and his friend kept talking, he turned to face the window and Jeremy couldn't really hear anymore.

He got into a groove with the Christmas cards and was just opening the second box when he heard a phone ringing. He could see that Rudy was still talking, which was when he realized it was his own phone ringing on the table in front of him.

Catherine was calling from the California hotel room she'd gone in on with a few other unmarried girls from the outer circle of sorority sisters. "Oh my god," she said when Jeremy asked how it had gone. "Let's just say it's a good thing no blood was shed." Catherine paused. "Jeremy? Can you hear me?"

"Yeah, fine. Go on."

"It's really noisy. Where are you?"

"Just at a coffee shop, working on the cards."

"Oh, good!"

"Getting there."

"So, Graciella, Ariella's mother, who is truly truly insane—manic-depressive, or for sure manic, at least—Graciella arrives from the Bahamas with her Iron Man bodybuilder boyfriend who's, like, never had to put on a suit before in his life and he's borrowed one for the occasion, only it's too small, and he's popped half the seams, so now they're hanging together with safety pins. Meanwhile Graciella's brought with her this enormous bouquet of the most phallic lilies you've ever seen in your life—these huge, red, patent leather–like things the size of salad plates with big fuzzy-yellow penises sticking straight up out of the center, and she starts parading through the reception hall pulling these things out of the bouquet one by one and sticking an enormous lily in each of the centerpieces. Which are, of course, these totally sweet, lovely little cottage-flower arrangements with, like, wheat sheaves and whatever, and Bill's mother—who'd, like, hand*spun* every sheaf of wheat—bursts into tears and starts rushing around behind Graciella yanking the penis-lilies back out of the arrangements. A full-on cat fight was only very very narrowly averted."

Catherine was, in her way, asking Jeremy to reassure her that there wouldn't be scenes like that at their wedding. He knew that's what she needed to hear him say, but she was so far away, and the Javaroma was so dense and busy with people and conversations and smells and clinking dishes and whirring espresso machines frothing milk and spurting steam, and to come out of that, to meet Catherine in *their* world—the world of their hypothetical not-too-distant wedding—would have taken a greater force of will than Jeremy possessed. He couldn't do it.

Catherine was right to be anxious. For weeks—actually, months— Jeremy had been breaking into night sweats, waking up in fits of panic over the impending wedding, all the details, the uncertainty of his future, the interaction that would be incumbent upon their respective families. Jeremy's mother adored Catherine, was entranced by all the things about Catherine that Jeremy knew were entrancing: her cosmopolitanism, her looks, her smarts, her style, her success. He and Catherine had been together five years. Five years since the night she'd stomped across the bar at Dingo's on a dare and demanded to see his ID, which he produced dutifully. She frowned at it, then at him. "It's fake, right?" she asked. He shrugged noncommittally. "How old are you really?" she asked. And in a moment of divine inspiration he'd had the wherewithal to say, "How old do you want me to be?" and then she'd had the balls to say, "Old enough to come home with me," and there was something so liberating about being the object of someone else's want—to be faced with someone who seemed to have a *plan* for him, for the night, for life—was so incredibly relieving he'd've done anything she wanted, which was basically what he'd been doing for the last five years. But in all that time Catherine's and Jeremy's parents had had very little interaction. Catherine was from Chicago, and Chicago was a very different Midwest from Des Moines. The difference between being from Chicago and being from Des Moines was like the difference between being from New York City and New York State. Jeremy had family in Rochester.

When Catherine came home to Des Moines with him for the first time soon after he'd gone home with her that night from Dingo's—when Jeremy was a nineteen-year-old sophomore at U of I and Catherine was a twenty-two-year-old first-year law student there—Jeremy's mom grabbed him the minute Catherine left the room, fawning, holding his face too close to hers as she inspected, cooing her irrepressible love and pride, all the while trying to temper it, trying to mock both herself and Jeremy to mediate the intensity of her adulation. "Oh, she's gorgeous. She's lovely. She's . . . what could she possibly see in *you*? What could she possibly possibly see in this beautiful, gorgeous boy of mine?"

From the couch, Jeremy's stepdad spoke without taking his eyes from the TV. "Sperm," he said. "Young, healthy sper-ma-ta-zo-a is what she's seeing. And good genes. He's got a strong jaw. And he's not going to go bald. She wants your seed, pretty boy."

"Frank!" Jeremy's mother chided, a stage whisper of reproach.

"What?" he said. "She's what? Five years older than you? Six?"

"Three," Jeremy corrected him. It was actually closer to four, but there was no need to advertise the point.

"Fine," Frank conceded. "She's old enough to be worrying. I bet you any amount of money she's worrying. I bet you all her little girlfriends are going to start getting married and popping out babies and she's going to want to get on the train fast or it'll leave without her. That's what I'll tell you. She'll want to get you married ASAP so she can rake in the wedding presents, pump out a live one, rake you over the coals with her through the crying and the no-sleeping and the diapers, and then she'll be out of there before you wash the baby shit off your hands. She'll find herself some guy closer her own age, with a *job*, a *trust fund, family* money, and she'll be done with you like that. Like that, my friend." This was the basic gist of the story of Frank's own first marriage, and Jeremy found it hard to begrudge the man his pain, even all these years later. Frank had a daughter somewhere in Arizona who'd called someone else *Daddy* her whole life and knew Frank only as a youthful mistake her mother'd once made, a mistake only redeemed by her birth, the way other early missteps can carry life lessons to abide by: one learns to live chastely, say, or not to party, or not to drink at all, after one's sorority sister chokes to death on her own vomit. Frank's bitterness was long-harbored, and Jeremy's mother, with her *Oh, Frank*, ministered to it like a bedsore, all balm and salve.

"Mark my words," Frank warned. "You marry that girl and in two years you'll be back here sleeping on the couch getting fat on carry-out Chinese food." The word *Chinese* got its stress on the *i*, accent on the first syllable; there was perhaps nothing Jeremy found as mortifying.

"Jesus, Frank," Jeremy'd said, trying to modulate his voice. Catherine was taking a shower on the other side of the house, but still. "We're *dating*—we're not getting *married*."

"Mark my words." Frank was a stubborn man.

"Jeremy?" Catherine was now saying through the telephone, into his ear, "Did I lose you? Jeremy? Wait, what . . . ?"

He said, "I'm here, I'm here," but Catherine was no longer with *him* entirely. In the background, in their sleepover-party hotel room, the girls were calling for her attention. She held the phone away from her mouth to answer them, but Jeremy could hear her fine. "A year," she said, definitively, then backtracked. "Eighteen months." She came back to the phone. "They're taking bets on how long it'll last."

The coffee hit Jeremy's bowels like a gut punch. "What will?" He hated the sound of his own voice, feared he sounded like Catherine's mother, who was known in her family for the "death voice," a catch of terror at the merest possibility something might not be wholly peachy.

"Ariella and Bill," Catherine clarified.

Jeremy couldn't tell if it was exasperation he detected in her voice, or something else. "*That* promising, huh?" He meant to inquire further but became aware of hearing his own name being called. Hardly an uncommon name, and plenty often it'd turn out to be for someone else, but this time it was coming from close by, a woman's voice, and it was a question, the name, as if it defied all belief to imagine that the person sitting there on his phone in the Javaroma might truly be Jeremy Bunn. He whipped toward the voice so quickly he sent Matisse doves flying like he'd just opened their cage. "Shit." Stumbling to collect them, Jeremy nearly toppled his half-full coffee cup, blustering all over the place. Meanwhile, Catherine started saying his name too, which only flustered him more. In the turmoil of the moment he hadn't even managed to look up and see *who* was standing there saying his name.

Getting things under control, Jeremy straightened, collected doves in hand, and looked out the window over Rudy's head onto the avenue. "C," he said into the phone. "Can I call you back? It's busy, and I just almost tipped my table over—"

Catherine, who was nearly always a step ahead of Jeremy in every way, was already saying, "Sweetie, it's fine. We're off to brunch anyway. I'll call you tonight, okay?" and then she was gone and Jeremy was free to turn around—pocketing his phone and clutching his doves—to contend with whatever he was about to have to contend with.

But he did not recognize the person addressing him in the Javaroma that Sunday afternoon. She had a round face and a head of thick dirty-blonde dreadlocks, and she was swaddled inside so much clothing she could have been nine months pregnant and no one would've known. She had on hiking boots, corduroys, and a long batiked skirt, and what looked like about eighteen Himalayan wool sweaters, the thick sleeves of which were pushed up to her elbows to reveal a pair of pale, delicate forearms poking out like corn dog sticks. "Jeremy?" she said again.

"Do I know you?" He tried to look apologetic.

She grinned broadly, and as her face spread, he could see the curled backing of her nose piercing peek out from one nostril like an unruly hair. "You used to date Karla?"

Jeremy didn't really know how to answer that, so he didn't.

"I've been away awhile?" It was apparent that this woman's every utterance would arrive in the form of a question. "Down in Guatemala?" She said *Guatemala* like a Spanish speaker. "I used to see you with her? Karla?"

"Guatemala," was all Jeremy could think to say, almost just to hear how it sounded in American English.

The girl laughed. She couldn't have been more than nineteen. "Not in *Guatemala*." She was, it seemed, going to correct his pronunciation by example. "Here . . . ? I used to see you with her here? Before I left?" She stuck her neck out in entreaty, like a Central American iguana.

"Oh, yeah?"

"I used to work here? I'm Becca?" She thrust out a corn dog stick so he could shake the hand at the end of it.

"Jere—" he began, then just shook her cold little hand in silence. It was conceivable that he'd once known her, in passing maybe, but he really had no memory of it. She took a long time relinquishing his hand, but he couldn't tell if that was because she was trying to warm up her own, or if they were in the midst of the kind of situation where she felt like she'd known him a long time from afar and was finally getting to meet him in person, was losing herself a little in the moment, like a starstruck fan.

"So," she let go at last, "you still live around here." It was the first declarative sentence she'd spoken, and it was wrong.

"Oh, no," Jeremy said, "I didn't . . . I, no, no, I live in Brooklyn."

"That's cool?" she said like it was a dream of her own. "I guess you're probably done with law school then, huh?"

"How do you . . . ?" She was freaking him out a little, and he was already thrown off, so he just floundered some more and then told her he'd dropped out. "For film school," he said.

"That's cool . . . NYU?"

"Oh," he said, "I mean, maybe. I just applied. I'm waiting, you know, to hear."

"What about Karla? What happened to her?"

"I don't know," Jeremy said. "I guess we kind of lost touch."

"I guess she must've had the baby, right?"

"I have no idea," he stammered. "Baby? I mean, I haven't, we . . . it's been a long time . . ."

Becca was figuring: "I left a year ago September, so last time I saw her . . . ? I don't know . . . But she was way pregnant before I left. Hard to imagine a baby coming out of someone so teeny, you know? I mean, she was, like, *all* belly."

"Wow." Jeremy couldn't quite get his head around the math. He was, he *knew*, not the father of Karla's baby. But just the surprise of hearing she'd had one . . . *Someone* was its father. "So she had a baby a year ago, then, you say?"

Becca's face broke out grinning again: "Why? Yours?" she teased.

"Um, no," he said. She looked at him like that wasn't at all the answer she'd expected, and Jeremy was thinking how horrendous it would be if he started spewing the details of his relationship with Karla here in the coffee shop she'd once upon a time patronized at least twice a day for her nonfat sugar-free *all*-foam no-whip mochas, but he was distracted by a sudden movement behind him. It was Rudy—back in his coat, and in the process of re-bundling himself for the outdoors—swooping around, waving, and speaking, it now seemed clear, to Jeremy.

"Scuse me?" Rudy was saying. "Excuse me . . . ? Hey . . . I'm sorry, but, hey could you—I've got to run, and the guy I was sitting with here, he left his stuff, but I've got to take off, and he's not back—could you just keep, like, half an eye, just so no one walks off with anything . . . ?"

Jeremy wasn't sure whether he responded or not, but Rudy clapped him on the shoulder nevertheless, said, "Thanks, bro," and promptly fled the premises.

In the course of that brief respite, Becca seemed to have assessed something in Jeremy's situation—Christmas cards in hand, table full of supplies—and when he turned back to her she was reaching up to touch his shoulder, saying, "I'll let you get back to your . . . stuff . . . ?" But before she spun off toward the counter, she locked her eyes on his in a way that seemed full of a certain meaning but not one he felt he could decipher with any certainty.

After that, Jeremy got deep into the dove cards in a sort of Zen trance kind of way and didn't come up out of it until a coffee cup was placed on his table, and suddenly there was Becca, sitting in the extra chair, one leg curled up under her, the other probably barely touching the floor. She took up the coffee cup in both hands and huddled herself around it for warmth. "You know, Splatt was saying he thinks Karla was—"

"*Splat?*" Jeremy said.

"Splatt." She pointed in the general direction of the espresso bar. "Two *t*s. Splatt was saying he thought Karla married that guy from the bike shop, over on—"

"I don't really know anything about it."

"You know, the guy at Spoke and—?"

"I didn't really know her," Jeremy said. "I mean, I didn't know her life. We just . . . I just didn't know her for very long or very well. I mean, I'm surprised you remember me. I wasn't around here with Karla very long, I mean."

She looked a little caught but smoothed her way out quickly. "Yeah, I've always had a memory like that . . . ? You know? Faces, names . . . ?"

"Right," Jeremy said.

"Yeah," she said, "good like that, I guess . . . ?"

"Right," he said again.

Becca looked like maybe she was out of things to say and was beginning to uncurl herself from the chair when a blur of movement erupted in Jeremy's peripheral vision, and his first, panicked thought was: someone's fucking with Jug's stuff! "Hey," Jeremy said, standing. "Hey, you!" He spoke loudly, a little too much like an overzealous rookie cop on TV. The guy looked over, which was when Jeremy realized it *was* Jug. He'd gotten his ponytail hacked off. It sat on top of one of his stacks of term papers, wrapped in wax paper like a burrito. "Hey, oh, sorry." Jeremy modulated his voice. Jug's face looked younger, innocent, worried. "Hey," he said again, "I—your . . . friend? The guy who was watching your stuff . . . ?" He was talking like Becca.

Jug nodded eagerly.

"He got a call, something important . . . an emergency maybe . . . He was, um, and he had to go, right then. He asked me to keep an eye on your things." And Jeremy didn't know if it was something in Jug's face or something in himself, but he felt suddenly like he had to say more. "He said, he said to say goodbye, you know, for him . . ."

A moment later Jug was back to riffling his papers, assessing his worktable. He was saying, "Thanks dude, that's nice of you," inspecting the state of his coffee cup, which he lifted to Jeremy as if in toast, and then started off toward the counter. He turned back after a few paces. "Dude, thanks for the message."

"No problem." Then Jeremy said, "Hey, nice haircut."

Jug reached up self-consciously and tried to smooth his hand down a ponytail he no longer had. "Thanks."

Becca was still in her seat at Jeremy's table, half unfurled, like she'd been frozen between sitting and standing. She wore a curious smirk. "You little liar," she said, her tone somewhere between condescension and flirtation.

Jeremy stared back at her blankly. He resumed his seat.

She kept grinning, slyly. "Yeah, next it'll be '*Karla*? I never slept with anybody named Karla . . . I never even ever knew anyone named Karla . . . My name's not Jeremy. In fact, I've never been here before in my life!'"

Becca was growing more and more pleased with her every word, and when she was done, she'd risen to standing, coffee cup still clutched between her palms. She looked at Jeremy hard for another second, eyes alive with merriment, and then she lifted her brow and cocked her head toward the back of the café—like there was a brothel in the storeroom to which Jeremy was being invited—turned, and stalked off.

Before he got back to the doves, and while Jug was still off at the coffee bar, Jeremy began to read a Christmas letter that had arrived the previous day from his cousin, Hedda. It was one of those holiday update-on-the-year-gone-by things: two sides, single-spaced, dot matrix printout on holiday stationery—not dissimilar to the Matisse-y doves, in fact—and in it Hedda had catalogued every movie she and her boyfriend, Warren, had gone to see since last New Year's, who'd liked it and who'd thought it so-so but nothing special. She went into some detail about a grocery store that was supposed to have opened in their neighborhood in Rochester but, in the end, hadn't, on account of some sort of building zoning code problem.

Jug was returning with his coffee as Jeremy moved on to Hedda's hobby update: Hedda and Warren were (in case anyone was worried) still enjoying TV, movies, music (Warren), video games (Hedda), travel, sightseeing, photography, and collecting snow globes. At this, Jeremy was incapable of suppressing his laughter, and he felt embarrassed, like someone who giggles at a funeral or in an emergency. Just as he was letting out a half-stifled snort, Jug stepped one leg over the back of his chair—as if that was, of course, how anyone would take a seat in a coffee shop—then turned, as he sat, to see what Jeremy was laughing about. He must have feared—as Jeremy would have, in Jug's position—that Jeremy was laughing at him, and it made Jeremy feel like a little kid, stammering, holding up Hedda's letter, trying to collect his face to explain what he was actually laughing at. Jug looked like he really wanted to believe Jeremy, wanted to put the pieces together and understand that he wasn't at the butt-end of a joke.

"I'm sorry," Jeremy tried. "I'm . . . it's . . ." and it seemed better, just then, to say too much rather than too little. "I'm reading—it's one of those Christmas letters, from my cousin, and it's killing me. It's like every detail of everything that happened to her all year. It's heartbreaking . . . it's just . . ." He was shaking his head, trying to convey the marvel, waving the letter like he was offering it to Jug, to read, as proof.

"Dude," said Jug. He crossed one leg over the other and draped an arm casually over the back of his chair. "My grandmother used to send out one of those that was priceless. Especially once she got to the nursing home, and the whole letter'd be full of the medical procedures of everyone there. She was, like, completely beyond propriety at that point, and we'd get holiday greetings and the details of someone's colostomy all in the same paragraph."

Jug and Jeremy were—both of them—relieved to have averted the awkwardness their misunderstanding might have caused, and they settled back into their respective projects. Jug returned to his grading, continuing to let out a bark of laughter every few minutes, wiping his eyes or holding a hand over his mouth in exaggerated pantomime of his amusement, and Jeremy went back to reading Hedda and Warren's Christmas letter. They were planning a trip to New York (*City!*) for Hedda's cousin Jeremy's wedding (*Yay Jeremy and Catherine! Congrats!*) and welcomed any tips or suggestions about things to do and places to see while they were there. Jeremy kept half-wanting to catch gazes with Jug just to be able to read some of Hedda's lines aloud, to say to Jug something like, *I'll read you mine if you read me yours . . .* It also crossed Jeremy's mind that if Jug lived in the Javaroma neighborhood, and if he'd been there awhile, he might've known Karla or would recognize a description of her, and be able, for whatever reason, to remember when she'd been pregnant or where she'd gone. Jeremy could've asked Splatt at the counter, he supposed, but that seemed potentially messier than it was worth.

Instead, Jeremy opened the third box of doves and uncapped his pen. *Dear Hedda and Warren, HAPPY HOLIDAYS! Great to know we'll be seeing you at the wedding. Hey, when are you guys going to take the plunge yourselves? (No pressure!)* Which was too inane to even write to Hedda and Warren, and way too mortifying to imagine holding open in front of Catherine while she signed her name. She might even refuse. *You know, why get married anyhow and risk fucking up a good thing? Because you and Warren have a good thing, right? Me and Catherine,*

*who knows? Some days I'm so grateful for her I could cry and some days
I think I've swallowed so much pride for her I'm going to choke on it in
my sleep and die like Jimi Hendrix, except without having done anything
first. So maybe I should wait until I actually* do *something before I choke
and die, except that I'll be too fucking old for it to even be impressive.
Maybe I'll wait to see if I get into film school before I decide to choke on
my own vomit and die, because—wonder of wonders!—I might actually
like film school, so I can enjoy that and then* after, *when I still can't
get a job, let alone make films, or pay the rent, when Catherine's had
our child and whisked it off to be raised by some count or baron she'll
marry in Monaco and erase all evidence of a first marriage—her* starter
marriage—*and tell the kid her biological father is a sperm bank,* then *I'll
go home to my mother's house in Iowa and choke on my own vomit and
die and be forever eulogized like Vicky Hrksta who couldn't possibly have
done fuck-all of anything in her nineteen-year life but learn to eat with a
fork, shit in a toilet, name the state capitals, tie a maraschino cherry stem
in a knot with her tongue, shoot green apple schnapps and play truth or
dare with the Pi Chi Tri Di guys, until she puked her guts out and woke
up dead. But until then, HAPPY HOLIDAYS! Love, Jeremy &*

Catherine called from the BART platform where she was waiting to catch
a train to the San Francisco airport. In New York it was long dark, long
evening, and Jeremy hadn't yet finished the cards or left the Javaroma,
though he also hadn't bought anything in hours, and Splatt-with-two-*t*s
was starting to send warning vibes in his direction that he'd better fork
over two dollars sixteen cents plus tax for another Javaroma Joe or saddle
up and move it along. Catherine must have been able to hear the anxiety
in Jeremy's voice.

"Jeremy," she said meaningfully, and he cringed in anticipation. "Jeremy, are you depressed?" She said *depressed* like it was a condition
brought on by poor hygiene. He pictured her on the platform surrounded
by eye-rolling Rama Llamas, sympathizing with their martyred Saint
Catherine over her cross that was Jeremy, a cross she bore with such
tenacity, such benevolent grace. He knew any second she'd launch into
another rendition of her Jeremy-rousing pep rally, chock full of, *honey,*

it's a stressful time right nows, and *so much is up in the air for yous*, and *things will settle down by springs*, and Jeremy thought if he had to hear it just then he might hurl himself at the plate glass window. It was street level, but it would still hurt.

"Yes, I'm depressed," he said to the phone. "Of course I'm depressed. I'm me. I'm your dreary lame-ass boyfriend who can't get his fucking life together and has no job and mooches off his girlfriend and lets her talk him into pretending that the next thing will work. I just have to find my calling, the fucking color of my parachute, and then it'll all be fine and we can have money and babies and be happy and fulfilled and presentable and our fucking Christmas cards will be cheery and bright because we're so cheery and bright that we can't help but just naturally pick out the cheeriest and brightest Christmas cards on the stand because it's just who we are—"

"Stop!" she was shouting into the phone, into his ear. "Stop stop stop stop stop!"

He stopped. He did as she said. His head throbbed like it was in a high-pressure vice getting squeezed. He couldn't see. The vice was so tight there were tears coming out of his eyes.

"I can't do this," Catherine said. "The train's coming. I have bags—" She was crying by then. "I have to get on a plane!" Her voice edged toward hysteria, and that always served to calm Jeremy down, to force him into reactionary stoicism.

"I'm sorry," he said. "I'm sorry. This wasn't the time. We'll talk about it when you get home." He kept going, let her keep crying, plowed on. "Have a good flight, get some rest, and I'll see you when you get home. Call me when you land, okay? So I can get up. So I'll be up by the time you get home. Okay?" He may have sounded like an automaton, but, he thought, at least a nice automaton, an apologetic automaton.

When she answered, her voice was soft and beaten. "Okay," she said.

Catherine hung up. Jeremy closed his phone. The vice had released him but left a dull pressurized ache through his skull, a pain he knew was brutal but couldn't access. He felt like he'd been pumped up with morphine while someone sawed into his frontal lobe, which—for reasons certainly only metaphoric—he seemed to be trying to hold in place with his hands.

When he finally looked up and opened his eyes, the first thing he saw was Jug, still there at his window seat, looking on patiently, like he was sitting vigil at Jeremy's bedside waiting for him to regain consciousness. Once his eyes were open, Jeremy didn't have the wherewithal to move quickly enough to avert Jug's gaze, so there they sat, looking at each other until Jug smiled, kind of apologetically, and said, "There's a bar down the block. Can I buy you a drink?"

Everyone in the bar was either gay or a tourist or both. This was Chelsea after all. Sunday, and still early enough—the place wasn't crowded. Jug and Jeremy sat at the bar, their bags and gear smushed at their feet. Jeremy ordered a beer—a Stella, on tap—but Jug gave him a look of such pleading pity that he didn't argue when Jug asked for two shots of Maker's and slid one in front of him. They'd officially exchanged names on the walk over, and Jeremy had been a little unnerved to find that Jug already seemed to know his, but then, he already knew Jug's. His brain felt too bleary to compute it all. Visions of Matisse-y doves danced in his head. He felt like he might cry and not be able to help it. And then, like that, he *was* crying, and he *couldn't* help it. He slung back the Maker's Mark; it ripped down his throat like a scream. Jug gestured knowingly to the bartender and a new shot replaced the empty.

Jeremy felt a hand on his shoulder—a kneading pressure, sympathetic and understanding—and when Jug spoke there was a laugh to his voice, like he knew how cliché he sounded when he said, "I'm a good listener . . . ?"

Jeremy coughed a sob, then was able to regain himself. "God, what a fucking mess—"

Jug cut him off. "Hey . . . it's okay. Really." The hand was back, kneading Jeremy's shoulder. "It's okay." And Jeremy knew something was a little off—the guy was being so *nice*—but he'd lost all capacity to judge, or trust his own judgment, or to think clearly enough to assess the situation. In that moment, whatever else was going on, Jeremy felt lucky: he was sitting at a bar in New York City, crying, and no one was laughing or pointing or telling him to take it somewhere else. Even the bartender seemed to be in on it, setting some extra cocktail napkins down by Jeremy's untouched beer, resting his hand atop the little stack—*Bob's Your Bar*—for a moment, as if in reassurance, before he pulled it away and continued his bartenderly business. Jeremy felt cared for—by strangers!—and that made him catch his breath and weep anew.

When Jeremy's tears subsided, Jug spoke to him gently: "Do you live around here?"

It sounded like a pickup line, and Jeremy almost laughed but managed to just shake his head, afraid to open his mouth for fear of more tears.

"I didn't think I'd seen you at the Javaroma before," Jug observed.

Jeremy collected himself. "No," he said. "Brooklyn. I, we, me and my girlfriend, we live in Brooklyn. Carroll Gardens." The effort exhausted him.

"Oh, yeah?" Jug said. "I thought Becca lived around here?" He gestured vaguely.

"Becca?" Jeremy felt confused. "No, wait. Not . . . *That*'s not my girlfriend—fiancée—not Becca. I don't know her. Becca. My fiancée's in California. For the weekend, I mean. Catherine. I live in Brooklyn, with my fiancée, Catherine, who's in California for the weekend. I don't know Becca. Or she knows me, or something, from when I used to be around the Javaroma at one point with this other woman . . ." There was something in Jug's face that made Jeremy think he wasn't yet comprehending the explanation, like Jeremy hadn't made himself clear, but he couldn't think of how else to say what he was trying to say. For all he knew that expectancy on Jug's face was just the way Jug looked, the way his face was put together. Had Jug struck him that way back in the Javaroma? Jeremy couldn't remember anymore. He tried again: "I used to hang out at the Javaroma with a woman named Karla—hey, maybe . . . you didn't know her, maybe, did you?" The whiskey was in his frontal lobe now. He'd meant to be explaining something else, hadn't he? "I'm curious what happened to her. We lost touch, I guess. Well, no, I mean, we—I went back to my girlfriend. To Catherine. My fiancée." Oh, it all sounded so tawdry! It sounded as bad as Jug and his Marilyn, but Jeremy couldn't make himself stop. "But, do you live around there—here? Maybe you knew her?"

Jug was shaking his head. "I'm on Twenty-Seventh, but, no, I don't think so . . ."

"She was pregnant, apparently . . ."

And then Jug got that same little mischievous look Becca'd had. "Yours?" he suggested, both bemused and coy.

"No! Jesus, no. I don't even . . . we weren't even really dating. I mean, no, I guess, no, we *were*, I guess. But we never—she was—*is*, I guess—a dancer. She had lots of issues, lots of body stuff, you know? Just, you know, lots of issues. It was, like, it was romantic—well, or not romantic, I guess, exactly, but it was about attraction—but it wasn't *sexual* . . . per se, that is."

Jug was nodding in a manner that almost seemed understanding, as though he, too, had had a fucked-up affair that wasn't even an affair, that had almost ended his engagement. Jeremy began to weep again in earnest, in gratitude, in desperation, because it was the only thing he had left in him. Jug said: "Another?" and raised his eyebrow at Jeremy's somehow empty glass.

Jeremy shook his head. Too vehemently. "I can't," he said, hoisting his hips to dig into the front pockets of his jeans, one and then the other. He pounded a twenty-dollar bill on the bar, with a couple crumpled singles. "That's all I'm good for."

"I got you," Jug said, and before Jeremy could accept or decline—or at least demur—there was another Maker's in front of him.

"Thanks," he said.

"My pleasure," said Jug. He stood then, shook out his Levi's, and patted down his own pockets. Finding a lump in one pocket, he unearthed the small fold of bills there, leafed through them, and set them down on the bar before him. "At least as long as *I'm* good for it," he said.

They drank for a minute in silence. Then Jug said, "So you're trying to find this . . . Karla? This old girlfriend-person?"

"Well, no, I mean, it wasn't, like, my *goal*, but then Becca was saying how she'd been pregnant and now I'm just, you know, wondering what happened to her and all . . ." God, he hated the sound of his own voice.

"I haven't lived here all that long," Jug said. "Just a few months, really. Since summer. I came to teach, just for this year, you know. I'm not really a New Yorker," he admitted.

"That explains why you're so nice!"

Jug laughed. "That's nice of you to say. I'm definitely not a New York—that much has been made clear to me." He sounded a little bitter, and Jeremy wondered what had happened to sour him on New York like that, but he didn't even have to figure out how to ask, because Jug just kept going. "I'm not quite cut out for this place, I don't think," he confessed. "I'm in that classroom, and, man, it's just not a world I *know*, you know? I mean, Omaha has its, like, downtrodden parts, sure, but . . ." Jeremy practically snorted his whiskey. "Omaha?" he said.

Jug's eyes seized with a kind of fear Jeremy knew well, like he thought he might be getting mocked but couldn't think fast enough to figure it out. Jeremy's own eyes bugged in reciprocal horror; he stammered, "No, I didn't . . . I wasn't . . ." Why couldn't he express himself tonight? "I'm from Des Moines," he got out, finally. "Born and raised. Des Moines, Iowa." He shook his head extravagantly, pantomiming his own wonder at the incredible irony of it all: two midwestern boys in the Big Apple.

Jug looked like he'd been granted a stay of execution. When he discovered he'd risen to standing in his alarm, he sat back down on his stool. "Des Moines," he breathed, like he knew the town well. His hand reached up then, instinctively, for his ponytail, and he grabbed at his neck awkwardly when he found it missing.

"Hey," Jeremy said, relieved to change the subject. "What inspired the haircut?"

Jug's hand went back to his head, feeling at his neckline—like a woman, Jeremy thought suddenly. Like a woman who's gone from long hair to short and can't quite believe it's not there anymore. He'd seen at least two of his sisters make the same gesture at various stages in their hairdo histories. Jug said, "Do you like it?"

Jeremy went instantly from relieved to undone: did he like Jug's haircut? He had no idea if he liked Jug's haircut! How could he have any opinion whatsoever of this near-stranger's haircut? But Jug was asking so earnestly—so midwesternly housewifely!—that Jeremy thought it would break his heart not to reassure the poor guy. "Sure," he said. "Sure. Looks like a good haircut." He craned to either side as if to inspect the quality of the barber's work. "I just, I just wondered what made you decide to cut it. Just tired of being a longhair or something?"

Jug chuckled sadly, as if recalling a bittersweet memory. He looked right into Jeremy's eyes like he was coming clean at last. "My kids were making fun of me," he confessed.

"Your *kids*?" Jeremy's brain clouded over with whiskey, a sudden fog that overtook everything, as his brain tried to morph this *Jug*—this random coffee shop guy sitting next to him at the bar—into a grown man with children, and a wife, and not some shithole studio apartment on Twenty-Seventh Street, but a *home* on Twenty-Seventh Street, with real furniture, and a couch with intact upholstery purchased *new* at a *furniture store*, and a bed—not a futon—but a bed, with a frame, and a headboard and footboard, like the beds Catherine pored over in the Pottery Barn catalogue . . .

"My *students*, my *students*," Jug was saying. "They'll probably just make fun of me now for cutting it off, but . . ." He shook his head. "There's no winning. If I make it through another semester alive it'll be a small miracle."

Jeremy shook his own head to try to clear it. "Another semester," he repeated. "So it's not great?" He wasn't sure what he was saying. He had this idea that Jug loved teaching, but why? Why should Jug love teaching? Why did he assume everyone who wasn't him loved what they did for a living? Why did he just *assume* that every single other human being was born knowing the frigging color of their goddamn parachute? He had to change his outlook. He had to *see* things differently, see *people* differently. "So, it's not—so you don't *like* teaching?" He knew how ridiculous it sounded the second it was out his mouth. Like every teacher on the planet *loved* teaching? As if it were downright shocking to hear that one first-year teacher in the city of New York hadn't quite taken to it. What was he, an imbecile? Jeremy sank his head into his hand on the bar, then realized that, from Jug's point of view, Jeremy probably looked like he was crushed beyond belief to learn that Jug wasn't the happiest schoolteacher in five boroughs. He lifted his head and tried to recompose his face into a look of benign cocktail-party-small-talk interest. He was a caricature of himself! They should never have let him *out* of Des Moines!

"I don't know. You know, maybe it's not teaching, per se. It might just be here. Or the school I'm at . . ." Jug was speaking to Jeremy as though

Jeremy were a perfectly normal human being. It was very disconcerting. For his part, Jeremy could think of absolutely no response to what Jug had just said. Nothing. Not one thing. He just sat there nodding. Jug kept on. "I just don't know that I'm doing *anything* for these kids, you know? I mean, I've got a master's in English from the University of Nebraska—what the fuck can I teach them? How to scan poetry? It just all seems so *remote*, you know. Like, I came here wanting to do something *relevant* and what I'm doing is so far from that it's laughable. *Relevant . . .*" He shook his head, out of steam.

Jeremy reached for his whiskey and tried to drink, but there was nothing left in the glass.

"You want another?" Jug offered.

"Oh, no, no," Jeremy said. "No, I've still got . . ." He lifted his now-warm beer as if in toast. "To relevance," he said.

Jug snorted. He lifted his whiskey. "To relevance." He drained the glass and set it down decisively on the bar before him. "Hey," he said, "you know, I have better beer than that back at my place. And I could use something to eat . . ." He looked at his watch as though to confirm the appropriateness of his appetite. "We could grab a few slices and go to my place . . . ? It's just a couple blocks . . ." The way Jug said *a few slices* Jeremy could practically hear the *of pizza* he was trying so hard not to say, the *of pizza* he'd weaned himself from upon entry into this city.

Food. Jeremy hadn't thought about food. But now that Jug mentioned it, food sounded good. Food was maybe exactly what he needed. "I got to stop at a bank machine," Jeremy said.

"There's one at Ray's." Jug confirmed, like Ray was a buddy of his, not a pizza chain.

"Then pizza's on me," Jeremy said. Or, rather, on Catherine. It was her money in the joint checking account; she was the one with a job.

Snow had begun to fall. By the time they pushed out of Ray's, a dusting of white covered the sidewalk. Jeremy carried the pizza box—its warmth glorious! its smell glorious!—and let himself breathe deeply: basil-y, oregano-y, blurbling melted cheese. And also: the crisp tingle of snow-flakes hitting his nostrils as though the air itself had crystallized. *This* was why people lived in New York. He felt a giddiness sparkling in his chest; the world sparkled around him. They walked uptown toward Jug's apartment, and for a few minutes Jeremy let himself think that being alive was okay, that being a person was sometimes a really nifty thing to be.

Jug's was a fourth-floor walk-up; he apologized to Jeremy as they mounted the stairs.

"Our place is five," Jeremy countered, "*and* it's in Carroll Gardens."

Jug turned to look at Jeremy a second before he continued the climb. "What were you doing at the Javaroma if you live all the way out there?"

Jeremy's solar plexus gave a little spasm of panic. What *was* he doing at a coffee shop that far from home? He liked it there. He had fond memories of being there with Karla, staring intently, longingly at one another across a tiny table over their sweet, steaming cups. The idea of doing the Christmas cards at Javaroma was the only thing that had made the task at all bearable in his mind. But he felt self-conscious telling that to Jug: was it weird to take such comfort in the sanctuary of a particular coffee shop? He felt suddenly afraid that nothing he did would ever make sense to anyone. The idea unsettled him profoundly and made him feel terribly alone. He'd already paused too long before answering. He heard himself breathing laboriously—they were only to the first landing! Jug would think he was seriously out of shape, panting by the second floor. "I just had some other stuff to do in the city." He was the worst liar in the world.

"Oh," Jug said. "Right, sure." And it took Jeremy a second to figure out why this response both calmed and surprised him so: Jug meant it. There was no sarcasm behind the words, not an ounce. Jug's *right, sure* was said with bolstering understanding. He was trying to make Jeremy comfortable, to put him at ease, and Jeremy's gratitude was so enormous he could have cried again, easily. He fought the tears, let them well in him as joy instead of sadness. Jeremy "Never-to-be-Esquire" Bunn let himself breathe in pizza steam, feel the old hissing heaters melt snowflakes from his eyelashes, and enjoy the taut pull at the back of his legs as he climbed. They rounded another landing. For a moment, Jeremy allowed himself to feel happy.

Jug's studio would have pleased Jeremy's mother. Clean lines. IKEA-chic. Nothing of real quality, but nothing ratty, and nothing out of place.

Jug gave a gentle tap to a spot on the wall and a tableside lamp rose from a dim filament into a warm and glowing light. It sat beside a Danish Modern reading chair that was probably faux but looked nice nonetheless. Jug gestured toward the kitchen-area counter for Jeremy to set down the pizza, then offered to take his coat. This involved a lot of steps: Jeremy heaving his bag from his shoulder, removing gloves, unwrapping his scarf, shaking snow from his hat. Jug hung the coat on a stylized chrome hanger and slipped it over a Lucite peg on the wall. Then Jeremy stood there feeling naked while Jug removed his own layers and got them onto a matching peg next to Jeremy's so that their coats hung beside each other, arms touching at the cuffs like paper dolls.

"This is a really nice place," Jeremy said.

"Oh, stop," Jug chided him. "It's a shithole."

"Are you kidding? This place is great."

"It was so gross when I got here," Jug confessed. "I just scoured it and covered the whole thing with white paint. Layers and layers. The dirt keeps seeping through though. So I just keep painting. If I didn't stay on top of it, I think the walls would be black by this point."

Now that Jug mentioned it, the place did smell kind of like latex, but it wasn't unpleasant.

Jug pulled a couple beers from the fridge, then seemed to wave them under the edge of the counter where their caps came off with a quick suck and fizz, landing in Jug's palm, and disappearing like scarves up a magician's sleeve. Jeremy thought of Jug swinging his leg over the Javaroma chair, and imagining him alone in this apartment, opening bottle after bottle—maybe even recapping the empty bottles just to practice smoothly prying them off again, until the metal refused to be refitted. Maybe you could even buy machines to cap beer bottles at home? Like from a homebrewers supply place. Jeremy wouldn't have been surprised if Jug had one, if such things existed. His smoothness was so practiced, it was impossible to imagine it being natural. He made Jeremy think of a professional ice skater.

"I love this," Jug said, passing Jeremy a bottle. "It's from a little brewery in Vermont I love. Really hoppy. I hope you like hoppy."

The beer was extremely cold and so sharp it hit Jeremy's nose like a dollop of horseradish. "Mmmmm." He nodded noncommittally. "Mmm." He didn't really have a clue how he felt about *hoppy*.

They sat on Jug's tiny, apartment-sized sofa and ate their pizza at the coffee table, looking out across the fire escape. Snow swept beneath the streetlights. Jug asked Jeremy about Des Moines and about Brooklyn and film school and Catherine. He was so nonjudgmental—so the opposite of his name!—it was easy to talk to him, to just tell him things. He seemed so totally, genuinely interested in what Jeremy had to say. "So how did you guys decide to get *married*, per se?" he asked, and it felt okay there in the glowing table light, with the snow falling all around, insulating them in this little snug box of an apartment, full of pizza and fuzzy with beer—and whiskey, he'd almost forgotten those whiskies, warm in his belly—it felt totally okay to tell Jug about Vicky Hrksta and the Rama Llamas and how he and Catherine had been together so long he almost couldn't remember them not being together, except the times they'd broken up, which had been so awful he didn't like to think about them. Awful mostly because he'd wound up back in Des Moines living with his mom and Frank, and because he loved Catherine, he did, and he knew—or at least he hoped really really fervently—that he'd love their life. Once he could figure out what the fuck to do with his own, he was sure he would love their life together. Everything had all just happened in such a tumbling, snowball sort of way. She'd been finishing law school when he was finishing undergrad; the whole time they'd been together she'd been in law school, so it was practically like he was already in law school himself. It made sense that maybe he *should* go law school. He'd applied to schools in every city where she'd applied for a job. They wound up in New York. But he'd hated law school. Hated hated *hated* it. And Catherine was working so hard, such long hours, paying back her own law school loans, they rarely *saw* each other that first year, it seemed like. But now she'd been at the firm two years, had things somewhat under control there, could think about the future a little. She was twenty-seven now, and—just like Frank said—her friends *were* all getting married and having babies, and it kind of seemed like the thing to do. Plus, their relationship had always taken a backseat to everything else in their life, and now was supposed to be the time when it started to come first, when they could actually focus on it, on each other. It was like they'd found each other years before, decided to mate for life, and then put their relationship on pause while they did the other things they needed to do. And this was all strange and uncomfortable for Jeremy to be saying, but Jug seemed to take it all in, like it made at least some amount of sense, which made Jeremy think maybe some of the things that never totally made sense to him might make more sense if he said them out loud to Jug. Like how the whole no-drinking thing that came out of the Vicky Hrksta tragedy was really part of a larger sort of pact Catherine had made with herself—and this was before Jeremy even knew her, years before—about how she was going to live a really exemplary life, a life that would somehow honor Vicky, or make up for the life Vicky didn't get to live or something. After Vicky died, Catherine promised herself and her parents and her psychiatrist and her sorority sisters that she wouldn't drink or do drugs or smoke, and that she would get all As, and wouldn't have sex until she was married, and—

Jug's eyebrows shot up. That was apparently where the line got drawn. Even this seemingly most-understanding-man-in-the-universe couldn't take that one in without registering unchecked surprise. Jeremy fumbled to explain. "It's not that we haven't had sex." He watched Jug for signs of relief. "We did, you know, to make sure we were good together. When we got engaged. When we knew we were planning to be together, you know?"

Jug was nodding, eagerly so, like he was really going to try to understand.

"It's a thing a lot of girls were doing," Jeremy went on. "A lot of her friends, anyway. I know it sounds weird. But, I don't know, at the time it . . . I guess it seemed like it was coming from the right place, you know? Like it was weird, but in good faith, or something?"

Jug was all over himself apologizing. "I didn't mean it was weird. I've heard of things like that. It's just, it's kind of surprising. Not in a bad way, I don't mean. Just different." Which was nice of him but didn't make Jeremy feel any less awkward about having just admitted to this person he didn't even know that he was basically someone who didn't have sex. Or someone who didn't even need one hand to count the number of times he'd had sex in his life. That he and Catherine had now been together for more *years* than the number of times they'd had sex, total.

All that was mortifying enough. But possibly even *more* mortifying was the fact that it didn't bother Jeremy all that much, not having sex. It made things easier. More manageable. Sex had become something he could put off in his mind, something he didn't have to figure out right away. He had so much else to deal with, and sex could wait, and that was kind of a relief. When he thought about it, he thought it was like how if you lived in Iowa, you didn't have to spend a lot of time worrying about not knowing how to ski, because skiing wasn't expected of you in Iowa. And you could rest assured that someday you would take a trip and go somewhere mountainous, and then skiing would be a relevant skill to acquire, so you'd take some lessons and figure out how to ski. Except the metaphor didn't really work, because skiing was one of those things, like languages, where if you didn't learn at a young age it was too late and you'd never be fluent. But who said he had to be fluent at sex? He and Catherine had lived for years without sex, and it was fine, and everyone talked about how once you got married you never had sex anymore anyway, and certainly once you had kids there wasn't time or privacy or anything to have sex anymore, so really he didn't see how, ultimately, it was going to be all that different from how it already was.

"Can I say something that might sound weird?" Jug asked. Like he'd have to ask! After all Jeremy'd just revealed—as if anything could sound weird after that. Jug said, "I was engaged, too, once. Or *essentially* engaged, anyway, and, anyway, when that ended, I was doing some hard thinking, some real soul searching . . ." He paused as if in dramatic reenactment of the hard thinking of which he spoke. Jeremy was curious to know if Jug's "essential" engagement had been with the short girl, Marilyn, but there was something in Jug's face that kept him from asking. He spoke with determination, and with sadness, like he had to get it out now or it was going to hurt him, physically. Jeremy waited; it was the least he could do. The guy'd been so nice.

Jug stared down into his beer bottle. Jeremy half expected him to lift it to his eye like an old-fashioned telescope, like he was Charles Darwin standing on the Galapagos rocks, gazing out over the origin of man. Jug spoke with his head bowed. "When that relationship was over, I had to ask myself a lot of hard questions, and, in the end—well, I don't know what *the end* is yet—there's no *in the end* yet. But right now at least . . ." Jug took a breath, then lifted his head and looked right at Jeremy, dead on, in the eyes, and Jeremy was too surprised to even think to turn away. "I don't think I'm gay," Jug said, "but I'm not *closed* to the idea. I haven't been. Closed to the idea. I'm not closed to it. And you're very . . . You're very beautiful. I find you very attractive, and I'm really happy you're here with me. I'm excited to be here with you, and I'd like to kiss you." And that was it—that was all the eye contact Jug could stand. He broke his gaze from Jeremy, looked down at his beer, tried to drain it, but rediscovered it was already empty and stood, suddenly nervous, like he'd used up all his wherewithal. But then, bottle grasped in his hand penitently, Jug looked up again like he'd found a last reserve of gumption. He said, "I'm so sorry. I understand if you want to leave. I just needed to say that. No—I didn't *need* to, I *wanted* to. I wanted to tell you that. I'm sorry." Jug looked like he might be the one to cry now.

Jeremy *did* want to leave. But he also *didn't*. The thing he kept thinking was that he *should* want to leave a lot more desperately than he actually did. It was warm and neat and beery and pizza-y and fresh paint-y and cozy in Jug's apartment, and outside it was snowing, and cold, and it was still New York. And even if all the trains were running, which they never were, it would take him at least an hour to get back to Brooklyn, where he'd have to walk eight more blocks home, past bodegas whose windows were stacked with grime-covered boxes of Spanish-printed laundry detergent, and Chinese takeout joints big enough to fit one cracked vinyl booth where drug deals went down twenty-four hours a day, seven days a week, rain, snow, sleet, hail, tornado, hurricane, blizzard, blackout. And then he'd have to climb five flights of creaking wooden stairs through corridors with baseboards so filth-encrusted that the corners were almost rounded like a half-pipe. The stairways never stopped smelling of fried onions, as though someone kept a saucepan of them perennially simmering like potpourri. It was enough to make him hate the smell of something as once-delicious as fried onions. God how he hated it there!

But here, at Jug's, the grime had been scrubbed from the baseboard corners, painted over, kept at bay. Jug was waging a losing battle, yes, but he was waging it! Jug would never make it here. He was a man who brought a stranger home and asked—earnestly!—if he could kiss him. He was the antithesis of New York, with his smooth skin and his shiny, shorn hair and his niceness! His goddamn niceness! Jeremy could weep for this man's freaking niceness! And then he *was* weeping—again!—and Jug was beside him, kneeling down on the floor at the edge of the tiny couch, one hand on Jeremy's leg, the other at his cheek, cupping his face, catching the tears. He kneeled there, his eyes huge with concern, his hand soft and sweetly cool at Jeremy's cheek. "I'm sorry," Jug was saying. "I'm so sorry. I shouldn't have . . . I'm sorry—" But Jeremy was talking at the same time, trying also to apologize, saying, "I'm sorry. I'm an idiot. I'm such a fucking idiot. I'm sitting here *crying*. I'm such a fucking asshole idiot," and he swiped at his face, his eyes, trying to slap away the ridiculous tears that just kept fucking *falling* out of his stupid asshole head. He swatted at his own face to staunch the tears, to slap himself into sense, but Jug grabbed his hands, grabbed both of Jeremy's hands in his own and pushed them down, away from his face, saying, "Stop, stop, please, please stop," grasping Jeremy's wrists in his hands and pushing them down, pushing them to Jeremy's side, rising from the ground with the effort, rising half to standing before letting his weight sink down onto the couch as he held—forcefully held down—Jeremy's hands, and, as if in a last resort to quell the sobbing, as though the tears were like blood whose flow had to be staunched, he leaned in with purpose, with determined, driven resolve for the last shot, the final spasm-crack of the defibrillator, he leaned in and pressed his soft, beautiful lips to Jeremy's own.

Everything went quiet for a moment, quiet and still, except for the tremor in their arms, Jeremy's shaking involuntarily, and Jug's shaking with the effort it took to hold Jeremy's shaking arms down. Everything still but their trembling arms, and then their lips, parting slowly, trembling too, their mouths opening to each other's mouths, their breathing sharp and shallow, mouths grappling, breath catching, the tentative, tentative reaching, mouth for mouth, breath for breath. Jug's tongue felt for Jeremy's, found it, and drew it out, solicitously, and then urgently. Jeremy didn't realize his wrist was free until he felt Jug's hand at the side of his face again, Jug pulling back then, out of the kiss, to look at Jeremy, his hand at Jeremy's temple, thumb brushing the tears away from his eyes. "My god, you're beautiful," Jug said. Jeremy choked. Coughed. The tears started flowing fresh. He let out an involuntary wail—not a wail of anguish at whatever he was crying about, because he didn't even know what he was crying about!—but at the fact that he was crying again. Crying *still*. That he was a grown fucking man sitting here crying. But Jug was unfazed, somehow still unfazed. He pulled back from Jeremy, moving deliberately, soothingly. He was saying, "Shhhhh, shhhhhh, you're okay, you're fine. You're so beautiful. Shhhhhh, shhhhhh, shhhhhhh." And he left that one hand at Jeremy's face, kept his eyes on Jeremy's eyes, while the other hand reached down for the waistband of Jeremy's Levi's button fly, one button, two buttons, slipping their holes. Not slipping easily, though, because Jeremy's erection was pushing at the denim, and Jug had to use his fingers to pull together the cloth to release button from buttonhole. Three buttons. Four. Jeremy closed his eyes. His breath came out ragged with tears, his body unloosing itself grotesquely there on Jug's miniature couch. He had no fight in him. His head fell back. Jug reached inside the cotton flap of his boxers, slipped Jeremy free of everything that held him in. Jeremy felt Jug's hand drift from his cheek to his neck, chest, diaphragm, into the soft heaving spot hollowed out below his ribcage. He felt Jug's tongue first, then his whole mouth. Jeremy moaned. There was nothing he could do. He came so quickly he didn't have time to think about stopping himself. He was coming and crying at the same time. Coming and sobbing and thinking, *I'm not gay if I'm crying. If I were gay, I wouldn't be crying, would I?* Thinking, god, it had been so long. So long since someone else had made him come. Such an eternity since he'd come in any way except spooned behind Catherine in bed, rubbing himself into the cleft of her ass as she fell asleep. So long since anyone had taken him in their mouth and cared to cause him pleasure. He wept openly. He wept like he was never going to stop.

It was close to five in the morning by the time he left Jug's apartment. If flights were on time—although the snow, still coming down, might be mercifully slowing things up at the airport—Catherine's plane would be landing soon, and depending on how long it took her—he couldn't remember if it was JFK or LaGuardia, or maybe even Newark?—he might be able to make it back to Brooklyn before she did. He humped his bag higher on his shoulder and tromped east toward Fifth Avenue through city streets as deserted as he'd ever seen them. His eyes were gritty, his head stuffy with hangover and crying. Fine, misty snowflakes fluttered against his cheeks, and he wanted to turn his face to the sky, close his swollen eyes, and let the cold numb the ache throbbing in his eye sockets.

In the enormous windows of a building at the corner of Twenty-Seventh and Fifth, hot-pink signs with white bubble print read: KINK. A little closer, and Jeremy could see, in finer print, on the building itself: museum of sex. He swallowed against the nausea, gulped at the cold air, then burrowed his face back down into his scarf. He turned down the avenue, tucked his head, and trundled on. If he'd headed west, he could have gotten the F-train. Now he'd have to take the R at Twenty-Third and change at Jay Street—if it was running. The trains were never running when you needed them. Especially in the middle of the night, or during storms, or when you were late. He'd probably wind up walking back to the F anyway. That's how it always wound up happening in this fucking city. But it was Monday-friggin'-morning! Didn't people have to get to work? When were the trains supposed to be running if not on Monday morning? He was already mad, and he hadn't even gotten to the station yet. This city baffled him. The world baffled him. He baffled himself. Catherine would know he'd been crying. Not that crying was anything particularly new. If she beat him home, she'd be annoyed, yes, but she'd assume he'd been out drinking, crying into his beer, she'd say. He had the sense that she felt it was beneath her to worry about Jeremy's faithfulness; to doubt it would be to admit their relationship was made of less than bedrock. If she did not question their solidity, then foundation-stone they were. It was practically a tautology, a closed and inescapable circuit.

The streetlamps were ringed with fog—gauzy halos of light. Jeremy's toes numbed inside his boots. The snow was three and four inches deep in some spots. Even Fifth Avenue shopkeepers hadn't come out yet to shovel their walks. A lone taxicab rolled past, and Jeremy watched its taillights disappear downtown into the haze, two pulsing red dots growing smaller and smaller until they were gone. Up ahead of him stood the Flatiron Building—that strange pie-sliver of a thing. To his left, the great trees of Madison Square Park stood dark against the lightening sky, limbs hung protectively over the street, catching the snow that turned their branches to silver filigree. This was what the Steichen photo should have looked like. This was how it did look in his mind.

AND THE NIGHT GOES OFF
LIKE A GUN IN A CAR

"He came to me last night." My mother jerks her chin at the orderly and dislodges her oxygen tube. I lean to nudge it back up her nostrils, and she grabs my blouse, pulls me close. A button pops. The woman is seventy-eight, with the grip of a barroom arm wrestler. "He's a fei-sty lit-tle rab-bit . . ." she sings, her shudder nearly orgasmic.

Behind me, Ken—my mother's feisty rabbit of an orderly—laughs. "You're too kind, Mrs. Russakoff." He's setting out her dinner.

"In the gable . . . in the . . . tuffet . . . The storm broke . . ." She is reliving something behind her eyes. "Lightning struck as he entered me—"

"*Mom—*"

The light glinting through the nursing home window is the grim golden gray of city dusk. "Oh, he was vast!" she marvels. I turn toward Ken's laughter behind me, and, unfortunately, awkwardly, meet his eyes. We're both red-faced. He shakes his head. My mother paints the mental images, and we're the ones who get stuck with them, like an attic full of godawful amateur acrylic and oil canvases we can't throw out for fear of hurting her feelings. Ken busies himself at the sink. In a world of tubby health care workers in cartoon print scrubs, it's just like my mother to wind up with a nursing home orderly who might as well be a Calvin Klein model. And only my mother has the power, through mere implication, to make me feel precisely as embarrassed as if I'd just lured Nurse Ken up to a skylighted turret in the old wing of the Riverview Home for a squalid, rutty tryst, thunder shaking the windows, the very walls around us trembling as we climax, simultaneously, and then crumple, spent, into each other.

My mother is—*was*—pseudonymously—Scarlett Beech, author of sixty-seven novels of wanton lust and ribald copulation. During her ten-year decline, she's stopped writing stories and tells them instead, from an ever-weirdening Alzheimer's-addled fishbowl. Which might be amusing if she didn't always manage to push buttons in such a way that her tales hit—freakishly, disturbingly—a pulse point of arousal, like the accidental brush of cloth against a nipple at just the time of month when that's all it takes to send a quiver through your pelvis, fallopian tubes fluttering like waking eyelids. Sitting at my mother's bedside, I feel myself go appallingly, thrillingly wet—a warm drop, like the pop and drain of a clogged ear—as though I'm ready to be thoroughly fucked by this attractive man in scrubs fussing nervously with my mother's boiled carrots.

When my father died this spring, I wanted to find a home for Mom near me, in California, but she refused to so much as discuss it. She said, "I will slit my wrists, Millicent." This was maybe six weeks ago. She'd wanted to stay in the apartment, on the Upper West Side, where I grew up, in Manhattan, where she'd lived her entire life. *Slit her wrists*? How was I meant to take that?

"So you're going to insist on being three thousand miles away from the place where I have a job and a life, a fiancée . . . ?"

"Such drama, Millie!" My mother never called me Millie. "We'll have *lunch . . .*"

"We can't *have lunch* if you live three thousand miles away."

"Irredeemable," she said. I think.

"Did you just say 'irredeemable'?"

Distracted by something at her feet, she folded herself down to whisk at the wheelchair footrest with a spotty, swollen hand. "Damn cuttlefish! Bottom-feeders . . ."

"The cuttlefish are back?"

She turned her head up at me in annoyance: what the hell did I think was swimming through the carpet if not cuttlefish?

"Time for a little Zyprexa?" I suggested.

"They won't let you have it."

"Let me see what I can do." I went to the kitchen for her pill.

"I do so look forward to the wedding," she said when I returned. I pushed the tablet through her lips, held her chin, lifted the glass, and tipped water in.

"Swallow," I said.

She swallowed.

"So now you're looking forward to it, huh?" I asked.

"Davey is a wonderful man." She grew moony. "So virile . . . very plum."

"Plump? I'm not marrying Davey, Ma. I'm marrying Kirk, Ma. Do you remember meeting Kirk?" Davey was a childhood neighbor I'd last seen when I was still in Underoos.

"Oh it's vague . . . Vaguely plum. Davey's a man like your father." And then, Zyprexa be damned, the cuttlefish seemed to return, and she bent forward again, swatting. "A broom, Millicent! Something! A shovel . . . Spoon them like . . . A net! Where is that net?"

"Why don't I bring Dad's fishing rod up from storage and we'll make an evening of it."

She snapped up. "Oh, Millicent . . ." She'd had it with me. "They're absolute shit." The ankle flicking resumed.

"Ma, you know where there's *great* fish . . . remember that market in Berkeley . . . ?"

"Millicent," she said, lifting her face, eyes narrow, jaw set, "I will slit my wrists."

When my mother is fed, washed, pilled, settled, and sleeping, I head for the bus stop. The dusty sunset has mutated into another summer-evening storm: premature darkness, the streetlamps like giant shower-heads. Weather lends a humility to this city, and it's not unbecoming. The streaked neon of lightning, industrial silhouettes revealed in each flash. Also flashing—in my mind, unbidden but hardly unpleasant—are images of furtive, urgent, lightning-bolt-lit turret sex with Nurse Ken.

And as I make my way down the wet Riverdale block—in this section of the Bronx that's hardly the Bronx, just up the Hudson from our old apartment, now sold—who's waiting under the bus stop shelter at the nursing home corner but Ken, who, from the look of his bumblebee shirt, must moonlight as some sort of a referee. In the dim streetlamp light, he squints to read a drooping newspaper. I know that if I'm forced face-to-face with him—if I have to see him squint like that to see who I am—I will blush instantly and say something so irredeemable as to render all future interaction too mortifying to be borne with any dignity. We may as well have already *had* our sex in the turret. And it may as well have been limply, dryly, awkwardly, shamefully terrible.

It's not *that* far to the subway . . . I can make it through a little summer rain. I pivot before he can look up and notice me. I could probably use a cold shower anyway.

The downtown train is a meat freezer on tracks. Sodden passengers board, and their glasses fog instantly. My blouse isn't drying so much as stiffening with cold. The safety pin I've got in place of the popped placket button becomes an icicle between my breasts. I take a corner seat. There's a discarded *New York Post* on the floor and I fight the urge to blanket myself in its pages. It's a long ride down to the Biggerstaffs.

Kirk's folks have generously been putting me up since we closed on the sale of my parents' apartment, and though I'm appreciative, I can't say I relish the thought of an evening with Stan and Muffy. Or, as some of us prefer, Man and Stuffy. Four months from Saturday I am to wed their son, John Kirkland Biggerstaff, whom I still cannot—after nearly a year of engagement—call *my fiancé*. The fiancé is about as close as I get. Man and Stuffy are the *future in-laws*. Kirk will inevitably be *the husband*, if I can, in four months' time, train my tongue around that word. It's certainly less odious than the thought of myself as *wife*, but *husband* evokes for me odd images of 4-H fairs; the warm, silty flank of a quarter horse; that fertile, loamy stink that rises from a pile of steaming, grassy horseshit. A photograph of me and Kirk will undoubtedly appear in the back pages of the *New York Times*' Sunday Styles section the weekend of our wedding. I'll be one of those brides who will "continue to use her own name," like another neo-Luddite resisting the latest update of Microsoft Word.

The subway peels into a station. I hear the doors shuttle open; my eyelids are too heavy to lift. My lashes may well be frozen together. A pounding racket of footfall sounds fast down the platform, and then I feel someone jump into the car before the doors clamber shut. There can't be a shortage of empty seats, but the new passenger doesn't seem to be taking one; I can feel the unmoving presence over me. My adrenaline rallies to potential danger, but I can barely muster the caution necessary to raise one reluctant eyelid.

And of all people in the world, who is it but Gabriel Weiselberg wearing a ridiculous orange poncho, beaming down at me, his mouth shaped into the most pleased and private of smiles, brown eyes giddy, eyelashes dewy with rain. (And don't imagine I'm not *well* aware of the restraint required of the daughters of romance novelists with regard to the use of words such as *dewy*. My utmost discretion is always in effect with regard to *throb, thrust, moist, member, mound, manhood*.) Gabe gives his poncho-ed body a shake, like a dog coming out of the surf, then slides silently in beside me. The warmth of him is miraculous, and before either of us speaks a word, I've gotten my arms wriggled up under the poncho and around his middle, where his abs, as always, are exoskeleton hard. A survival instinct propels me toward his core heat, though this is where my hands always go on Gabe. His body is a body that needs to be touched. Or rather, a body that I, in his presence, cannot keep my hands off.

Gabe kisses the crown of my freezing-wet head. "When'd you get to town, pretty lady?"

My voice says, "May . . ."

He pulls back.

"My father died. I just put my mother into a nursing home in Riverdale . . ."

And his lovely weathered face opens entirely in sympathy, and then his arm is around me, pulling me back in. "Oh, Millie," he says. "You should have called. I could've helped . . . Why didn't you call?"

I shake my head a little, lift my shoulders as if to shrug. "You're busy. Your dissertation . . ." The truth: *You have a girlfriend, Gabe; I have a fiancé.* Gabe finished his doctoral coursework seven years ago. He may never *not* be "finishing up." ABD, he jokes, means Anything But Dissertation. I tell him that a PhD is like his own personal ERA: a worthy lifelong cause. Success, per se, might remain elusive, but what peace of mind to know you've spent your life fighting the good, right fight. *Right, right*, he says, *right, peace of mind*. Gabe is, at any given time, an alcoholic, insomniac, exercise junkie, Ritalin-popping transcendental meditator/videogame addict. He says, *I could write a fucking dissertation on peace of mind.*

Now what he says is, "Aviva and I broke up."

I lift my head. He's inscrutable as always. "I'm . . . sorry?"

He's nodding soberly. "It was a matter of time."

"You're in the platitude stage then."

"Yeah," he says, like he hasn't quite heard, and hugs me closer. "Hey." He perks up. "Means I have an apartment to myself though . . ."

"I'm staying with Man and Stuffy."

"Well I wasn't suggesting you bring me *there*!"

"It might look a little funny if I didn't come home . . ."

"You're really going to get married, aren't you?"

Again, all I can muster is the helpless suggestion of a shrug. My wedding at this point feels inevitable as aging, as determined as the end of a book.

Gabe pouts. "And you're really going to go monogamous on me, even before that?"

"Look," I say, "it's entirely possible that I just fucked my mother's rest home orderly in a hospital gable in the middle of a lightning storm, so I don't honestly have any *idea* what I'm doing . . ."

"Are you serious? You're not serious. You *are* still getting married?"

"Apparently."

"I almost feel *bad* for poor old Biggerstaff."

"Kirk's a big boy."

"So the name implies. You just want to be Millicent *Biggerstaff*."

"I'm *not* changing my name."

"I've got it! You marry him and take his name. Then get divorced, marry me, and I'll take *your* name!"

"All that to be Gabriel Biggerstaff?"

"All that to compensate for my tiny, tiny ashen penis."

I laugh.

"Now, now," he chides, "easy on the schadenfreude."

In his high school yearbook, Gabe was voted "Most Likely to Have Trouble Fitting In." The man has—and not unseriously—contemplated abandoning his doctorate entirely to pursue a career in pornography. It may well be his true calling.

"Anyway," he says, "I think I have VD."

Something hollows behind my ribcage. My ears and jaw go tingling numb. "*What*? *VD*? Who says *VD* anymore?"

"*ED, ED*," he's saying. Apparently I have misheard. "*E*-D," he says one last time.

"*ED*?"

"Erectile dysfunction."

"Okay, no," I say, flat out. "Okay, the last time I saw you we had sex seven times in twelve hours. You do *not* have erectile dysfunction."

"That was *months* ago. What do you care, anyway? You're getting married. To *Biggerstaff*."

And all I can do is burrow closer and hang on.

The train doors open. Forty-Second Street. They close again.

"Where are you going anyhow?" I ask.

"Barbecue."

"Nice weather for it."

"Hey, actually—you remember Marco, from college? He was part of that whole Eighth Street scene . . . ? Big communist . . . ?"

"Vaguely."

"The guy we bought the pot from that time . . . ?"

"*He's* a communist?"

"Totally. I ran into him last week. Works for them now. His fucking business cards are like: Marco Hausman, Communist Party. Come on, Mill, come with me! They might even have a washer/dryer. You could dry your clothes. There'll probably be other folks from school, maybe. Otherwise, what? You're just going home to Man and Stuffy?"

"Twist my arm."

"You know I don't like that rough stuff you're into." Gabe lifts an orange wing, points a finger to the center of my chest. "That's dangerous," he says of the safety pin over my heart.

"So's riding the subway with your breasts hanging out."

"Touché."

I mock kick him and miss.

"Millie, Millie, Mill, Mill, Mill," Gabe coos, and I close my eyes again until we reach Union Square.

Fourteenth Street is streaky with neon glare. We turn into a bodega and I wait up front while Gabe chooses beer from the back coolers. A wiry little leather-tan man in an undershirt is checking out at the register with a pack of Parliaments and as many pieces of Bazooka gum as he can buy with his leftover change. On the counter beside the Bazooka bin is a cardboard stand, a flyer stapled to it—"MISSING," with a Xeroxed photo of Brenda "Bebe" Cleveland: "D.O.B. 3/18/60; hair: blond; eyes: hazel; height: 5'1"; weight: 160; ID marks: tattoo of a green dancing bear on left ankle, Steal-Your-Face skull on right hip. Last seen: 5/16/05 Penn Station."

The outside door swings open then, and I have to squeeze aside for a bunch of high school boys who pour in posturing like upper-middle-class hoods. The Bazooka buyer looks up at the *bing-bong* of the door chime and takes me in with the sweep of his glance before he resumes counting change. I watch the candy racks, delirious, like I'm stoned, the packages bright and fake as props, cartoon renditions of junk food: blue-razz-fizz, all Juicy, Spree, Zing, Mmmm.

"You know, that could be you," says a man's voice. I look up. It's the Bazooka buyer, unwrapping a dusty-pink chunk and feeding it into his mouth while the cashier corrals the rest of the pile into a baggie and rings up the sale.

"Excuse me?" I say. "Were you talking to . . . ?"

He turns to Brenda Cleveland's flyer, then back to me. He wags a finger between us, me and Brenda. "Could be you, you know," he says again.

"O-kay," I say, wary, speaking like he's a child, a slow one. "I suppose it could be any of us, missing, sure . . ."

"No, no," he says, "Look at that. Cut the hair, change the clothes, could be you, no question, for sure." He's going back and forth now, me, the photo, me, Brenda "Bebe" Cleveland. Now the cashier's doing it too. "That for *sure* could be a picture of you."

I peer a little closer. It's hard to see much of anything on a black and white Xerox of a photograph. "Well, I *guess*," I say finally. "It's *not*, but . . ." And then this seems as dumb a thing as any to say since it's obviously exactly what I'd say if it *were* me and I was about to get found and didn't want to be. So I'm standing there trying to figure out how to convince these men that I'm not a missing person, and of course anything I do makes me look guiltier. When Gabe swings into the counter with a six-pack of Anchor Steam and another of PBR—"We'll go high and lowbrow at the same time," he's saying—the men both look like they're ready to jump and wrestle him to the ground if he tries anything funny, this guy in the orange poncho, clearly my captor. When he pays with cash—to cover his tracks, of course, leave no trace—I imagine the cashier noting the surfaces on which Gabe may have left his fingerprints. And those on which I, Bebe Cleveland, may have left mine. When we exit through the chiming door, I'm ready for the SWAT team surround and ambush.

On the street I tell Gabe I've been mistaken for a short, plump, forty-five-year-old, dancing-bear-tattooed, missing Deadhead.

"Now, Milly, what have we said about flashing the tattoos to bodega clerks?"

"I do not look forty-five!"

Gabe drapes one beer-laden hand over my shoulder and, half-tripping us both, pulls me to him. "Not a day over forty-four, gorgeous."

"Ow, ow, ow, ow ow ow!" There's a sharp tearing pain at my chest like I'm being stung by a swarm of bees. I try to duck away from the pain, stumbling under Gabe's arm, sending him reeling to keep his balance and save the beer. I'm swatting at my chest until I realize that's worse, like the bee is trapped there, and then I realize: the safety pin! I stop flailing and freeze. Of course it's the pin, open, tearing my shirt, which I pinch away from my body to inspect the damage: a cluster of red-hot pricks and jagged trails like seismographic markings in my cleavage. I re-clasp the pin, fan my shirt against my skin to cool the spot.

"Oh," Gabe says, "good, right, just leave it there. I'm sure it won't open again."

"Do you have a better suggestion?"

Gabe just stares me down.

"This," I say, "is why you and I cannot have a relationship."

His face spreads in a signature magnanimous grin, arm rising to take me in again. "Honey," he says, "come to Papa."

"And that," I say, snuggling in, "would be another."

Marco Hausman and his communist bride share the rooftop apartment of an un-renovated brownstone on Twelfth Street. I'm nearly grateful to mount six flights of stairs if only for the blood circulation and attendant body heat the climb stimulates. Gabe rang the bell from the street below and announced us as "Gabriel Weiselberg and long-lost surprise guest," and I wonder who Marco imagines might be climbing these steps toward his home. As we reach the final landing, a door flies open at the end of the hall and a thinner, less-imposing, no-longer-dreadlocked version of Pothead Marco throws open his arms and cries, "Millicent Russakoff! My god! That's incredible—you two are *still* together!" If our lives were a novel by my mother, this is the moment when Gabe and I would look at each other and realize—At last! And before it's too late!—that we've actually been in love all these years without ever really knowing it.

Gabe laughs. "As *if*!"

"I can't believe you remember my *name*," I tell Marco. He wraps me in an enormous hug and doesn't answer, just pulls back as he lets go and looks at me like I'm his grandchild, and possibly also a little bit insane on top of it. He says, "Let's go find you some dry clothes." It's unclear to me if he understands that Gabe and I are not a couple.

We are pulled into the apartment, a shop-worn IKEA display room, communists sold separately. An interior door opens and a woolly-poncho-clad woman with long gray hair steps out, closing the door behind her. "Mr. Zimmerman took a shit in the middle of the floor," she announces, her skinny bare arms flying up from beneath the poncho in a grand gesture of throwing in the towel.

"Baby," Marco coos, and then he's raising an arm that seems to span the small room and draws her to him. "Gabriel, Millicent—my bride, Letitia."

She is ten years his senior, at least, both beaming in-love-ness like they've been irradiated with it. Letitia takes one look at me, says, "Come," and pulls me through a throng of short, dark, spectacled Jews in threadbare suit slacks and sneakers, and into a bedroom where I am outfitted in someone's old Levi's cords cinched at the waist with a strip of Guatemalan macramé. Letitia waits while I unclasp the safety pin at my chest, then trades me my blouse for a green T-shirt from some kayaking outfit in Oahu. I tug the shirt on. "My boyfriend-fiancé-person-type-person is a kayaker," I tell her.

"Really?" she says, with more interest than I'd expect. "Marco didn't tell me."

"Oh," I say, "there's not, I mean, I don't even know if he knows I'm . . . Oh! Not *Gabe*. Gabe and I aren't . . . He's not the—I mean, we dated in college, but we're just friends, essentially, mostly, anyway—my . . . the . . . the person I'm getting married to is someone else. In California."

"Oh, oh, oh," Letitia is saying, "I'm sorry, I just assumed, I guess . . ." I let her lead me back into the party. From there she points me toward a propped-open door leading onto a wooden rooftop patio. There's a free-standing tent, beneath which a man who may very well *be* Fidel Castro is flipping burgers on an enormous gas grill. A table of potlucky foodstuffs is suddenly the most inviting spread I've ever seen, and I start piling a plate with beet salad and couscous and something that looks like Chex Mix with peas.

"Turkey burger?" offers Fidel, and I open a bun to accept. I have to say that I find great comfort in knowing that whatever else is going on in this horrendous war-riddled world tonight, at least one rooftop in New York City is populated with communists eating turkey burgers. Across the table I hear one person ask another, "So what have you been up to?" and the second answers, "Oh, you know, waiting for the revolution . . ." and I remind myself, again, to be grateful for small gifts, for little things that—even if for the briefest flash—make the world seem less irredeemably horrific.

My father is dead, my mother's sex-crazed with dementia, I'm about to marry a semi-professional kayaking dilettante for personal reasons I don't myself entirely understand, in a country being run by a war-mongering, election-stealing brat with Jesus up his ass, in a world bent on self-annihilation, and there are very few things these days that offer much solace or hope, but drinking PBR on a wet Manhattan rooftop with my sweet ex-boyfriend and a bunch of raving pinkos is one of them. Gabe and I huddle together, sharing a beer, and then another, as Marco tells us the love story of Marco and Letitia, which involves a city council election, two feral cats, a potentially toxic waste-disposal plant, someone's irresponsible roommate named Bob, an ostensible case of mistaken identity, and Bob Dylan playing "Simple Twist of Fate" on a makeshift stage at a Triple-A ballpark somewhere in the middle of nowhere.

"Gabe says you're getting married, too?" Marco asks, leadingly.

I nod, make a face I imagine to be a sort of slapstick version of terror.

"You're getting married, but you're *not* marrying Gabriel here?" Marco guesses, like we're playing charades now and I'm not allowed to speak.

I nod, miming guilt, miming shame. I have lost count of the beers; we seem to be through what we brought, drinking whatever we find in the cooler.

Gabe says, "I'm no kayaker . . ."

Marco is confused. He points at me—*you*—and mimes a paddle—*dip right, dip left, dip right, dip left—kayaker?*

I point at myself, shake my head, no. Not me. *Kirk*, I want to say, but I'm at a loss as to how to indicate him without words. I tap my heart.

"You *love* kayakers . . . ?" Marco tries.

I shake my head again, wave away my last gesture. *Start again.* How to mime fiancé? I hold out my left hand where a ring would be if I were a person who'd wear such a thing. I indicate this invisible ring, the band around my fourth finger. I put an imaginary diamond on it, a rock the size of a golf ball. I try to make it shine. I admire it, hold it to my heart, smile, bat my lashes. Then I reenact Marco's paddling.

"You're marrying a kayak!" Marco cries.

Hurrah! I lift my arms, hands clasped in victory.

"Um," says Marco, "and, um, why, exactly?"

"Because I love it," I declare. "And it loves me."

"And what about children?" he asks.

"None yet," I say. "But we hope to have a whole fleet someday. An armada of a family."

And then Letitia is calling Marco inside, the telephone receiver clasped in her hand: *for you*, she's mouthing.

"If you'll excuse me," says Marco, hopping to his feet in one motion like a Russian dancer. He scuttles inside.

I lean my head against Gabe's shoulder. "Why *am* I getting married, Gabe? Do you remember? I feel like I had a good reason once . . . I can't remember what it is. Did I ever have a good reason?"

Gabe looks at me sternly—the paternal Gabe-mode I've always had a weakness for. "Because you love him," he says. "And he loves you."

"But is that any reason to *marry*?!"

Gabe's shrug is kindly, but it's a shrug nonetheless.

"Why *do* people get married?" I ask. "I mean, *real* people. People like us. People like Marco and Letitia. People who do it for good reasons, not bad reasons."

"Do we know they did it for good reasons?"

"We're giving them the benefit of the doubt. We're *assuming* they had a good reason. Or she needed a green card. Or they did it for health insurance."

"Those are good reasons?"

"They're *understandable* reasons."

"And so what are bad reasons?"

"Okay," I say, "bad reasons to get married . . . One: fear of loneliness. Two: fear of future loneliness. Three: fear of dying alone."

"Four," Gabe says, "fear of fear."

"Four," I say, "to quote-unquote ensure stability. Five: to please your parents. Six: to displease your parents. Seven: to have children. Eight: to ensure that splitting up would cause an enormous legal, logistical, emotional hassle."

"That's a bad reason?" Gabe asks.

I have no response to this.

"I mean," he clarifies, "what if getting married is like getting a tattoo? You have a realization, some understanding of who you are or how the world works or what means something, or something like that. And so, you get some symbol of that emblazoned on your body so that you can't ever forget that once you knew something. Or with the idea that if a time ever comes when you regret that tattoo, you'll know that you've betrayed the person you once wanted to be . . ."

"What if you just realize that you were young and stupid? That the Grateful Dead weren't the answer? Or Winnie the Pooh didn't know The Way?"

"Exactly." Gabe's nodding vigorously. "Which is why there's tattoo removal. And why it's painful and expensive and a huge pain in the ass. Or ankle, arm, stomach, that lower back thing everyone's got now . . ."

I give him a pun-appreciating snort. "Do you know why Marco and Letitia got married?"

"Because they love each other . . . ?"

We sit sipping our beers a minute. Then I say, "Why can't we be in love, Gabe?"

"With each other?"

I'm nodding. "It could be nice . . ."

"I know," he says, "I don't know." And that's enough to remind me a little bit of why I'm not in love with Gabe: the only thing he ever seems to *know* is that he doesn't know.

"We *should* be," I say. Now I feel guilty for not being in love with him.

"We could try . . ." he suggests, though I'm not hearing the commitment in his voice.

"I don't think it's something you can *try* at."

"I know," he admits.

"It *should* be," I say.

"It should."

When Marco returns to us, he's got fresh beers, and somehow that seems like the perfect invitation to say, "Marco, why did you and Letitia decide to get *married*, I mean, you know, like not *why each other*, but why *married*, per se?"

He's nodding at me thoughtfully, like he's heard this question before and is going to wait politely while I finish garbling out the question before he makes it all clear to me at last. "I think," he begins. "I think a few reasons. I think partly out of a crazy, intense, emotional desire to just get up there in front of everyone you know and say, 'Oh my god I love this person so much I can't stand it!' you know?"

Gabe and I nod, as if we do know, and I'm surprised we don't burst out laughing at each other right then, but it seems we're both too eager to hear what Marco has to say next.

"I think, also, that it had something to do with having both been people who never did the"—he mimes air quotes—"right thing. And this idea that there could be something radical in the act of getting married if it was people like us doing it, you know?"

Our nods are growing less nod-like by the second, but Marco seems oblivious. "Why?" he asks me. "You having jitters?" And the lack of irony in that word alone makes me feel certain that whatever Marco and Letitia's reasons were, they're not likely reasons I'd consider *good*. He's lost me, and my brain switches into hibernation mode as he launches into some kind of manifesto about the power of reclaiming tradition, and all I can think is, *If the* communists *are this full of shit, what hope is there?* And then I can imagine Kirk, looking up from one of his environmental philosophy tomes and peering at me over his glasses, saying, *And where exactly did you get the idea that it's the* communists *who are supposed to be* less *full of shit than everyone else?*

Then, on the rainy rooftop, Gabe's voice takes on that obsequious tone I can't stand, and he's asking a question like Marco's some great, all-knowing sage, and Marco—perfectly happy to play guru—is saying something about making peace with the past. Gabe would defend himself later if I were to accuse him of sycophancy. He'd say that's how you get someone like Marco to really talk: treat him like the Buddha. *He didn't seem to be having any trouble talking*, I'd reply.

"You know, I've had a lot of lovers," Marco says, and what he sounds like is one of the bodice-ripping louts from the seamy depths of my mother's oeuvre, "but then someone comes along who makes you forget the rest of them, or not forget, but just not care anymore. Someone who makes going back not even cross your mind."

Gabe shoots me a look of astonishing smugness, as though every point he's ever made has just been scientifically proven right.

"Oh, so that's supposed to be the ultimate test, then? If I were *really* supposed to marry Kirk—"

Gabe's hands go up in surrender. "I'm just saying . . ."

"Or maybe, you're kind of working your way through these"—Marco's searching for a word—"these *others*, so that you can make peace with the past and go on and marry your . . . what's his name? Kurt?"

"Kirk," Gabe and I say in unison.

"Maybe you need to make peace with, say, the Gabe part of your past before you marry Kirk?"

I think I liked Marco a lot more as an insufferable pothead. "Apparently Gabriel and I have quite a lot of peace to make." I lift my beer bottle to Gabe for a toast, and though he clinks me, his heart's not in it. "Hey," I say, "maybe I could look up CJ Hultman and make some peace with him too before I get married . . ."

Gabe snorts, then sighs, exasperated. "I can't believe you're still talking about CJ Hultman."

"CJ Hultman from school?" Marco says.

"Mill spent one night with the guy in, like, 1980 and *still* hasn't gotten over it."

"It was 1992, thank you very much, and if what you mean by *hasn't gotten over it* is *has incredibly fond memories of what remains one of the most extraordinary sexual experiences of my short life*, then fine, yes, you're right, I haven't gotten over it."

"We'll look him up," Marco says. "We'll call him. He's back living in the Village again. I run into him all the time. We'll invite him over."

"No," I say.

"Why not?" Gabe and Marco sing back at me.

"Because."

"Come on, Mill, it'll be good for you," Gabe says. "You're exorcizing us."

"Shall I make the pun, or would you like to do the honors?" I reply.

Gabe just shakes his head.

"I think," I say, standing shakily, "I think this would be an appropriate and wise juncture for me to take a bathroom break." I plant a kiss on the top of Gabe's head and make my way as steadily as I can manage toward the apartment door.

The bathroom, of course, is occupied. I'm second in line behind a woman who looks very, very angry. She acknowledges my existence and then allows the brooding to subsume her once again. I lean against a wall. Beside me is a little built-in telephone shelf, and below it another built-in bookshelf, upon which, among other things, is a 2003 Manhattan phone book. I pick it up. Casually—which is difficult when it comes to the somewhat drunken handling of a New York telephone directory—I flip through to *H*. No listing for Hultman, CJ. The bathroom door opens; it's the angry girl's turn. Christopher? Charles? No, definitely Christopher. But Christopher what? Christopher James? Christopher John? And there it is: Christopher John, Barrow Street. Before I think about it much more than that I've picked up the phone. I tell myself I'm just checking, out of curiosity, to see if it's really him. I'm expecting the machine. He won't be *home*. That possibility doesn't really cross my mind somehow, until someone's saying "Hello?" and there's no question that it's him: that little twang of Southern drawl that once weakened my knees threatens to melt me once again.

"CJ?"

"Yep."

"Wow," I say. "Hi, I, I don't think I expected you to be home."

"Who's this?" he's saying.

"Oh, I . . . I don't know if you'll remember me. It's been a long time. My name's Millicent Russakoff . . . ?"

"Millicent! Hey, wow. I didn't know you were still friends with Marco."

"Marco?"

"Oh, the caller ID," he says.

"Oh, right," I say. "Yeah, wow, yeah, I just, we were just here, and your name came up. I was talking to Marco, and, I don't know if you knew him, Gabriel Weiselberg? We were just talking and somehow . . . your name came up and Marco said, *CJ Hultman, he lives right down here. We should call him up and invite him over*, and then I came inside and there was a phone book sitting here and there was your name and I don't know why I didn't think you'd be home but . . ."

"Wow," says CJ. "Millicent Russakoff. It's been a *long* time . . ."

"Yeah," I say, and it seems clear at that moment that we're both having a very acute memory of what exactly it was that transpired between us that long time ago. It involved an almost-exhaustive transpiring of bodily fluids. And though it was only one night, in my memory what transpired just kept transpiring and transpiring and transpiring. There's a marked pause on the line before either of us speaks again, and when we try to it's at the same time. We laugh, try again. Finally, I stay quiet. "You go," I say, and he says, "So you're at Marco's?"

My head's gone slow; it takes a second for me to remember who Marco is. "Yes! Right, yeah: Marco's . . . Big communist . . . ? He used to deal, at school . . . ? He got married, I mean, he's different than he used to be . . . I don't think he deals anymore. Well, I don't know . . . I guess maybe he might . . . I guess . . ."

"I *know* Marco," says CJ.

"Oh! Oh . . ."

"And Letitia."

"Yeah! Letitia!" I am a moron. "So, you should—I mean, if you're not doing anything—you should—if you wanted—you could, I mean, you *should*, come over . . . There're people you'd know I bet . . ."

"Right," CJ says, "and I do already know you and Letitia and Marco . . ."

"Right! Letitia and Marco," I cry, like we've just figured out we have mutual friends. I'm a disaster, absolutely flailing, but understanding that I'm tripping doesn't seem to have any relation to figuring out how to balance.

"Right . . ." CJ says again.

"No," I say, determined: "You should come over. It'd be great to see you. They're at—oh, wait, you probably know where they live . . . ?"

"I know where they live," he echoes, and I must be sounding saner, because the sound of his relief is audible.

"Well, so you should come over, if you want . . ." I'm going for flirty, unclear as to my success.

"Well maybe I just will," says CJ Hultman.

When I hang up the phone, it's a minute before I realize the bathroom's vacant, and I remember what I was standing here for in the first place.

Marco and Gabe have regressed to lying down on the roof, looking up at the stormy sky, debating whether more rain's in store tonight.

"I called him," I announce.

"Who?" they say.

"CJ Hultman."

"No way!" Gabe sits up, then regrets it immediately and lies back down, and his vulnerability in that moment reawakens all my love for him. I slide down to sitting and lift his boozy head gently into my lap. "I think you're right," I say, stroking the damp hair back off his face. "It's time to deal with my unresolved issues."

"Great," Gabe mutters, and I'm sure if he could he'd get up and get away from me, but his own inebriation is holding him down with not much choice but to submit to my mothering. Gabe, lovely as he can be, has a definite tendency toward childish petulance, and he's not above a hearty pout. This is probably, in part, why we get along so well: selfish only-children galled at the other's sense of entitlement and simultaneously enthralled and reviled by the mirrors we inadvertently hold up to one another.

We stay there on the roof for a time, quiet, watching the sky. Marco extracts a pack of cigarettes from the pocket of his cargo shorts and offers them up. I take one and get it lighted for Gabe, then hold it to his lips so he can inhale. We could not, I don't think, add up the number of cigarettes I've held for him to smoke in the last seventeen years if we tried. This is the order of my thoughts right now: 1) When my mother dies, Gabe will be the closest thing I have to family; and 2) what about Kirk?

When the raindrops start falling again—huge and heavy, like someone's taking aim and firing them down from the sky—we scurry back under the party tent, and I sneak a look in toward the apartment and catch sight of someone standing near the door who might very well be CJ Hultman.

"Okay, kids," I say to Gabe and Marco. "I think my past awaits me . . ."

They both peer in, squinting, then give up, and stagger back to supine.

I head inside with what I hope looks like boldness, at least to the drunk or unattuned.

CJ Hultman seems somehow diminished, in the way of great homes you've known in childhood which turn out, upon re-visitation as an adult, to be relatively modest and unassuming. He looks much as I remember him looking, and yet all of these attributes strike me as shockingly un-awe-inspiring. It's disconcerting. He's a good-looking guy, thick brown hair tamped down by the rain he got caught in on the walk over, pleasant face, average height, slumpy posture, burrowing as if to hide a bit of himself in the depths of his jeans' pockets. CJ Hultman is extraordinarily *regular*-looking. I'm finding myself at a loss for words. "CJ Hultman," is what I manage. I have this odd sense that our phone conversation half an hour ago never took place and he just happens to have shown up at this party by chance.

"Millicent Russakoff," he says, but the smile cracking on his face is not the smile of the man who's populated my sexual fantasy life for the last decade and a half. It's more the smile of someone who's saying to himself, *I definitely remember the name, but if I saw her on the street I'd've walked right by.*

"Wow," I say, "it's been awhile . . ."

"Yeah." He smiles. Sincerely, not creepily. "Maybe since that night . . . ?"

"You know," I say, beer fortified, and ready to wrangle my demons, "it may not have been even the slightest bit of a big deal or of any deal at all to you, but that night blew my nineteen-year-old mind. That night was . . ."

It's only a momentary pause, but CJ jumps in. "I re*mem*ber that night," he says, like he's defending himself against an accusation of Alzheimer's. "I think about that night sometimes, in the times when I let myself lie back and think about things like that . . ."

And though I'm pretty sure what that means is, *Totally, that night was hot, and I think of it sometimes when I jack off*, what I come out with in response is, "So have you been here in New York since then? Since college?"

"I got married, and we lived in North Carolina awhile," he says, "but otherwise I've been here."

"Oh," I say, so nonchalantly it's patently absurd. "You're married."

"No, not anymore. I moved back to the city when we split up." He's smiling at me in a way I can't quite read. Nervousness? Predation? Insanity?

I don't even know what it is I'm about to say in response when there's some commotion outside; the rain has started to pour down at a velocity greater than the tent can handle. I catch a glimpse of Gabe lurching toward the apartment door. "Hey," I say to CJ, "do you need a drink?" and before he can answer I've grabbed his arm and am herding him though a closed door off the main room that, by process of deduction, has to be the kitchen. I close it behind us.

Though CJ looks mildly alarmed, he almost doesn't look quite alarmed enough for someone who's arrived at a party only to be secreted away by some chick he hasn't seen in fifteen years who may as well have just admitted to harboring an obsession with him that would outlive all dogs and most cats. "Wow it smells in here," CJ observes.

"It's cat pee," I say, defensive by proxy. "They put their cats here—Marco and Letitia—I mean, not that they're the cats, I mean Marco and Letitia must've closed their cats in here for the party. To keep them from getting out on the roof."

"Yeah?" says CJ, though it almost sounds like he hasn't heard me.

To inhale in this kitchen is like putting your nose to a jug of ammonia or turpentine or nail polish remover and drawing in deep. My eyes water. In the dim light—only the stove-hood lamp is on—CJ looks a little frightened, like he'd like to be led out of this room as passively as he was pushed into it. I open the fridge, and the brightness inside is comforting, like a safety light flashing on in the dark late at night in a part of town you don't know so well: jarring, and then a relief. There's a lot of food in the fridge—Fresh Direct boxes and lots of bottled water—but no booze. "I think maybe all the beer's outside in the cooler," I say, then immediately regret that I've offered him an escape hatch.

"I'd take one of those waters there," he says, and as I pull two out, I feel another wave of relief. Almost enough to make up for the loss of the fridge light when I shut the door. I hand CJ a water bottle and struggle more dramatically than necessary with the plastic safety seal on my own. The rain is pelting the roof over our heads with such force it sounds like hail.

"So," I say, "so, you were married. Wow."

"I guess . . ." He smiles. Toasts me a plastic, sport-capped-bottle toast.

"Can I ask you a question?" I say. "We were actually just having this whole conversation earlier tonight, about getting married. And I was asking Marco why he and Letitia got married. I don't know, I guess I'm just curious, you know? Like, why *married*? I mean, I get love, and all that, but still, you know, why *married*?"

"Is that a question?" CJ says. "Are you asking why I got married?"

"Oh, yeah. But only if you . . . I mean, only if you want to answer it. I'm sorry, I'm . . . that's . . . I've had a bunch of beer . . . I'm being kind of censor-less, I'm sorry."

"No, no," he says, "no that's cool." And by this he does not mean *that's hip*, but *that's okay*, and the surfer dorkiness of it serves to temper my unease. I wait, suddenly mellow, eternally patient, for CJ's explanation as to—*drum roll, please*—why marry?

"You know," he says, "it feels like a pretty modest reason, really." And I go jittery again at his use of "modest," which casts light, I feel, on his intelligence, his worth, his—*god help me!*—viability as a mate. "I think it was really because, like, there we were, in this relationship, and we loved each other, and there wasn't any reason to break up, and it's not that getting married was the next step in some scheme of expectations, it's more like in order to get at the other things we had to do together . . . like there was work we had to do together, and in order to do that work, we had to have gone through that stage and said 'I do,' and dealt with the real, imminent possibilities of everything that culturally and historically, and, honestly, emotionally goes along with that. You know? It was like: we had to get married to get on with our relationship and figure out that we shouldn't be married."

I am standing with the cool water bottle pressed against the side of my face, and it's not until CJ finishes that I realize I'm giving myself an ice cream–type headache. He stops and takes a swig from his own bottle.

"That," I say, "was honestly very possibly the single most understandable, sensical case for marriage I think I've ever heard. Hands down."

CJ lets out a *ha!* of laughter.

"I'm serious," I say. "That actually makes sense."

"Well," he says, shrugging, waffling, looking like he wants to climb back into his own pockets, "we *are* divorced now, so I don't know how *good* a case it makes, but . . ."

"But you had to get married in order to get divorced in order to know what you know now, right?" I remind him.

"Well, sure, I guess if you can make yourself think that way, sure . . . It kind of assumes what I know now is worth something . . ."

"It's more than you knew before," I say.

"Touché," he says.

"Why are men always saying *touché* to me? Am I a confrontational person?"

CJ's eyeing me uncomfortably. "You know," he says, "could we . . . ? Do we need to stay here?" And I wish I could claim that for even a moment I thought he might be asking me to leave with him. But this is no proposition; he's just begging for release from the cat-piss room, the desperation flooded through his face like love. It's this beseeching look that I remember, viscerally, when I see it now, again, after fifteen years—the look he gave me that night, all night long, like he couldn't believe where he was, what he was doing, and with whom, and how astounding I was, how astounding we were together. And here it is again, right there on his face as he's asking me, please, to take him away from the kitty-pee stench, and my beery head's wrestling to reconcile this image in my memory with what's going on in the moment, when there's an explosion. Lightning strikes the roof over our heads, plunges through the kitchen ceiling, and rips open a cavernous illuminated hole, the thunder so loud it appears to be shaking the lighting jagged, as though lightning might be a sleek-edged lightsaber beam if not for the jarring of the thunder around it. The bolt shoots down at us, aimed to cleave CJ Hultman from me once again, this time for good, and it's another second before I understand that the room is still whole, there's just a skylight above us. We're merely seeing the lightning flash through the skylight, yet the blast somehow manages to hurl us into each other, me and CJ Hultman, forcing us to enact another horrible scene out of my mother's pseudo-literary imagination, because *of course* his hands are, defensively, at his chest, but as we're thrown together his hands are suddenly, *of course*, at *my* chest, crushing my nipples against the soft cotton kayak tee, and for the second time tonight my pelvis drops out from under me in a rush of wet warmth. And then the crash is over, the dim dark back as it was,

CJ Hultman's body up against mine like we've been struck and charged by that lightning, and now we're fused to each other in an embrace so absurd I'd laugh if it weren't so fucking arousing at the same time. The confusion of the moment lasts long enough for me to notice the small-ness of CJ's body, how delicate it seems beside me, and I wonder if he has actually changed, if he really did used to be bigger. And because it's this night—this surreal, pinball ricochet of a night!—and I seem to have no filters or borders or boundaries left, I don't even think before I say, "You're smaller than I remember," and CJ, without pulling himself away from me, says into my hair, "Great. Thanks," and then I'm backpedaling, "No I don't mean . . . I just mean I remembered you as bigger somehow," which does nothing to ameliorate anything, only it doesn't seem to mat-ter, because what CJ Hultman appears to be doing now is moving his hands around my back like he's going to slide them up under my shirt or down into my borrowed pants or over the worn corduroy of the ass, pulling me into him like my body remembers him pulling me into him, him into me, and his hand is coming across the small of my back and I'm desperate with the physical *need* for him to reach his hand down the back seam of the butt of these Levi's, to fit the back of his hand into the cleave of me, and draw me up onto him like fifteen years may have gone by but the body remembers everything, when suddenly he's letting out a cry of alarm, a shriek of fear, jumping backward, leaping away from me like he's been stabbed by my safety pin, but I've taken it off, there is no safety pin! "What's going on?" I cry, and I'm practically trembling with fear and want and confusion, and the look on CJ Hultman's face is utter revulsion and what he's saying, I realize only gradually—he has to repeat it four or five times before I have any idea what it means—what he's saying is, "I'm terrified of corduroy."

"You're *what*?"

He's scrambling in embarrassment. "It's weird," he's saying, "I know it's weird. I always have been. It just really creeps me out. Just the whole . . . Algh, I can't, I really, I just can't even talk about it or think about it, it's the texture, something, it just makes me go all . . . it's like nails on a chalkboard. Like that. I just can't even stand to think . . ."

There is, very distinctly, a man in front of me, physically reeling in repulsion, but I cannot put this together with what he's saying: corduroy. "Are you kidding?" I say. "You're kidding."

He says: "I'm not. I'm sorry, I'm really . . . Can we just get out of here? Could we please just . . . the smell's awful. I have sinus problems; I really can't breathe here. Do you mind if we . . . ?" And then he's pushing open the door, out into the light, like Dorothy stepping into Oz, and I just stand there in the cat pee, feeling strangely reconciled, and let him go.

When Gabe has seemingly vomited everything he could possibly have to vomit into Marco and Letitia's toilet bowl, I corral him downstairs and put him in a cab home, then hail one for myself. The rain has stopped again, and the air feels warmer somehow, not muggy warm, just summery. My clothes—my own clothes—have not only been tumble dried but someone has replaced the button on my blouse! Sewn a new button right into place! Letitia? The communist elves? It feels like a little miracle.

It's close to midnight when I land back at Man and Stuffy's, unlocking the door bolts with the infinitesimally slow motions of a novice thief, but my caution's for naught, it turns out. As I gingerly ease open the door, I hear music. There's low light coming from the archway to the living room, and I follow the muted call of operatic voices. Pausing in the arch, I'm privy to a sudden tableau of Man and Stuffy on their plush velvet sofa, Stuffy leaning into her husband, stocking feet tucked up under her skinny behind. They're both clutching fistfuls of tissues and each other's hands as if demonstrating a seated square dance promenade, with improvised bouquet. The music is coming from the stereo speakers, at which they gaze, enraptured. Stuffy looks up as I appear, then turns away, as though ashamed. Man takes up the charge, looks to me over his wife's head and stage whispers in a craggy voice thick with tears, "*La Bohème*. On the radio," waving me away impatiently, imperatively, with a puff of tissues, as if to say, *I'm sorry you had to see us like this . . . Go, run, save yourself!* I back away, practically bowing my apologies, and retreat to Kirk's childhood bedroom-cum-guestroom.

Though I was sober compared to Gabe, I'm not actually sober at all;

I'm keyed up and exhausted at the same time. I turn out the light, pull off my clothes, and huddle down into Kirk's teenage twin bed with its striped boy-toned sheets: navy, mustard, hunter green. If I could stop my feet from making time with the opera in the living room I feel like I might be able to fall asleep, but then the music stops and I hear Man and Stuffy shutting things down, heading off to bed, and still my feet won't stop conducting Puccini under the sheets. There's a phone on the bedside table, and I pick up the receiver and think to call Kirk, but he doesn't pick up, and I get my own voice on the outgoing recording sounding lispy and cloying, and instead of leaving a message I press seven to see if there are any voicemails. The first is from Sharon, my mother's college room-mate, and I don't make it any further than that.

"Millie. Millie, it's Sharon. I'm so excited for your wedding, darling. So happy for you. That there might be a joyous event after such hardship you've been through. Since your mother won't be able to, I want to make a toast to you at your wedding, Millie. And, because it's me, you know how I express myself, in music, always, and I want to make you a toast in song." Sharon is a folksinger from before there were folksingers. The woman anticipated being a Joni Mitchell knockoff twenty years before there was such a person as Joni Mitchell *to* knock off. She married a tycoon. Never worked. Never had kids. I'm the closest thing she has to a daughter, and we're not particularly close. Except, it seems, when my life occasions a folk song. "I'm writing a song for you, for your wedding"—Sharon's voicemail goes on—"and I've just finished a draft of it. I want to play it for you. I want to know if you like it, if you'll *approve* of my song to be performed, by me, at your wedding. So I'm going to sing it for you, honey, and you call me and you tell me what you think, okay? I call it 'The Song of Millie's Life, So Far.'" And then there's the knock of phone against table, the hollow thunk of a guitar body, a few chords, shaky and vibrato as an old lady's handwriting, and then Sharon's trembling soprano coming twinkly with static through the telephone wire, verses, choruses, and all:

I'm a girl from the city, like my mother before me
But I've left to see the world. Now I'm a California girl

My childhood was happy, I was free and on the loose
Running, jumping, laughing, playing Duck, Duck, Goose

As a teen I dated lots of handsome boys
But none made me happy. Not one brought me true joy

Oh the pain of youth,
And the comfort of age
I look for answers as I grow up wise and sage

One sad day my father had a stroke and left this world
Now it's just me and Mama, Daddy's own two girls

But Mom's health's not good herself, she's declining rapidly
She's not long for this world. She cannot remember me

Oh the pain of illness,
And the comfort of death
I look for answers even when I am bereft

But I've met myself a good, strong man who kayaks the oceans blue
I love him, and—what luck!—he loves me too!

So now I've found a special friend with whom I'll share my life
We'll live happily ever after. He's Kirk, and I'm his wife.

Oh the pain of loneliness,
And the comfort of love
I have found the answers in the arms of my true love

Oh we'll live happily ever after and have children by the score
I have Kirk and he has me—how could we ask for more?

I hang up and dial Kirk's cell phone. It takes him awhile to pick up, and
when he does, he's clearly in a bar.

"Where are you?" I say.

"Saturn. Where are you?" It's a lounge. The Saturn Lounge.

"Your folks'."

"How *are* Man and Stuffy?"

"They're awake!" I marvel. "It's midnight, and they're in the living room, weeping over *La Bohème* on the radio."

"Sweet Jesus," says Kirk. Then he says, "Did you—?" and I know exactly what he's asking so I'm already answering. "I just did."

"We can't have a wedding," he says.

"I know," I say. Then I say, "Why were we having a wedding in the first place?"

Kirk says, "I don't know. A party seemed like a nice idea . . . But seriously, Mill, now? What's the point? Your father's gone. Your mother won't know the difference between being at our wedding or being on the *QE2*. I'd honestly do just about anything to avoid sharing a meal with my parents, let alone standing at the feet of some justice with them hovering over my shoulder telling me not to slouch . . ."

"Why are we getting married?" I say.

"Mill," he says, "if you don't want to get married, we don't have to get married." And, god, his patience is astounding. He says: "I've said this before, and I'll say it again if you need to hear it again. The way I feel about you is, I think, the way people who get married feel, but whether we actually get married or not doesn't really make that much of a difference to me."

"I know," I say, "I know."

"Okay," Kirk says, "but easy as I am, I'm putting my foot down somewhere, and I am not, never, ever, going to get married in any kind of ceremony or reception or anything where Sharon sings that song. Or any song. Baby, I love you. But I am not marrying you in any anything where that woman sings, 'He's Kirk and I'm his wife,' okay? I mean, I draw the line somewhere, okay? That's where I draw the line."

I don't even realize I'm crying until I try to speak and all that comes out is a heave.

"Mill?"

I gulp some air. "We could go to Vegas . . . ?"

There's a second, and I know he's thinking, plotting. Then he says, "Does that mean call in the morning and start trying to cancel things?"

"Will you still marry me anyway?" I say.

There's another long pause, and I'm not sure if I breathe during it or not, but finally Kirk answers, and the magnitude of my relief is, I'm sure, testament to something.

I don't claim to understand a thing more about it than I ever did, but for what it's worth: Reader, I married him. What happens next remains to be seen.

Acknowledgments

The stories in this collection have appeared in print and online, some in slightly different forms—some more than slightly. "You Were My Favorite Scarecrow" first appeared in *Virginia Quarterly Review*. "The Church of the Fellowship of Something" was published originally in *StoryQuarterly*, then in *Made in Michigan 10th Anniversary Short Story Anthology* (Wayne State University Press, 2016), and it also appears, much altered, within my novel *Our Lady of the Prairie* (Houghton Mifflin Harcourt, 2018). "Don't Sweat the Petty" was published on *Five Chapters*. "And the Night Goes Off Like a Gun in a Car" (whose title is the last line of Spencer Short's poem "And I Have Mastered the Speed & Strength Which Is the Armor of the World," whose title is itself a line from Frank O'Hara's "Poem: There I could never be a boy") appeared in *Glimmer Train*. "Win's Girl" appeared in the *Cincinnati Review* and in *The Best American Mystery Stories 2008*. "Alone and Clapping" was published in *Chattahoochee Review* in a different form as "How Other People Make Love." "Home Is Where the Heart Gives Out and We Arouse the Grass" (whose title is taken from James Galvin's poem "Leap Year") first appeared in *Glimmer Train*. "We Shall Go to Her, but She Will Not Return to Us" originally appeared in *The American Scholar*, but some snippets of it first existed in "BABYLAND," a piece of "tag-team fiction" cowritten with Kevin Brockmeier for *The Journal News*. "Unity Brought Them Together" appears in Platypus Press's digital shorts series and in their Shorts 2020 print anthology. I'm deeply grateful to the editors and publishers who gave such good homes to these stories along the way: Ted Genoways, Malena Watrous, and M.M.M. Hayes and the *StoryQuarterly* Stegner Fellow Guest Editors, M. L. Liebler and Michael Delp, Dave Daley, Linda Swanson-Davies and Susan Burmeister-Brown, Michael Griffith and Brock Clarke and Nicola Mason, Otto Penzler and George Pelecanos, Mark Fitten, Sudip Bose, Michelle Tudor, and Peter Barnfather, and all the folks behind the scenes at these presses and magazines who keep literary publishing alive and thriving. And to everyone at Wayne State University Press—especially Annie Martin, who has made me feel so very very lucky for this chance, and so very much at home. Thanks, also, to Jen Anderson at Clearing Blocks Editing Services for excellent and extremely thoughtful copyediting. I am giddy with delight to see these stories published with such a stunning cover photograph (of the stunning Laurel Snyder!) by dear friend Sonya Naumann (www.sonyanaumann.com) from her gorgeous series *The Thousand Dollar Dress Project* (www.thousanddollardress.com). And a big shout-out of thanks to Josh Ritter and Rural Songs for the use of the epigraph lyric from "Kathleen," and to Erik Gilbert at Duchamp, Inc. for making all that happen. I am incalculably grateful to the friends and readers who've helped me with these stories at all stages, but this book's been so long in the making—twenty-two years!—that I no longer remember for certain everyone who read and gave me notes, so if I've left you out, please forgive me! But I *know* I owe huge thanks (for either reading drafts or listening to me blather on about fictional characters) to Allison Amend, Erin Ergenbright, Michelle Forman, Cody Greene, Katie Hubert, Laurel Snyder, Sarah Townsend Reiser, and Vinnie Wilhelm. I want, also, to try to express the enormity of my gratitude to Eric Simonoff for a *quarter-century* of agenting and friendship. My parents, Myra and Tony Nissen, gave me their love and support, and that's with me always, in every story I tell. And I want to give buckets of love to Bunski, who's not quite ready to read these yet but very enthusiastically asks me to tell him what my stories are about and says he thinks they sound cool, even if I know he wishes they were a little more magical . . . Jay Baron Nicorvo, the most astonishing reader and editor and husband I could ever have dreamed of, has the whole of my heart and gratitude, always. Our wedding may well be the only one from which I haven't filched details for these stories . . . or have I? Sometimes I can't remember what's fiction anymore and what actually happened. I would be remiss here if I didn't thank everyone who ever invited me to a wedding, and if I neglected to beg their forgiveness for scribbling notes on the back of my program during the ceremony and copying down conversations overheard in the ladies' room. I hope I haven't inadvertently, in these pages, unconscionably insulted anyone's Great Aunt Myrtle.

About the Author

Thisbe Nissen's first story collection, *Out of the Girls' Room and Into the Night*, won the John Simmons Short Fiction Award and was published in 1999 by the University of Iowa Press. She is also the author of three novels, *The Good People of New York*, *Osprey Island*, and, most recently, *Our Lady of the Prairie*. With co-author, co-collagist, co-chef, and co-conspirator Erin Ergenbright, Thisbe created *The Ex-Boyfriend Cookbook: They Came, They Cooked, They Left (But We Ended Up with Some Great Recipes)*.

Thisbe's education accrued at Hunter Elementary and High Schools in New York City, Camp Whippoorwill, the Green Mountain Guild at the Killington Playhouse, Wilderness Ventures, NOLS, Oberlin College, the Sierra Institute, Wheatland Vegetable Farms, and the Iowa Writers' Workshop. Now a professor at Western Michigan University, she works with undergraduate, MFA, and PhD creative writing students.

When not writing, Thisbe can usually be found quilting, collaging, taking photographs, or tending flowers and vegetables on the old farmstead outside Battle Creek, Michigan, where she lives with her husband, writer Jay Baron Nicorvo, their son, cats, and chickens.